CW01336610

Copyright © 2023 Alexia Onyx

ISBN: 979-8-9860020-7-1

Cover design by Cassie Chapman/Opulent Designs
Full editing services provided by Lunar Rose Editing Services
Interior formatting by Shannon Elliot

All rights reserved.

All rights reserved. No part of this book may be reproduced or used in any manner without the prior written permission of the copyright owner.

This is a work of fiction. Names, places, characters, events, and incidents are the product or depiction of the author's imagination and are completely fictitious. Any resemblance to actual persons, living or dead, events or establishments is purely coincidental.

COME OUT, COME OUT

ALEXIA ONYX

This one is for my chronically sad babes.

Please remember three things:
It's not your fault.
You don't have to pretend it doesn't hurt.
You deserve someone who will hold your hand when the darkness takes over.

With love, Alexia

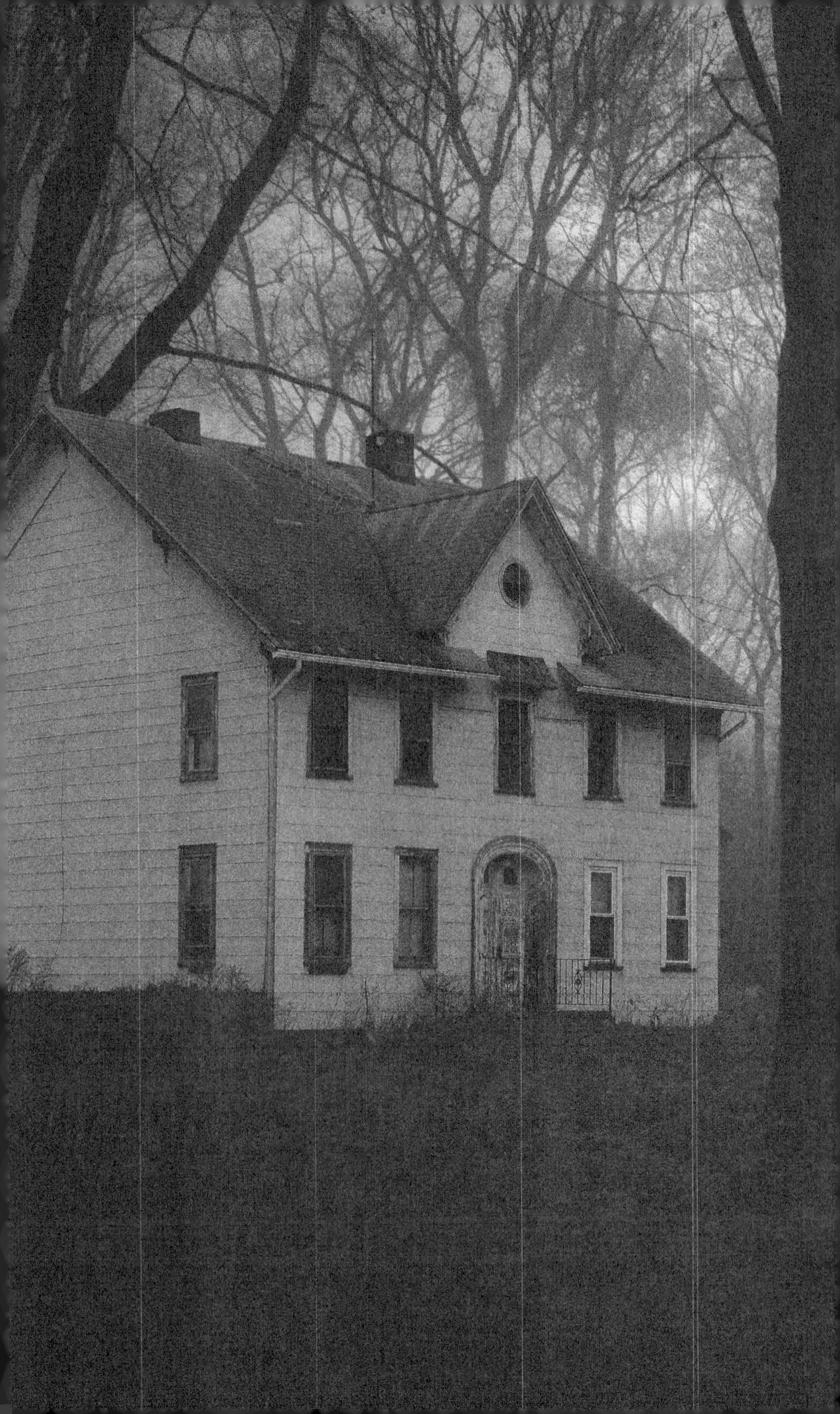

Before Reading

The topics explored in this book are very personal to me and Skye's struggles are written from my own experiences and perspective, I know this will not be universal, but I wanted it to be realistic. Topics including suicidal ideation, death, loss, depression, self-harm, and drug and substance misuse are discussed and shown on-page in this book, please keep that in mind before reading. You will find warnings and resources on the following pages if you need them.

A full list of content warnings is at the front of the book and there's a chapter-by-chapter breakdown at the back of the book for those who want to avoid certain triggers.

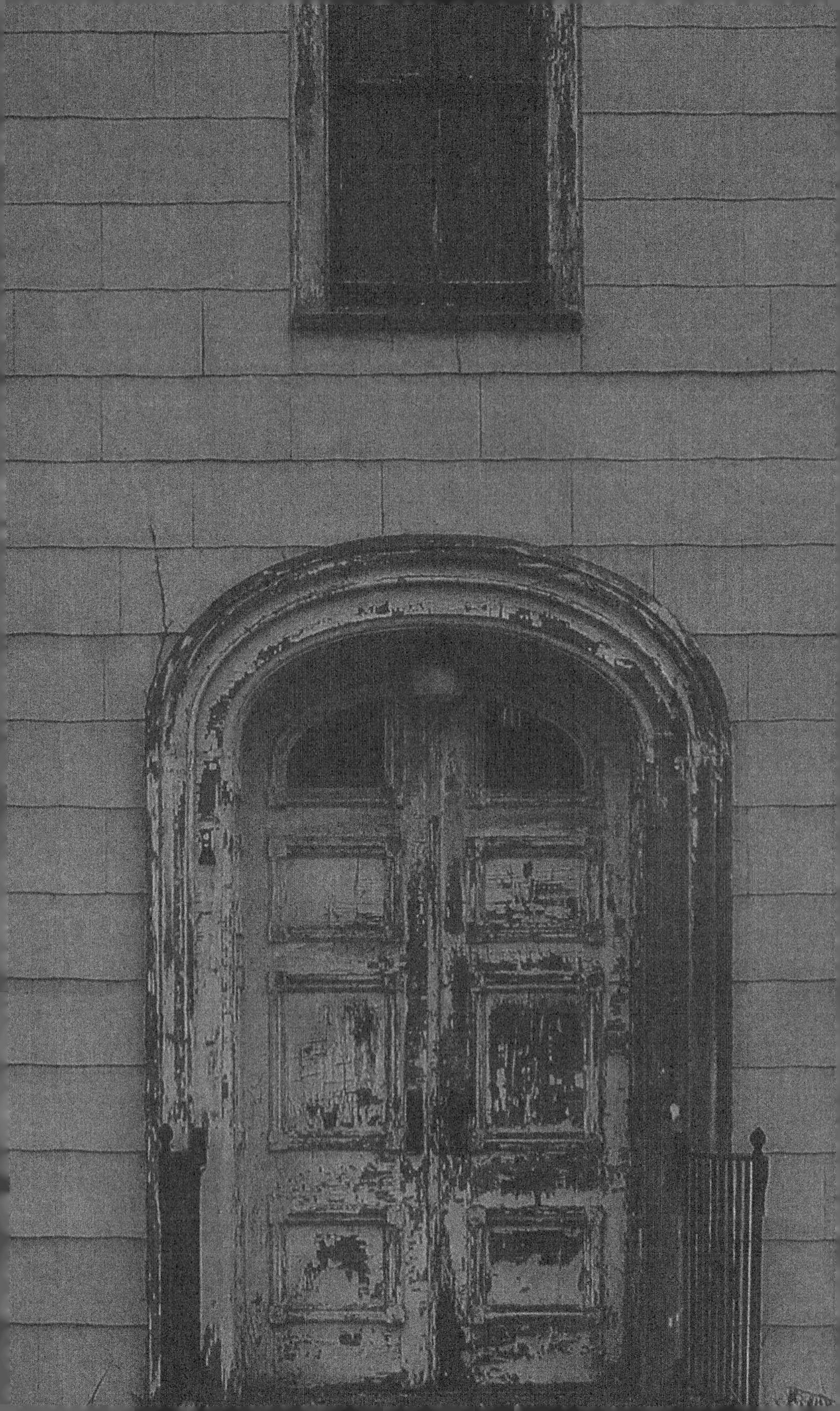

CW

This is an adult dark romance that contains graphic and explicit content as well as serious mental health themes. The content of this book is only intended for adults of legal age.

- Suicidal ideation
- Death by suicide
- Self-harm
- Grieving parent (death of their adult daughter), grieving sibling
- Substance misuse (cocaine and alcohol)
- Depression
- Mention of cops
- Blood and gore
- Murder
- Death, loss, and grief
- Head injury
- Bleeding out
- Mutilation (carving)
- Vomiting (non-pregnancy related)
- Mention of past homophobia
- Predatory landlord
- Break in
- Self-defense
- Feelings of abandonment
- Sensory overstimulation
- Negative self-image (non-body related)
- Isolation
- Attempted drowning
- Haunting
- Anti-religious rhetoric
- Unprotected sex
- CNC/roleplay
- Sex in life-threatening situations
- Sex with an injured person
- Knife play
- Penetration with an object
- Large, non-human dildo use
- Possessive/jealous partner
- Degradation
- Slut shaming (fake)
- Rough blow job
- Spitting
- Edging
- Chasing
- FMC hooks up with someone other than the MMC (before they are together)
- Sexual fantasies about someone other than the MMC (before they are officially together)
- Masturbation

Please note that while Come Out, Come Out includes sexual activities that are loosely inspired by kinks, they are not accurate representations of BDSM and are not meant to act as a guide for engaging in such activities.

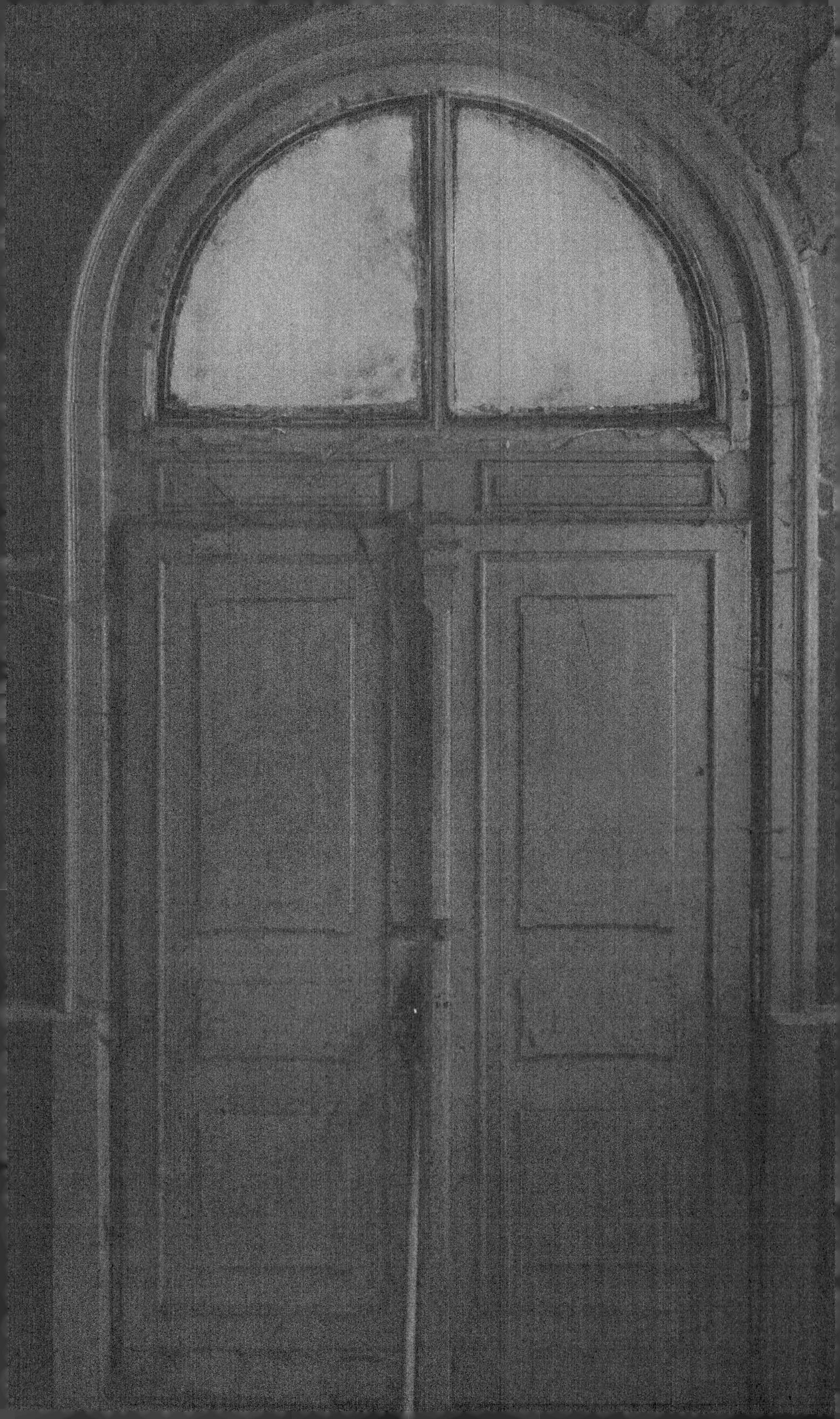

Resources

Your mental health and safety matters to me. Please make note of the resources below if this list or any content in this book is triggering for you:

» **Dial 988** for the Suicide & Crisis Helpline or visit their website for more resources
» For support after losing a loved one to suicide, **call 1-800-646-7322** or visit the Friends for Survival website
» **Call 1-800-662-HELP (4357) for SAMHSA'S national helpline** or visit the Substance Abuse and Mental Health Services Administration website for more resources

The Essentials

I Miss You - Blink 182
I'm Not Okay (I Promise) - My Chemical Romance
Somebody's Watching Me - Madelyn Darling
Haunted - sped up + reverb - pearl, fast forward >>, Tazzy
under the weather - Corpse
Lake of Fire - Nirvana
Lonely Day - System of a Down
Can You Feel My Heart - Bring Me the Horizon
Heavy - Peach PRC
Serotonin - girl in red
California Dream' - The Mamas & The Papas
Born to Die - Lana Del Rey
Send the Pain Below - Chevelle
Until the Day I Die - Story of the Year
Dead Girls - Penelope Scott
Where Did You Sleep Last Night - Nirvana
808s and Goth Bitches - Kiraw
Another One Bites the Dust - Queen
(Don't Fear) The Reaper - Nightshade, Satin Puppets, Lyndsi Austin
As the World Caves In - Matt Maltese
Say Yes to Heaven - Lana Del Rey
Good Looking - Suki Waterhouse
Should I Stay or Should I Go - The Clash
In the Room Where You Sleep - Dead Man's Bones

Listen To The Full Playlist

CONTENTS

Prologue...1
Chapter 1 - Aiden...3
Chapter 2 - Aiden...27
Chapter 3 - Aiden...35
Chapter 4 - Skye..49
Chapter 5 - Aiden...69
Chapter 6 - Skye..77
Chapter 7 - Aiden...87
Chapter 8 - Skye..95
Chapter 9 - Skye..105
Chapter 10 - Aiden..113
Chapter 11 - Skye...123
Chapter 12 - Aiden..139
Chapter 13 - Skye...161
Chapter 14 - Aiden..171
Chapter 15 - Skye...179
Chapter 16 - Skye...191
Chapter 17 - Aiden..203
Chapter 18 - Skye...213
Chapter 19 - Aiden..221
Chapter 20 - Skye...229
Chapter 21 - Aiden..237
Chapter 22 - Skye...247
Chapter 23 - Skye...253
Chapter 24 - Aiden..265
Chapter 25 - Skye...279
Chapter 26 - Aiden..287
Chapter 27 - Skye...299
Chapter 28 - Aiden..311
Chapter 29 - Skye...321
Chapter 30 - Skye...331
Chapter 31 - Aiden..343
Chapter 32 - Aiden..351
Chapter 33 - Skye...363
Chapter 34 - Aiden..369
Chapter 35 - Skye...375
Epilogue..381
Acknowledgments..385
About the Author..389
CW by Chapter...390
Black Cat Statistics...395

PROLOGUE

I always found the notion of death romantic; I never could have predicted how right I would be.

Come out, come out, wherever you are

CHAPTER ONE

Aiden

December 13th, 2019

Everything changes tonight; I can't sit here drowning in my grief any longer.

Drowning. The word brings back an onslaught of memories I wish I could erase, but then I would be getting rid of a piece of her. As devastating as the last time I saw my sister was, I could never let it go. I tried; *god* did I fucking try. I moved across the country, putting nearly three thousand miles between me and this place and the memories that cling to its walls like old tobacco. Five years–five *long*, achingly lonely years–away from my support system and nothing's changed. The second I stepped foot in this house, it came over me like a plastic bag meant to suffocate, leaving no way out. My first

COME OUT COME OUT

instinct was to struggle, to run back to New York, but my need for familiarity was so much greater. I walk these halls and breathe in the decay and yearning my parents have allowed to grow here. It's everywhere like the most persistent mold. Spores have spread and toxins weep from the photos of me and her. *All I see is my loss.* Smiling faces and rosy cheeks run into streaks of red; the once-innocent faces oozing blood and death. I stop in front of my sister's door, my forehead resting against the spotless wood kept clean by a mother's love. Instead of Becca's obnoxiously sweet perfume, I smell iron and rot. My parents' refusal to let her go is pungent; it turns my stomach.

    I don't want to blame them, can't really. I didn't do anything to heal the gaping wound she left either. I ran, yes, but the memory of Becca followed. My grief has festered within me, in the space that the thrumming connection to my sibling used to occupy. That volatile twin bond that used to buzz between us has flatlined. Sometimes, late at night, I grasp at straws, clawing in the darkness for the string of fate between us that was once pulled taught. Instead, it's limp and dangling from my wrist like a wrought-iron chain that's dragging behind me with every step I take. There's no escaping the heavy burden of her loss. The oppressive metal of it is fused with my bones.

ALEXIA ONYX

Every time I look into my own reflection, Becca's gaze follows me, watching me live with little to show for the extra years I got while she decomposes in the ground. I begged my parents not to put her there, in that hard box, in the cold soil of the earth amongst people she doesn't know. They told me Becca loved nature, that she would want to be there. Parents trumped sibling; I can't even bring myself to visit. I don't think I could bear the idea of her resting beneath where I sit. So close, yet so far.

The funny thing is, I can be *here*. In the eye of the storm, allowing myself to get torn up in the violence of it.

Instead of avoiding the very spot where my sister killed herself, I can't seem to stay away. It's like the last piece of her soul resides here and, still, five years down the line, I can't bear to leave her alone. I already failed her. That truth was brought to light under the fluorescence of the liquor aisle at the market down the street.

"Aiden?" The familiar voice of my sister's best friend called in disbelief. "Umm, hey. Didn't expect to see you here." The comfort in her eyes had dimmed with somberness when I finally met her gaze. Did she see Becca there, too?

"I'm here for the next month, visiting for the holidays." The need to escape the conversation I knew was coming drove me to grab one of my least favorite beers.

COME OUT COME OUT

"Oh, I know. They told me you were coming. Just didn't think I'd see you out in the wild. They were so excited to have you home it's practically all they've talked about every time I've stopped by to check in on them." Megan is a good person. The best I could have asked for to watch out for my sister–and now my parents, apparently. "I can't imagine how hard it's been for you, between losing your sister and...whatever it was that you had with Nate."

"What does Nate have to do with anything?"

"Well, everything, doesn't he?" I'll never forget the confusion and then the pity in her eyes. I know that look so well, the one where I'm the one out of the loop. "You know, how he and his friends were commenting on all her pictures. How they were telling her ..."

The clank of nearly-shattered bottles meeting the metal shelf had her retreating before she finished the sentence. "What do you mean commenting on her pictures?"

"They had been cyberbullying her for months before she . . . She never told you?" And then I saw it, the regret I felt too, of not knowing exactly what was going on in Becca's head. "She said she would. I assumed she did. I even blamed you for a long time–I'm so sorry, Aiden–but I did, I blamed you for not putting a stop to it, for not saving her."

Despite the last few years of my life flipping on its head, that part stuck out the most because I blamed me too. More so every minute.

"Shit. You really didn't know? It's still there for everyone to see. Your parents never deactivated her profiles."

It was there amongst the violating cold of the freezer aisle that I realized I was even more of a failure of a brother than I'd ever realized. How could I have been so oblivious?

Maybe the answers of what to do next are below the now-cold water, etched into the porcelain. I test my theory and submerge myself, not bothering to take off my hoodie and jeans. My knees jut out of the water but I manage to flatten my shoulders against the bottom so my upper body and face are completely underwater. My clothes become heavy, weighing me down, and I give myself over to sinking into it.

I listen to the muted sound of the water as it sloshes against the tub, straining my ears in hopes that maybe I can hear her pleas for help that I somehow missed. Of course, there's nothing down here but the faded stains of that one black bath bomb Becca tried that one time. My smile comes and goes in seconds. Inside my head, I'm calling out to her; we never had that twin telepathy thing people talk about, but maybe some fragment of her spirit is still out there waiting for me. No matter how hard I concentrate, my screams into the void go unanswered. I force my eyes open and peer up through the blurry surface.

"Fuck," I yell, letting the water rush in until it cuts me

off, but I don't stop it from flooding my lungs when movement catches my eye. My heart pumps violently in my chest when a figure takes shape above me. Hands plunge beneath the surface; they're warm as they dig into my chilled skin.

"Aiden!" My mother's panicked voice breaks through the moment of confusion. "What are you doing?" Anger and fear make her voice crack as she shakes me.

I sit up and take a deep breath. "I was just . . ." An explanation evades me. "I'm fine Mom." I cover her shaking hand with mine and hold her gaze. "I promise."

"And if you're not, it's okay." Drops of water flick in every direction as she runs her fingers soothingly through my dark brown hair. "I'm here for you, Aiden. *We're* still here. Don't go chasing ghosts, or I'll lose you too." Reluctantly, she lets me go and leaves the bathroom with a pleading look over her shoulder.

When most people visit their hometown, they catch up with old friends and hit the bars. That's for people who come back on happier terms. I'm attending my own pity party and lighting up a joint in memory of my sister. She wouldn't have approved but when I flick the lighter and blow out the first puff of hazy smoke, I can hear her scold me so clearly that it sends a chill down my spine. That echo of her is why I've gone through the majority of my stash that was supposed to last my entire visit. Anything to be close to Becca again.

The ironic thing is, I feel closer to her than I have in a long time. We had a fine relationship–but weren't attached at the hip like most twins. Becca and I were worlds apart. I'd loved her of course, but our lives were just too different for us to have that typical twin dynamic. She was a straight-A student who never put a toe out of line. I'd always been the rebellious one with a knack for disappointing my parents and drawing the attention of the sexually repressed jocks who hated themselves more than they hated me. Where Becca was a try-hard, eager for everyone's validation, I was perfectly fine with being an outcast.

At least I thought so. That was before I was well and truly on my own in this fucked up world. Before, I'd always known that when things got really bad, when I just needed a bit of comfort, I could bust into Becca's room and throw myself on her bed, sending her papers flying. She'd roll her eyes and huff, but she'd let me stay and be my silent comfort. We weren't really the kind of siblings that talked about things, but we were there for each other in our own way—or so I'd thought. In the end, I guess Becca didn't feel like she could come to me when she needed it most. I wish she would have told me about Nate. Finding out from Megan five years after the fact was a punch to the gut.

COME OUT COME OUT

Dazed, I'm transported back to that night when I found her. I remember it too clearly—a bathtub filled with red, her limp wrist dripping with beaded bracelets, dangling over the edge, my sister's eerily pale skin, and her vacant eyes no longer looking just like mine. If there was anything in my stomach, the memories would have forced it out of me. Instead, misery sits idly in the empty pit.

Stinging pricks my eyes and the tissue in my throat constricts. I punch my fist into the water disrupting the unwanted detour down memory lane. What-if's plague me as the I run through the last year of her too-short life for the millionth time. I'd had my head stuck way too far up my own ass to have noticed. Even if I hadn't been a twenty-three-year-old selfish prick, it's unlikely I would have known anything was wrong. After I'd decided to go to junior college instead of the state university with her, we became even more distant than before, both caught up in our own lives.

"You're a fucking selfish bastard," I remind myself under my breath.

It was all made worse by the fact that I'd introduced the shitheads who are to blame into her life. To think this all started because I didn't want to fuck Nate anymore. For me, Nate had been a conquest. Outcast tops star football player and ex-bully. What a fucking high *that* was! And then I got bored. Nate had nothing else to offer besides his body and I didn't like the idea of being someone's dirty little secret either. The saddest part was, he didn't even hide that we were hooking up because he was afraid of the homophobia—he'd finally come out after high school—no, he was afraid of his reputation. He hadn't changed at all, other than the fact that he finally admitted why he'd relentlessly harassed me for damn near a decade.

It'd been a badge of pride, fucking him, having him wrapped around my finger. *Now it makes me sick.*

When the tides turned and I finally humiliated him— his words, not mine—he couldn't handle it. Bullies were always so fucking weak when it came to their own suffering. I tried to be as mature as possible about it when I told him it was over. I'd been ready to put everything between us in the past; I guess you could say I'd fucked all the resentment out of my system. I could have been petty, thought about it, actually. Maybe I should have been. Would that have stopped him from having the balls to go after my sister? I'll never know, but I can make him pay. I won't let him have the final point in this twisted fucking game he's playing. We're way past petty.

I grab my phone off the floor, careful to hold it off the side of the tub so it doesn't get ruined. I quickly find Nate's profile and scroll through the most recent photos. Predictable

COME OUT COME OUT

as ever. He has no worries about laying out his entire life like an open book–the better to show it off. There's even a photo of him standing outside the same old house he's been renting with his frat bros since college. Some people really can't let go of their "glory years." They might have graduated, but not much about their lifestyle has changed from the looks of it. Luckily for me, he only lives a few minutes away, perfect for a late-night visit.

Before I realize what I'm doing, I find my way over to Becca's profile. I increase my screen to full brightness and stare at the last photo she ever posted until my vision blurs. Holding my breath, I move on to the reason I'm on here in the first place. I click the comment icon and start scrolling. The first few remind me how much Becca was loved by those she chose to surround herself with, but it doesn't take long to find what Megan was referring to. The arrogant sons of bitches didn't even feel guilty enough to remove any of it. Photo after photo I find a stream of vile comments. They attacked her looks, her sense of humor, her relation to me, everything. When I get to about a month before she died, all the comments are turned off on those posts. She'd tried to protect herself, but at some point, she'd given up and let the floodgates remain open. With a barrage of comments under each photo from Nate and several of his friends that I immediately recognize, I can't imagine how many notifications she was getting a day—how incessant their torment was. And this is just one social media platform. I can't stomach checking the rest, don't need to. I've seen enough to know that those motherfuckers are going to pay.

    I shoot up to my feet, sloshing water over the sides of the tub and onto the floor where my sister's fluffy lavender bathmat should have been, but it'd been soaked through with blood so it had to be tossed. I take off my sopping clothes, dry off, and dress quickly. I pull on a black cut-off tee and black jeans, then lace up my old, reliable combat boots. I reach under my bed and grab the hidden whiskey I never finished and shove it in my back pocket, ignoring the awkward bulge. Slipping on Becca's old silver rings that I wear out of habit every day reminds me of one more thing I need to grab. My hand stills only for a fraction of a moment before I take in a lungful of air and step into her room. Her bed is made perfectly, and nothing's been moved an inch—even the book she'd been reading is laying open. I fight the urge building to let my anger get the best of me and walk straight to what I want. Carefully opening her jewelry box, I reach in with gentle fingers and grab a single silver earring with a red butterfly hanging from it. This pair was Becca's favorite; I leave one for her. Before the museum of memories locked in here prevents me from finishing what I started, I exit and make a beeline for the front door.

COME OUT COME OUT

"Aiden, honey, where are you going?" My mother looks over the top of the couch, her brow creased with worry.

"Be back later," I shout over my shoulder without stopping and grab my keys off the hook by the door. I need to get in the car before I lose my nerve.

Ready or not Nate, I'm coming for you.

He thinks I made a fool of him before, he has no idea what I'm capable of. I'd let everything he's ever done go. I found it within myself to write him off as being a wayward kid who hated himself so much he needed to take it out on someone else. But then he'd taken one of the most important people in the world to me. *It was simply unforgivable.*

Flashbacks of those nights when I let him sleep in my bed, his body pressed against mine, made my skin crawl now. There was a brief moment in our time together that I thought I might feel something, there was a part of me that wanted there to be more when he'd subtly bring me back to his room to "smoke" after the party wound down, but it never ended there. He'd clutch at my clothes, pull me into him, smother me with his long-repressed need. For a while, I ate that shit up. Being wanted by the person who told you they were disgusted by you, tasting the sweetness of their desire and lies on your tongue had been a heady experience. It felt like power, but he was toxic through and through. He never claimed me, he never defended me—not that I needed it, but still—and he never touched me with the reverence I deserved. I could never have loved someone like him, could never have given him more than just my cock. And for that little bit of self-awareness, I'm grateful, especially now.

He might not have acted alone, but he was the main reason my only sister, my twin, was dead. It was nauseating that I ever found any kind of pleasure in his company.

I know there's no sense in dwelling in the past. Hell, I've been doing it for weeks and it's made no difference. The only thing that gives me any semblance of peace is the idea of taking out those fuckers who bullied and harassed her endlessly. In-person. Online. Day in. Day out. There's only so much one person can take, didn't they know that? *They did, though.* We *all* inherently know that. *They just didn't care.* I remind myself of the painful truth. The clarity affirms my decision as I turn the key in the ignition and make the short drive to the isolated house I'm far too familiar with.

I park a bit down the dirt road, grab the whiskey bottle from where I stashed it in the trunk, and take a few long swigs to keep me warm as I stalk toward the looming house in the distance. Within three minutes I'm rounding the side of the house and creeping past the rear windows. With a final sip, I set the bottle on the cigarette-laden patio table. As always, the back door is unlocked, so I let myself in.

The fall of my heavy boots punches up at me from the dirty wood that's sticky with beer and fuck knows what else. A death march. I ignore the ominous sound and follow the direction of the obnoxious voices that are accented by the whisper then splash of a lint-covered ping-pong ball sinking into a cup. It reeks in here. Irritability pitches my anger higher. I'm already suffocating under the weight of it, but it's the only force keeping me going. Without it, I'll collapse under the agony of loss and never get back up.

The familiar sting of cheap cinnamon and whiskey crawls up my throat and my sister's ashen face and empty eyes take up residence in the forefront of my mind. It was my lifeline after I lost her, the only thing that dulled the ache threatening to tear me apart. I force the image of her away, focusing on the knife in my pocket that's as sharp as her razor blades. Between uneven breaths I repeat the names I found most frequently in her comments.

Nate.

Rob.

Richard.

The three pieces of shit I came all the way out here for in the damn-near middle of the night. The historic house has unsurprisingly been poorly taken care of. It gives serious *Am-*

ityville house vibes with its prominent balcony and the countless large windows that follow you with curious eyes as you approach it. You never escape its looming presence.

When I round the corner, Rob and Nate come into view. They see me and are confused, then recognition flickers across their objectively handsome faces, their sculpted jaws clenching and eyes hardening.

Nate's hazel eyes widen as they track the changes in my face after so much time apart. He's trying to reconcile the Aiden who once stared at his chiseled body with desire with the one standing in front of him who only looks at him with absolute hatred. "What are you doing here?" He runs a hand through his white-blonde hair and swallows nervously—we both know there's only one reason I'd be here after not seeing each other for five years. His freckled cheeks redden just slightly with distress, but he corrects it with a macho façade that he forces into place. His muscular shoulders roll back and he stands taller. "Get out of my house."

I snort a laugh; he might tower over me at 6'5" but that's never intimidated me, even considering the fact that he's put on quite a bit of muscle since I last saw him. Still, I'm not unaffected by him. The speech I'd rehearsed in my head falls apart on my tongue now that I'm in the same room with him again. I struggle to think straight with the anger and bitter memories thickening the air around me.

"You're fucking pathetic. Do you know that? What kind of loser bullies a woman?" I stand, blocking the entrance and exit to the kitchen. "You went too far, Nate. You never should have fucked with my sister."

Rob mimics Nate's posture. His pale skin is now covered in tattoos and he's grown a hideous, thick copper mustache, but otherwise, he looks the same. "He asked you to leave nicely. Get the hell out, or we'll take a little trip down memory lane." Rob looks over at his friend with an obnoxious smile on his face, but I take note of how his hand tightens around the beer pong ball in his palm. "Remember that one time we tossed him the dumpster in seventh grade?"

Nate's brow furrows and he shakes his head.

I clap loudly, bringing their attention back to me. "Oh Rob," I say through a strangled laugh. "As much as I'd like to sit here and take a leisurely stroll down memory lane, I did come here for a reason. Thanks for reminding me what a piece of shit you are, I'm going to really enjoy this." Staring right into his blue eyes, much brighter than my own, a sneer overtakes my lips. My hand tightens around the knife at my back and with it, any lingering qualms about making them pay are squashed. *They* started this. *They* brought this upon themselves with every decision they made to keep harassing my sister.

Three long strides and I'm driving the kitchen knife I'd brought from home into Rob's muscular stomach.

"What the fu—" His words fail him as he falls to his knees.

I pull out my knife with a grunt and catch Nate's olive-green eyes. "I'll give you a head start, for old time's sake." Adrenaline pounds through me and a maniacal smile spreads across my face. This feels so fucking good. This feels like a release of so much of the venomous agony that's been poisoning me for half a decade. It's finally caused the rational part of my brain to become necrotic. I let my murderous intent take over and the reward center of my brain lights up like the goddamn Las Vegas strip. This is the best I've felt in years.

I'm not ready for this euphoria to end. I decide to play with him a bit. After all, he's owed a bit of torment for all he's done. *A taste of his own medicine.* "Twenty, nineteen, eighteen . . ." I start counting down and he just stares at me. His eyes are glassy and his lips tremble despite how he clenches his jaw, holding on to that last bit of fragile masculinity. I'm excited to tear it to shreds. "Are you going to just sit there and start crying, or are you going to put up a bit of a fight?" I taunt, "I'd get moving if I were you." Fear wins out and a tear breaks free as his eyes dart around in panic, uselessly searching for the best path to freedom. "Fourteen, thirteen . . ."

COME OUT COME OUT

Finally, he takes off toward the front door, his socks sliding across the wood floor. He might have been an athlete in his prime, but he's lost his touch. My muscles twitch with anticipation.

"Ready or not, here I come," I yell as I take off in a sprint, my boots giving me traction while Nate's an unsteady, flustered mess. I nearly tackle him and fist the back of his thick platinum hair, pulling him against my chest. The familiarity of this position isn't lost on me. I've fucked him like this more than once. *How fitting.*

"Please, don't do this, man." His breathing is uneven as he drowns in snot and an onslaught of tears. "Aiden, come on, I thought I meant something to you. You can't kill me."

"Oh, but I can," I grit out between clenched teeth. "It's too late to turn back. You should have thought about that before you tormented my sister. You just couldn't help yourself, could you?"

"I didn't know she'd kill herself. It's not my fault."

"Don't you fucking dare! It is your fault. Take some damn accountability for once in your life, Nate."

He doesn't; he just continues pleading for his worthless life through those pretty plump lips I used to love seeing wrapped around my cock. Any affection I ever held for him is gone. The moment I knew he had any part in this, he was dead to me. He showed me who he was when we were kids; bullies never change, not really. I never should have let him back in my life.

With that clarity, I raise my knife. "Rot in hell." Blade meets skin as I slash across Nate's throat, cutting off his unmoving pleas. Warm blood pours over my arm and sprays across my face. It's the best release he's ever given me. I pant with exertion and satisfaction, but it's not enough.

I release him and he hits the floor with a thud. I follow the snail-like trail of red to find Rob bleeding heavily and hyperventilating in a corner that he managed to crawl to. I grip a fistful of his shirt and force him upright. Once I ensure he's looking me in the eyes, I drive my knife to the hilt into his stomach to finish what I started. He starts crying. I'm unmoved. Guys like this are always happy to dole out the torment, but they can't take shit. They're weak. They're pathetic. And now, they're getting exactly what they deserve.

Looking down at his limp, bloodied body, I breathe a little easier. I take a second to wipe off the handle of the knife with the only clean part of his t-shirt then head for the staircase leading up to the bedrooms. Unfortunately, no one else is home. Looks like I'll have to wait for our boy Richard. How inconvenient. After a few minutes, I begin pacing what I'm pretty sure is Richard's room. I was supposed to be in and out, so no one would know I was here. I should leave before someone finds the bodies; I just left them there thinking this would be quick work.

But I don't leave. My need to finish this, to avenge my sister, is too strong.

"Bro, what the fuck?" Several voices echo in the entryway, so Richard takes me by surprise when his wide frame darkens the doorway. His brown eyes round with shock and his lips part. He takes two startled steps back, but I'm on him and covering his mouth before he can say a word. He's much shorter than me, so he's easy to overpower as I drag him into the room.

"Don't act so surprised to see me, Richy. Karma always catches up with us." He mumbles something unintelligible beneath my fingers. "Don't waste your last few breaths; there's nothing you can say to defend yourself. You deserve to bleed out all alone like my sister, you sorry fucking excuse for a human", I hiss into his ear. "But first, I want you to hear you apologize."

Richard shakes against me and pisses himself. Sweat pores from his brown hair and his skin immediately flushes with embarrassment. When it gets on my shoe, I jab the knife deep into his side. "Say it." I peel my fingers back just enough to let sound out.

ALEXIA ONYX

"I'm . . . I'm sorry," he yelps between ragged breaths.

The empty apology only makes me angrier instead of soothing the aching loss that rakes over the hot coals of my insides. "Do you even know what you're apologizing for?"

He shakes his head side-to-side frantically.

"You killed my sister." I stab into his side again and twist the knife. "You and your *brothers*," I spit the word, "drove her to death. You're a bunch of pathetic cowards who wasted their lives making other people miserable. Not anymore."

Several sets of feet pound up the stairs concealing the muffled voices. There's nowhere for me to go; I lingered too long.

"We called the cops; they'll be here any minute." I don't have a face to put to the voice, but the jumpy tone tells me they're terrified of what they'll find.

Richard whimpers as I rip the knife from his side. There's nowhere to hide. I can hear them right outside in the hallway, a few more steps and they'll be standing in the doorway, witnessing me covered in their friends' blood.

"Don't fucking move," The brunette guy in front demands as he holds a hammer high over his head.

I can't help but laugh. Do they really think that would stop someone hellbent on murder? I have no interest in killing them, they aren't part of this. But I'm also so far gone that I don't really care one way or another. If this guy thinks he's going to hit me over the head with a hammer and I'm just going to take it, he has another thing coming. *What's one more?*

The shrill scream of sirens blares from out front. They weren't bluffing. That's too bad for me. I guess it doesn't really matter though, it's not like I have much going for me. I haven't really been living since Becca died. I've been getting by for this long by the skin of my teeth.

That line of thinking is interrupted by a voice coming through a megaphone. "Come out with your hands up. Nobody else has to get hurt."

Liars. The most important person already got hurt. I'm already hurt. I turn my gaze to the two men standing in the doorway and they make a break for the front door. My head becomes cloudy and it's as if I'm floating outside my body as I tackle the brunette and shove the other guy, trying to barrel my way through the door. Hand on the knob, I pull it open. At the same time, a searing heat erupts in my side. I turn and see the knife plunge in again, and again. Color me surprised that Richard found enough strength to get off his ass. He's pale, sweating, and unsteady on his feet. He might have gotten me, but that fucker's not walking out of here either. I'm so consumed by pain and shock that I don't feel the next wound as distinctly.

Sluggish thoughts crawl their way to the front of my splintered mind.

Was this a mistake?

What did I really think was going to happen?

I guess I didn't.

My poor parents.

I hope I get to see my sister again.

Numbness spreads from my limbs and into my torso before I slip into that cold darkness, which honestly feels like the best sleep anyone could dream of. Better than a night spent in a luxury hotel with the air blasting. *It's so peaceful here.* The relieved sigh that slips through my lips releases the last bit of life left in me; I can feel it in the hollowness of this body I've called home for twenty-eight years.

My little wraith

CHAPTER TWO

Aiden

January 15th, 2020 - One Month Later

Ever so slowly, light flickers back in, like when you wake up in a hospital bed. But there's no softness beneath my back or relieved faces staring back at me. Thoughts begin to whir to life like a computer booting up and it takes several seconds for me to recognize the bare walls around me. I honestly didn't expect there to be anything after death. I've never been religious and never hoped for something better to be waiting on the other side. This definitely wasn't something better.

The air in here feels dead. The place looks especially morbid thanks to the built-up grime in the grout. The white walls are dirty with old fingerprints and flecks of dried blood, and the air is stale with death and abandonment. I turn in a circle, taking in what's become of the house I died in. *The house I killed in.*

The magnitude of that reminder is like another plunging knife, but I don't regret it. They got what they deserved. They may not have been the ones to run the blade down my sister's wrists, but they did everything they could to drive her to that point. If this was my punishment, then so be it.

I move to explore the rest of the house, but my eyes catch on the rust-brown stain on the floor. Kneeling down, I press my hand to it. For what reason? I'm not sure, but I somehow know that's the last connection to the life I once had. I run my fingers over the textured wood, but confusion sparks when I realize it's not cool against my fingertips like it should be.

Dots connect as I piece together my circumstances.

I'm able to see and touch things, but the sensations are all wrong, like I'm here but I'm not.

I died, but I'm not gone.

Does that mean that I'm a ghost?

Quickly, I make my way over to the closest bedroom I remember having a mirrored closet. I stand right in front of it and take in my reflection. I look exactly the same, down to my worn combat boots, which I guess is a relief, but I feel it in my bones. I'm dead.

Great. I'm a fucking ghost. I guess what they say is true, 'ain't no rest for the wicked'. But if that's the case, then where are those other fuckers. I can't be the only one stuck here.

"Come out here, you fucking cowards," I yell, but only my own raspy voice echoes back at me from every barren corner. As I wait for something, any clue that the others are here, a distinct sense of solitude fills the air around me. I should be relieved. I am, I suppose. I don't have to spend whatever this is with them. I don't understand it, but I guess it doesn't really matter. It is what it is. I can only hope that there's somewhere worse than this and they've ended up there.

Resigned to acceptance, I decide to explore the rest of the house. Random pieces of furniture were left behind—a couch in the living room, a desk in one of the bedrooms, the beer pong table of all things—but otherwise, it's been wholly abandoned. The buildup of dust and dirt unfortunately isn't any indication of how long it's been since I died; it's not like it was kept clean before. It could have been a few days or months.

I walk over to the cracked window in Nate's room and peer out. Heavy, gray clouds fill the sky, and wind rustles through the trees. It smells like late winter, but I can't really be sure. I died on December 13th, so it's maybe been a month or two.

A month or two of no memories. A month or two of

my parents mourning me on top of Becca. A month or two of lost time with no idea why. I don't have the energy to invest in all the questions other people might be preoccupied with. I'm dead that much is clear, so it really doesn't fucking matter. What does consume me once again, is my loss.

Becca.

The thought strikes me that my circumstances may apply to her too. What if she's been home all along? She could have been watching me drown my sorrows in the very bath where hers caught up with her. Guilt sits heavy in my chest amongst the hope. Despite everything, that possibility is comforting. Maybe she was never gone forever. I might never know. My fingers find the red butterfly that dangles from my right ear; this and her silver thumb rings were the only things I could bear to take from her room. I'm glad I snagged the earring on a whim before I left.

With that small comfort to steady me, I keep walking, forcing my feet forward, to distract myself.

After touring the rest of the house, I spread myself out on the couch and watch the day pass by through the window. I always thought it was odd how people would say your life flashes before your eyes when you die. I didn't experience that, but now, sitting here with nothing but time, I let myself wade through the past. Almost like revisiting an old favorite movie. I fast forward through the shittier parts, I'll revisit them later—what else do I have to do—but right now, I need to remember the good. Laying here reminds me of those days when Becca would let me crash her movie marathons with her friends. They'd pile a bunch of blankets and pillows on the floor, then set up an array of the best damn snacks I've had in my life. The movie line-up was always solid, too. It was usually a mix of rom-coms and period pieces–Pride and Prejudice (2005 version, of course) or Moulin Rouge were always included and I was secretly thrilled. Becca knew that though. She also saw that sometimes, even a loner needed some company. She'd been a good sister.

GONER

Whoever implied that death was peaceful clearly hadn't fucking experienced it. In reality, it was absolutely maddening. It's Hell.

Time is a muddy thing that clings to me and distorts my sense of the world around me—of which there is very little of, might I add. I attempted to leave this house behind, I'd hoped to go home and see if my sister might be there, but I wasn't able to. I made it off the porch and down the patch of dirt that served as a driveway, but when I walked into the tree line, I ended up right back inside the house.

Determined as ever, I tried a few times more, but any time I would push the boundary, near-shattering pain coursed through me like my insides were being torn apart and my head was going to explode. I don't know what's worse, that or the endless emptiness and isolation.

The lack of any and all stimulation is getting to me, and yet, there's no escape. For who knows how long, it's just been me and my thoughts. I relive the last moments of my life over and over again. The suction of my knife in their organs, the sharp slice of the blade ramming into me, and then the hollowness of my last breaths.

As the reality of my situation sinks in, I even start to hope my sister isn't still here, lingering in this fucked up space between life and death. I would never wish this miserable existence, or lack thereof, on her. I hope she's somewhere better. She has to be. Becca was kind; fuck whatever religious zealots had to say about taking your own life. If there was a God, he should have protected her. She might not have believed in anything either, but Becca was undeniably a good person. That had to count for something, didn't it?

My gut turns as memories of my sister in that bathtub flash across my mind for the millionth time. I would give anything for a distraction. Instead, I'm stuck with the discomfort my emotional turmoil causes without the physical relief it craves. I give it a pathetic shot, pacing around the house as if I don't know every single centimeter by now. And when the frustration mounts, I find myself throttling the knob of the front door and making my way outside to pace in the open air. At least it's a change of scenery. But no matter where I go, the stillness and silence that presses in around me never give me any space. It's just me and my misery.

Come out, come out, wherever you are

CHAPTER THREE

Aiden

February 17th, 2020 - One Month Later

Over the last . . . fuck who knows how long, I've been trying my best to track each sunrise, but even that proves difficult at times. My existence just seems to stretch on and on, no matter how much I wish it would end. But then, the cleaning crew shows up and life—or death, I guess—becomes infinitely more interesting again.

They do a full scrub-down of the long-empty house. I follow them from room to room with the rapt attention of someone watching the best movie they'd ever seen—my boredom has reached painfully unprecedented levels, so it's truly entertaining. They removed the evidence of neglect and the flecks of blood that had dried in the kitchen's grout. The rogue stains on the wood floors of the entryway and bedroom were too far gone, but nobody but me would know what they were from as small and blackened as they were after all the time that's passed. When they finish, lemon and bleach linger in the air. It's a welcome change from dank moisture and dust.

    What feels like a few days later, the owner of the property—an average-looking man with a shaved head and nasally voice—and four women enter. He's ready to rent it out again. Two of the women—Sarah and Elle—have that classic California girl look: blond and thin. However the other two are more my type. The one named Ava has shaggy plum hair that brushes her shoulders and thick legs that are a testament to the resilient stitching on the ripped black pants she wears. The other, Skye, has a similar build to the Ava, who's attractive enough, but it's Skye who utterly captivates me. I'm immediately sucked in by her sad, disinterested brown eyes framed by thick cat eyeliner and short, jet-black bangs. Mid-length hair falls across her chest where the Nirvana logo is prominently displayed. *Would you look at that… We already have something in common.* I smirk shamelessly as I continue my perusal of her delicious body down to the black and white platform sneakers on her feet. I can't help but become momentarily fixated on how her voluptuous ass peeks out from her denim, high-waisted shorts and fishnets. I'm grateful she can't see me because that means I don't have to worry about looking like a complete ass drooling over her. Everything about Skye draws me forward as they walk through the viewing. The tension in her shoulders and the flexing of her hands at her sides makes me wonder whether she can feel me there, always just a few steps behind her.

Everything about her has me salivating, from the knowledge that we share a favorite band to the confident, 'I don't give a shit about anything' attitude. But what makes her exactly what I need is the heavy melancholy that clings to her. Its tentacles reach for me, and I let them wind their way around my limbs and sink their tips into my skin. As they spear into me, it sparks something I've never felt before, a powerful and raw need for another person. I feel her inside of me down to the very pit of my soul. It shivers, aching with the need for more of her. What I've been allowed is far too small of a taste. I want to drink her sorrow until I'm wasted off it; I want to consume her every worry and delight in the sourness of it; I want to dig my way into her head and put down roots she can't ever pull out.

For the first time in forever, I feel like I have purpose—even if she hasn't acknowledged my presence. I know with all surety that she's the reason I've been stuck here waiting. The truth of it settles deep within me, temporarily soothing the unfamiliar ache that pulses through me with every step I take.

"The listing said it's available on the 30th. Is there any chance of moving that up?" Skye asks the landlord and her soft, husky voice is so alluring that I nearly miss his response.

"Yeah. I could have you in as early as next week if you take it." He shrugs and keeps walking, leading us downstairs toward the front door. "Just let me know as soon as you can, I have a few other interested groups."

I roll my eyes at the lie but keep my attention on Skye as she makes eye contact with her roommates, having a silent discussion I want in on. I need them to move in. I hope they see the charm behind the peeling exterior. My stomach turns with hunger. I'm ravenous for her. I'll wither away if she doesn't come back. I pray and plead to whatever higher power has put me here that she'll sign that lease.

A week later, she shows up and fills the emptiness around me with her all-consuming presence. Despite the heaviness of her innate sadness, I feel lighter than I have since Becca's death. I start to think that maybe my misery is over, but then the reality of my situation sinks in. The torture is just beginning. My true obsession with her and the reality that she doesn't know I exist, and most important, the fact that there's nothing I can do about it.

Or is there?

If I'm forced to remain a ghost in this house, I might as well lean into it. I'm not proud of it, but desire can drive you to uncharacteristic things.

It starts innocently enough. I'm just looking for acknowledgment. I move things around in her room, lay next to her in the bed while she sleeps, and close cabinets and drawers when she's cooking. But I never get the reaction I'm looking for. Either she's purposely ignoring me, or she simply hasn't noticed, too lost in the haze of a steady mix of drugs and alcohol that I have watched her ingest on a daily basis. I don't know which is more frustrating. While she's numb, I'm on fire with desperation.

With no other options, I shift my attention to her roommates. Maybe she'll finally notice then. Or, at the very least, I'll have something else to focus on. I need an outlet after all this time sitting in purposeless isolation. I start out small, tame – moving their things around and opening doors and drawers that should be closed – the same tricks I've tried with Skye. They too write it all off with barely a second glance.

Do these women truly have no survival instincts? Haven't they seen horror movies?

I know Skye has; they're her favorite. I've spent countless hours at the end of her bed watching them with her. When those tactics prove ineffective, I go for the real scares — opening their doors when they've just laid down in bed and pulling their blankets off. That, they can't ignore. I grow bold, breaking dishes right in front of them, slamming their vanity mirror shut while they're brushing their teeth. I even dare to take a phone out of Ava's hand and throw it against the wall. That's the final straw; they call a roommate meeting.

"I already emailed the landlord," Sarah starts, "he told me we could break the lease if we find someone to move in here. He tried to convince us to stay with a lower rent offer, but there's no way I'm staying in this creepy ass house."

"I agree with Sarah. We can't live here, it's not safe." Elle's eyes shift around the room as she wraps her knit blanket tighter around her shoulders.

"Shocker," Skye mumbles under her breath, ignoring the glare Elle sends her way.

"I don't want to be here anymore either. Do you think we can find someone quickly?" Ava pulls out her laptop from under the coffee table.

"Let me get this straight, you all can't stand the idea of being here because you're being haunted, but you want to trick someone else into living here when it's quote, unquote, not safe."

"It's either we stay here, or we get someone else in. What other choice do we have?" Sarah gets defensive. I make a mental note to make sure the rest of her time here is downright miserable for even suggesting they leave in the first place. Right now, I'm too busy trying to stop the bleeding wound that's opening up inside me as my connection to Skye is being forcibly removed. I'm going to lose her. This is the end.

"You know what, I'll make it easy for you." She stands. "I'm staying. You're all free to go somewhere you feel safe, but I like it here. I'm comfortable and I'm not moving my shit again." The other women call after her, but she ignores them as she goes up to her room.

After they've all cooled down, Ava goes up to talk to her.

"I've made up my mind; I already emailed the landlord and let him know I'll take the lower rent offer. He gave me an even bigger discount since it's just me."

"Skye, why are you so adamant about staying here? I don't want something bad to happen to you." Ava scoots closer to Skye on the bed and grabs her hand.

Sky allows it, but her arm is rigid. "This ghost hasn't bothered me or hurt me yet. Why would that change?"

"Well, clearly, it's been devoting all its attention to the three of us," Ava insists.

"I appreciate the concern, but I'm not leaving. I'm

COME OUT COME OUT

comfortable here, I feel *at home* here. It's been too long since I've had that. I won't give that up because some restless spirit is getting some kicks out of messing with you all, I'm sorry." Skye holds her roommate's eye contact, making herself clear.

Ava lets out a long sigh but realizes she can't tell another grown woman what to do. "Just take care of yourself. Promise me you'll call me if something happens. You'll always have somewhere to stay with me."

"I promise." Skye's eyes fall to where their hands are connected. "It'll be fine."

When her roommate leaves, she relaxes back into the bed with a look of contentment on her face. I think she sees the opportunity that's presented itself—relief from the pressure to always pretend.

I have a front-row seat for the show she puts on for her roommates. Before she opens the door, she takes a deep breath, draws her lips upward like some puppet being controlled by marionette strings, and rolls her shoulders back—as if strengthening her spine will better bear the weight of the burden she's about to undertake. Her mask is a heavy one, the role demanding.

She's always *fine* around them. There's nothing to worry about, she tells them as she cuts herself behind closed doors to ease her suffering. Work is good. Classes are going

- 42 -

well. She's buried with work and always racing to meet deadlines, she can't hang out. *Sorry.* Meanwhile, she's drinking until she's too tired to worry anymore and her lips and heart go numb.

They buy the act. Just like most shallow friendships of convenience, they never pry, because if they do, they'll see that she's rotting from within. Regardless, I'm falling for her. My heart belongs to a living ghost who has one foot on the other side of the veil at all times and is slowly creeping closer. *My little wraith.*

I often wondered if I was the one haunting her or if it was the other way around.

I see right through the facade. I'm eager to destroy the mask, get under her skin, and taste her brand of intoxication. I'll make myself sick with it, I don't care. I just want to be with her, to be *seen* by her.

GONER

March 13th, 2020 - One Month Later

Now that her roommates have moved out, I get to see so much more of her. And, god damn, is she tragically beautiful. I get my wish; the mask quickly falls away, the curtain closes, and the show's over.

COME OUT COME OUT

She lets herself be free, and in turn, she's free with me. Without the pressure of judging her, she allows herself to stay up and sleep in as late as she wants to. She blares her music and dances around the house half-naked, and she spends more of her time creating, even when she's not working for clients. I love it when she takes her laptop out on the porch with her morning coffee and just sits there designing for a few hours. It's incredible to watch her take basic images you wouldn't usually look twice at and create layers upon layers until she has something beautiful. I love it, but it also makes me miss my own art. It'd turned into something far darker than ever before after Becca died – all heavy black ink and eerie imagery – but I still loved the pieces I made, even got one tattooed on me. I stroke the lips and long tongue that drip down into the word "ART" on my arm.

All the days aren't like that, though. Sometimes, she wakes up and curses the fluttering of her lids, the air that fills her lungs, and the pulse of her regretfully pumping heart. On those days, she doesn't get out of bed other than to go to the bathroom. It's a relief when she even remembers to eat or drink water. Those days seem to go on forever as I fixate on the rise and fall of her chest, aching with the need to dry her tears and pull her closer until she's absorbed into my own body and I can protect her from everything that has and will ever hurt her. But no matter how much I wish it were possible, I'm forced to sit there, helpless to care for her other than simply being there, which she's still utterly oblivious to. Those days are almost, *almost*, as bad as when I was trapped here on my own.

But today is one of those lucky mornings where the haze has cleared and she isn't numb yet. We slip into our own routine and I'm thoroughly enjoying it. When she gets out of bed after an hour of scrolling, she takes off the tiny bra and shorts she always sleeps in, revealing her creamy skin that's flushed with proof of life. Her body is delicious with her heavy breasts, round stomach, pillowy arms, and lush thighs that I desperately want to feel pressing into the hardness of my own much narrower hips. Everything about her body is soft, the complete opposite of the barbed wire she keeps around her heart.

I spend the next thirty minutes watching the boiling shower water lick across her skin and redden her ass like I want to. Standing stark against the steam, she's a soon-to-be fallen angel basking amongst the clouds.

Each day, I'm more determined to save her from the fall.

I peer through the flimsy shower curtain as she lathers up her hands and sweeps the slick soap across her arms, then her legs, and finally under her stomach. On a gasp, her eyes droop closed. I shift forward from where I sit on the bathroom counter, suddenly needing a better view. With each fleeting touch, her long lashes flutter against her cheeks as she becomes more and more sensitive. I watch with rapt attention, my gaze homing in on the moment her nipples pucker and her back slowly arches into the warm air. Her panting breaths mingle with the steam and I stick my tongue out in a failed attempt to catch them just to have the smallest taste of her. Her brow furrows and her eyes squeeze closed in pleasure as she pinches and tugs her nipples, moaning at the attention of her own expert hands. I nearly drool as I watch the water droplets drip from the dusky pink tips of her down-turned breasts. I follow their descent to the river that runs between the glistening lips of her cunt as she starts to rub and tease her clit. All I want is to drop to my knees and drink from her greedily like she's the fountain of youth.

It's a fucking glorious sight to behold, her pleasure. When her lust-filled gaze stares through the open curtain, I let myself fall into the fantasy that she knows I'm watching, that this is part of our little game.

"Yes, yes, yes. Oh god, right there. Yes." The words are rushed and slurred as she pushes herself closer to an orgasm. Her intent brown eyes hold me captive and I can't help but indulge myself by participating. I pull out my cock and stroke it slowly — grateful I can still feel my own touch, if nothing else. Her mouth falls open on a whimper and I imagine how it would feel to ram my cock past those pouty lips and into the warmth of her throat. I fist myself tighter, almost painfully, when I think about how those needy moans would feel vibrating around my throbbing cock. I fixate on her fingers when she pinches her clit. Her eyes squeeze shut and her jaw clenches as she comes, reminding me that my girl likes a little pain with her pleasure.

    What I wouldn't give to actually experience it.

My Binxie boy

CHAPTER FOUR

Skye

March 13th, 2020 - The Same Day

I can still hardly believe that the landlord is letting me stay here even though he's only getting a third of the rent since I'm here by myself. I contemplate his motives as I chug the rest of my beer and take a bump of coke off the edge of my house key. Maybe he knows he can't rent out a haunted house – something he conveniently left out when he rented to us – but part of me suspects he has some cam set up in here so he can watch me and jerk it. Maybe he's selling videos of me finger fucking myself to recoup his losses. Whatever. Let him. What the hell do I care?

All that matters to me was that I have a roof over my head and nobody bothers me. As fucked up as it is, it kind of turns me on thinking about the possibility of a cam watching me. Now I'm intrigued by the idea. My gaze flits around the bedroom, searching for some clue of it. I don't see one. *But I can still pretend, right?* That quickie in the shower didn't quite take the edge off and this is more fun than doing that project I've been putting off. I check my calendar and confirm I have a few more days before it's due to the client, then take another bump.

    I peel my oversized cropped sweatshirt over my head in a mock striptease. I run my fingers over my sheer lace bralette, my nipples harden under my fingertips immediately. I roll the straps off each shoulder and run my fingers over my bare breasts in a way that makes my back arch. I stare into the mirror like there's someone standing behind it watching me. A shiver runs down my spine at how real the sensation feels. I turn around so the imaginary voyeur can see my fantastic ass as I inch my joggers down to reveal a black mesh thong. I bend over and slap my own ass so it sends a jiggle through both cheeks down my thighs. I always love the way it looks when other women do it.

    Fuck. Women, everything about us is so hot.

    My legs shake with need; I can barely stand it now. Crawling up onto the bed, I lean back on my forearms and rest my feet on the frame spreading my legs open so I'm entirely on display. I slip my fingers into my panties and pull them to the side. My pussy glistens in the reflection. I need to touch myself so badly that I altogether abandon the idea of watching myself in the mirror and fall back, using one hand to hold myself open as the other fingers play and pick up a rhythm that has me panting. In my mind, I can still see it all. A mysterious stranger that's a million times hotter than my middle-aged landlord watching the feed of the camera that's so conveniently placed in front of my bed. They fist their cock and tug it in heavy strokes as they watch me rock my hips to meet my fingers. I let my moans echo off the walls of this old, empty house suddenly wishing there was someone here to hear me, to put their hand over my mouth, to suffocate me 'til I'm on the verge of passing out.

My left hand leaves my pussy and cups my mouth, muffling my cries. I press harder and upward, mostly covering my nose. My breath becomes shallower. It's so fucking heady. My fingers pump faster, crashing desperately into my pussy as I chase my orgasm before I pass out.

I should probably be more concerned about the tightness in my chest or the fact that I feel like I'm levitating. But I'm not. The blow and beer chase those worries away before they fully form and all I feel is the pounding of my own heart. The steady bass that pumps through my speakers accompanies the sucking rasp of my failing breath in a symphony of chaos. *I'm so close.*

I crash back down to reality when I hear the door slam loudly downstairs.

My hand leaves my face, but the fingers inside me freeze right where they are. Hot fear courses through me like lava. The shock immediately clears my head of the cocktail of drugs and alcohol. The ghost has been dormant since my roommates moved out. Could it be turning on me now that they're no longer here to torment? I really hope it's the ghost and not some murderer. I sit in complete stillness for what feels like an eternity. Nothing else happens, but something feels *different*. It feels like someone is here with me, like the house is holding its breath just as much as I am.

The door bouncing against the wall frays my nerves as I want for . . . something. "Hello?" I call out in a trembling voice before I can think about how bad of an idea that is. It's such a naive-girl-in-a-horror-movie mistake. God dammit. I've watched all the classics; I always thought I'd be a final girl. Guess I was wrong.

I sit up silently, putting my clothes back on quickly. My eyes search everywhere for some kind of weapon. I grab the sheers I recently used on my DIY haircut from my vanity. These will do. My cat, Binx, meows his dissent as I prepare to leave the room, but he remains crouched down on his haunches and staring at me with wide, green eyes.

A deep breath rattles my chest as I work up the courage to peek around the corner of my open door. When I see there's no one immediately outside I creep forward to try to see over the bannister to the living room. Nothing. Maybe it was just the wind that blew the door open. If someone broke in, wouldn't they have gone directly to where the music was blaring from? If the ghost wanted my attention, wouldn't it have done more?

Seconds pass as I hold my breath and strain my ears, waiting for any sound to confirm or deny whether someone is here.

I can't sit up here and ignore the fact that best case scenario, my front door is inviting any weirdo to walk in, or worst case scenario, a potential murderer is lurking around my house waiting to kill me. My pussy wakes up a bit at the first idea and I scold myself. What the fuck is wrong with me? A lot honestly but that's nothing new. Coming from a family where nobody wants to talk about emotions unless it's an outburst of explosive anger, I learned to keep everything locked up inside, apparently that really fucks a person up. And when that emotional repression makes you lose your interest in opening up to or investing in other people? Well then, you're really done for. I've gone through several therapists who can confirm that I'm a difficult case who continues to get in my own way. Honestly, I'm just fucking tired.

I refocus and start down the staircase, careful to avoid the two stairs after the first landing that groan whenever I step on them. The door is wide open and the wind is whistling through the trees. It bounces off the wall as I stare into the darkness that is the woods outside the house. I do a quick sweep of the porch then come back in, slamming and locking it behind me.

I let out a laugh at my own expense. I should really stop watching scary movies, but I won't – no way I could give up my regular rewatches of the Ring and Midsommar. My heart is pounding like it might actually claw its way through my chest. Cold sweat coats my skin uncomfortably. I need a damn drink.

I walk back through the living room towards the kitchen, but as I step onto the freezing tile floor, my stomach drops and true fear spikes through me. The hottest guy I've ever seen is sitting at my kitchen table drinking straight from the bottle of dark rum I'd left out. My eyes travel over his tattooed arms on display, thanks to his sleeveless black tee, that has a bleeding hand covered in thorns holding a rose on fire in the center. On one arm, fluid ink creates a marbled effect that reminds me of an oil spill. The dark ink is a striking contrast to his pale skin. On the bicep of his other arm sits a pair of open lips with protruding fangs over a long tongue winding out, bleeding into long drips down his forearm, forming the word 'ART' on his wrist. The drips flow down onto the back of his hand to an eye in the center of an intricate spider web. I continue my exploration, briefly landing on the one that says 'GONER' on his throat, then the thin hoop that accents his otherwise symmetrical nose, and finally I find his gorgeous blue-grey eyes framed by messy brown hair drinking me in with equal parts desire and something that looks like shock. As if he isn't the one who broke into *my* house? I'm both startled and intrigued by his audacity.

There go those stellar self-preservation instincts.

He doesn't move or say anything to me, he just sets the bottle on the table and rakes his eyes over me in a way that makes heat flush up my neck into my face. My mind is stumbling over itself, processing the fact that someone broke into my house and that this person is unbelievably fucking hot. When he leans forward and hangs his ring-laden hands between his legs like he belongs here, words finally find their way to my mouth.

"Who the fuck are you and what are you doing in my house?" I half-yell over the music that I forgot to turn off. On second thought, I pull the sheers back out of my sweatshirt pocket, pointing them in his direction.

He looks up at me through the unruly hair hanging in his face. "It sounded like a party, thought I'd crash it." He shrugs like he didn't break and enter into a single woman's home in the middle of basically nowhere.

I take a step back when he sits up straight. "What are you even doing out this way? We're, like, at least half a mile from the next house and there isn't anything else around here. There's literally no reason for someone to be in this area."

The left side of his unfairly plump lips turn up, equal parts flirtation and danger. The seduction of his smile causes a chill to spread over my skin and my heart to start pumping faster. But it's not fear, it's so much worse. *I want him.* "I was out for a walk. It's peaceful out here."

"You really expect me to believe that? You're just out here for a casual stroll. Give me a fucking break."

The intruder picks up the shot glass I'd set out for myself and pours rum almost all the way to the rim. I shift on my feet momentarily. I can feel my anxiety creeping back in and I can't have that. *If he was going to kill me, he would have already done it, right?* I weigh the pros and cons of having one shot — just to take the edge off.

I have a high tolerance, it'll be fine. I reason.

I sigh and take a seat across from him, not dropping my sheers. This might be questionable but I'm not letting my guard down yet.

His blue eyes narrow on them and he has the gall to smirk. "Thinking about using those on me? I thought those were just for you?"

The question stumps me for a minute, and I quickly search the blades for blood from the last time I brought them across my ankle. Nothing. A weird thing someone could guess, unless he meant using them to stab me. Fear turns my stomach momentarily, but then Binx finally turns up, winding through my legs. He doesn't react negatively to the stranger sitting at my table – he barely takes note of his presence at all – which slightly puts me at ease even though it probably shouldn't. But animals can usually sense people who are going to harm you, right?

Our fingers touch briefly, his hands are a bit chilly and I feel the electricity of our clear mutual attraction zip through me. I try to ignore it. It's one thing to take a shot with a stranger who broke into your house, it's a whole other thing to fuck them. The spicy rum burns down my throat as it makes its way to my empty belly.

The intruder pours another, his intent eyes daring me to deny him. It's then that I notice the dark navy polish on his nails. *Hot.*

My leg bounces under the table. I want to feel numb so badly. Losing myself in the all-encompassing feeling of someone's body on mine is such an easy way to escape my thoughts, to disappear, even if it's only for a little while. But I also don't want to end up in chopped-up pieces beneath my floorboards. If I'm going to be taken out, I want it to be on my own terms.

His raspy voice breaks through my indecision. Somehow, it's a balm on my nerves; there's a familiarity to it. "Just drink it. Unless you want me to leave? I will if that's what you want?"

My gut twists and my leg bounces faster. As much as I know I should tell him to get the fuck out and not come back, I find that I truly don't want him to leave. How sad that I'm that lonely and desperate. Another reason to just take the fucking shot.

It tastes like bad decisions.

"You can stay for now. But if I say you have to leave, you leave. Got it?"

He holds his hands up in feigned innocence. "Of course, pretty girl."

"Ew. Another rule, don't fucking call me that."

"God, I love that fucking mouth." Tenderness softens

his gaze.

"Nobody asked you." I'm embarrassingly at a loss for words.

"Cute." He scoots his chair closer to the table and turns to face me head-on. "Take the shot already."

The command laced in his tone sends a flood of heat between my thighs that only worsens as we stare at each other. He's unfairly pretty and I'm positive he knows it when he runs his tongue across his lower lip without breaking eye contact. I rub my thighs together and pray to any divine entity that he can't see me shifting beneath the table. I don't need to give him any ideas. I take the shot, hoping it will also chase away the desperation for his touch that's starting to take over my mind.

"Should we play a drinking game?" The intruder's gaze searches the room.

I huff a laugh. "Don't tell me you're some kind of frat boy or something."

"Absolutely fucking not." He grimaces. "But what else are we going to do, sit here and stare at each other?"

"I mean, you could leave?" I suggest and my stomach protests as my pulse skyrockets.

He simply deadpans and leans forward so his elbows are on the table and his arms are stretched toward mine. My attention is again drawn to the hand tattoo; the web and eye are so detailed they look like someone somehow copied and pasted the real thing to his skin.

Eventually, I give in. "What do you propose we play?" I realize I'm subconsciously mirroring his posture; our fingers are only a few inches away from touching. My pinky twitches and his gaze follows it so briefly I almost miss it.

He smiles widely. "Never have I ever. Each round, the loser has to take something off." A thick, dark brow raises in challenge.

This fucker. "Wow, how original." I laugh and a small smile breaks free despite myself. I try to recover my air of indifference by rolling my eyes, but inside, my heart flutters and wetness drips between my thighs.

"Never have I ever fingered myself."

I scoff. "Fucking cheater. Are you that desperate to see some tits?" I take off my sweatshirt first; at least I still have a bralette on.

He shakes his head and takes another shot.

"Never have I ever broken into a stranger's house."

His jaw ticks but he removes his shirt.

My throat dries at the sight of the smooth planes of his body. He's toned in the way that naturally slim men are. He has abs and pecs, but they aren't puffed up with layers of bulk.

"Never have I ever," his eyes pierce through me like a hook in a fish's mouth, "wanted to fuck someone who broke into my house."

My mouth pops open, but no sound comes out. I can't even deny it, I'm soaked. I remove my black joggers, leaving me in just my bra and panties. "Fucker."

"There we go, progress." He leans forward, elbows on his knees. "Honesty is good for the soul, love."

"Never have I ever been so desperate to fuck someone that I make them play an immature drinking game." I level him a glare, but my smile gives away my poker face.

"Desperate is a strong word, but I'll let you have this round." The metal tinkling of his belt being undone has my heart pumping. Maybe I'm the desperate one. His dick is hard when he stands in just his black briefs. He laughs when he catches where my stare has drifted but picks right back up where he left off. "Never have I ever—"

"Fuck it." I stand and wrap my hand around his neck, bringing his mouth to mine in an urgent, needy kiss. He tastes like spice and danger, and it makes my pussy throb with each swipe of our tongues.

Abruptly he breaks away from me and rounds the table. Determined, he slams us up against the fridge, shaking the bottles inside from the force of it. My legs lift and lock around his narrow waist and my drenched panties are pressed against his stomach.

"I'm no quitter, baby. I play fair and square." He grinds into me. "Never have I ever wanted a stranger to fuck me roughly 'til I come so hard I can barely speak."

All I can hear is my thumping heart and harsh breaths and I try to tamp down my desire. But I can't. I pull off my lace bralette and the cool air pricks at my hardened nipples.

His hand grips under my chin as he leans back, looking his fill. "I can't wait to bury my face between those." He leans forward and grinds into me again. "Your turn, love."

"Never have I ever, ah—" I'm cut off as he grinds harder, his torso forcefully pressing into my sensitive pussy. "Oh my God, please, just fuck me."

He pinches my cheeks together painfully, causing tears to spring to my eyes. "Are you forfeiting?"

"Yes." I force the words out against his hold.

"Then I get to pick the next game. It's my favorite one." A wicked gleam sparks in his eyes, but it only amplifies my need. "But don't worry, I'm going to fuck your needy little pussy first."

The next kiss is hungry, like he's been waiting to feast on me for so much longer than a mere half hour. He doesn't hesitate to dig in. Lips suck and tease along my skin, paying special attention to my collarbones, breasts, and the tops of my thighs. It feels like forever and no time at all has passed as I lose myself in the possessive hold his body has on mine. I'm sweating, panting, moaning with need. I can't wait any longer.

"I need you inside me." My fingers find their way into his briefs and his dick springs free. Pre-cum glistens at the head of his cock. My hand strokes reverently up and down the shaft and I turn my gaze to his. "Fuck me before I regain my sense of preservation and kick you out." I spread my legs wider in invitation and wrap my hand around the back of his neck to pull him closer.

He slides us over to the counter so my ass rests on the ledge, pulls my panties to the side, and then lines his cock up to my entrance without hesitation. "Self-preservation is over-rated. Don't you agree?"

I nod and thrust my hips up making my intentions clear. "Prove it."

"With pleasure." He groans as he slams into me.

My assumption was right, he does know how to use it. I have the fleeting thought that there's a distinct chill in the air that creeps up my spine and clings to my skin despite our closeness, but then his cock hits that spot inside me, making my thoughts scatter, my toes curl painfully, and my head falls back. Immediately, his hand latches around my throat and forces my gaze to his.

"Look at me," he thrusts deeply into me to punctuate the command, "I want you to see me."

I grip his arm and nod in eager understanding as my mind zeroes in on the way my pulse thumps excitedly against his palm. The part of my brain that processes fear went haywire long ago because all I can think is how goddamn hot it is that this person I don't even know holds my life in his hands. I don't know anything about him, he could easily cut off my oxygen or snap my neck. Just the thought makes me impossibly wetter. All the doctors I've seen over the last two decades had every right to be seriously concerned about my mental health. It's the first time I fully agree.

A searing pain brings me back to the moment as he bites down on my nipple and tugs. I wind my fingers in his hair and grind my hips, encouraging him to do it again. He does. It should be unsettling how well he seems to know me already, but it's such a relief to sit back and let him take control of my pleasure. I lean forward slightly, forcing his palm against my throat and he adjusts his grip to apply more pressure on each side.

"Do you like that? When I decide how much you can breathe?" He pauses and licks the sensitive space between my neck and chin. "Tell me." His touch lightens ever so slightly.

"Yes. Don't stop," I gasp out. I tighten my fingers in his hair and shift my hips against him, my pussy clenches around his cock the same way he grips my throat.

Placing a sloppy kiss on my lips, he slips his hands behind my knees, opening me wider and hitting even deeper. My head softly bumps against the wood cabinet in rhythm with the punishing thrusts of his hips. Releasing his hair, I dig my nails into his lower back, enjoying the movement of his muscles underneath my fingers.

"Music to my fucking ears," he groans, referring to the snap of his hips against the fat on my thighs and ass that nearly drowns the garbled moans he's driving out of my constricted airway. "Come on, sing for me, baby."

My eyes flutter momentarily, his touch becomes lighter, and his icy gaze holds me here. I whimper at the absence of that delicious pressure.

"You can do better than that." A devious smirk is the only warning I get before he starts pounding into me without restraint. A strong finger presses and teases my clit with a masterfulness that has an endless stream of begging falling from my lips as I come violently around him. My breath stutters, my eyes squeeze shut, and my jaw tenses as I cling to consciousness that this mind-bending orgasm is trying to steal from me.

"I told you to keep your eyes open," he grinds out between clenched teeth. Instead of spilling into me like I fear, he pulls out, drags me off the counter, and forces me down to my knees in front of him.

I look up at the man I should be afraid of, holding his stare, and stick my tongue out expectantly. Cum coats my tongue and throat and I swallow every last drop, never breaking eye contact.

"Now this." He points to his lower abdomen and the base of his cock that's still dripping with my release. I lick it all off without any hesitation. The way he takes command of my mind and my body is the most peaceful I've felt in years, maybe ever. It's a drug I want to hit again and again, and I fully intend to chase the high.

Who the fuck is this man, and where did he come from?

My little wraith

CHAPTER FIVE

Aiden

MARCH 13th, 2020 - The Same Day

Every fiber of my being was frantically screaming at me to keep my hands on Skye and never let her go. I remind myself that I'm still able to feel the warmth of her for now as I pull her back up to her feet. Her full brown eyes drink in my body; she's not ready for the night to end either. It's time for another game.

"100, 99, 98 . . ." I pause my counting, "I would run and hide if I were you." Her mouth falls open as she looks around for her clothes, but I'm not about to let her cover up that beautiful body I plan to mark as mine. "You don't need those. As soon as I find you, I'm going to fuck you. Now run." I emphasize my point by slapping my hands against her ass

COME OUT COME OUT

and kissing her roughly. My hand on her neck pulls us apart and urges her out of the kitchen. "97, 96, 95 . . ." Skye's rushed steps on the wood and up the stairs narrow down the hiding places. I distract myself from listening any further, so there's still some thrill in our little game when I finally finish counting. "Ready or not, here I come." It feels right to pick up where I left off with the game I started last time I was hunting in this house.

For having been a ghost for several months, I certainly didn't move discreetly. Operating in the limitations of having a corporeal form was already foreign to me; she'll definitely know I'm coming. *I hope it makes her wet.*

As quietly as I can, I enter her bedroom. My eyes scan the space I'm more familiar with than she could ever guess. Immediately, I notice that her duffle bag, usually under her bed, is sticking out slightly. My smile is so wide it's painful as I creep around her room, pretending like I don't already know exactly where she is. I can feel her eyes on me in the mirror and I fight the urge to meet her gaze, continuing my aimless perusal of her dresser. Despite the lingering chill in the air, my cock hardens by the second. I'm eager to sink myself into her, but one final tease is worth the wait. I walk pointedly toward the bedroom door and at the last second, I turn back and grab her ankles from under the bed.

"Wait, no!" Skye shrieks in surprise as I flip her on her back. My erection is painful as I watch her tits and stomach bounce with the force of it.

"Are you okay?" Concern flares within me, overriding the excitement.

"Yes." She breathes heavily and lets out a delirious giggle. I want to capture the sound and take it back to Hell with me to keep me company. "Then, what's the matter?"

"It's my turn to pick the game. You're an intruder, right?" She watches me closely, and I nod my agreement – in her eyes, I am. "I want to feel like your helpless victim." Self-consciousness flickers across her features for a moment, but when I don't object, she continues, "I want you to scare me while you fuck me."

I'm in awe of how much she trusts me, and I don't hesitate to agree even though I've never done anything like this. *For her, I'd do anything.* "Run."

Skye's breath stutters and her eyes grow wide as I loom over her, repeating myself in a low tone I've never heard from myself before. This time, she scrambles back until she's out from beneath me and takes off at a run. I count to ten in my head and start after her; I've always been a fast runner.

"You can run, but I'm going to get what I came here for." Before she can descend the stairs, I wrap my arms around her waist and pull her back against me. "Too slow," I grit out against her ear. I want to revel in the sensation of her plush body pressed against mine, but I'm making her fantasy come true right now. Skye struggles a bit, but there's no real fight in her; she wants this.

I fist her hair and push her down to her knees on the top step. My lips tickle her ear as I whisper, "Do as I say, and you won't get hurt. Put your palms on the stairs two steps down, now."

Slowly, she eases forward. I can feel her battling her self-preservation. When her palms are flat on the wood stairs, I loom over her. "Hold on," I command. My cock jumps at the sight of her white knuckles wrapped over the step's edge and the quivering of her arms as she holds herself up with adrenaline coursing through her.

"What are you doing?" Fear and excitement raise the tone of her voice.

"Fucking you within an inch of your life," I answer simply as I part her cheeks for an unobstructed view of that perfect cunt of hers. It glistens with her arousal as I wrap my arms around her thighs and pull her ass back against my face. The moment my tongue swipes through her delicious pussy, all I can think about is quenching my thirst as she fills my mouth. Her distinct taste fills my mouth, a faint sweetness that's a perfectly distilled essence of her sweat mixed with the berries she ate earlier. And paired with the lingering scent of the orange and almond notes of her perfume—I groan as I flatten my tongue to eagerly devour every inch of her.

Skye's moans and cries are music to my ears. The melody accented by the creaking of the decaying wood. I could eat her out forever, but I know that her arms will become tired soon, and I don't want her to actually get hurt, so regretfully, I withdraw my tongue. She whimpers her frustration.

"Don't let go; we wouldn't want you to snap that pretty neck." As the words leave my lips, I lift her legs and wrap them around my waist, then slam into her slick pussy. *Fucking glorious.* This is everything I'd hoped for. I thrust into her again and she cries out.

"You're out of your fucking mind." She groans as her pussy tightens around me. I nearly lose myself over the panic mixed with pleasure that deepens her voice.

"You have no idea." I slam into her again.

"You feel so good, don't stop," she pants between a gasp when her fingers almost slip. "Oh fuck, I'm going to come."

"Don't you fucking dare!" I slow my pace, pulling almost all the way out until she whines in protest. Finally, I give in and double my efforts, slamming into her hard and fast, knowing that even if she doesn't hold on, I would never let her fall. I pump into her like a man who's lost his mind, and I suppose I have. I'm lost in the ecstasy that is *her*. Skye's deliciously fat ass bounces off my stomach, her raven hair slithers on the stairs below her, and her arms become pink and shake as I pound into her. She's entirely at my mercy and it's the best reward I could ask for. She cries and whines from below me, but I don't soften my thrusts. She likes this, needs it. My girl craves the call of death. *My little wraith.* She wants to risk her life. Wants to be taunted on the edge. She wants me to scare her, to hurt her, more than she does herself. *I can set her free.*

As if in agreement, she tightens and pulses around me as she orgasms for the second time tonight. Two more times than I ever thought I'd get to experience with her. The satisfaction of that truth flows through me and burns hot as I pull out and coat her ass in my cum. *Mine.*

Skye collapses on the stairs, her arms weak from the exertion and her limbs loose from her orgasm. I reach around her waist and lift her against me, helping her to her bathroom. Once the water is hot, I pull us in there together, and it's everything I've dreamed of, just being with her in the silence. I lather her soap in my hands and discreetly cup them around my nose, greedily inhaling as much of the intoxicating scent as I can, then begin to spread it over her warm skin. My fingers tingle as I glide them over her back and arms, then gently caress her breasts. I'm lost in the sensation of being able to touch and feel her, combined with the heat of the water pounding down on me. It's everything that I've been missing. She leans into me, letting me care for her as if I'm someone she's known forever, someone she can trust. *I knew I was made for her.*

I'm completely wrapped up in the moment and savoring every second. When she lets me lay next to her in her bed, I watch her drift off and when she finally falls asleep, my mind wanders, fantasizing about all the ways I'd fuck her on every surface of this house that has been my prison but had suddenly become my sanctuary. I don't know how this is possible, but I'm not one to complain. My plans are forming so clearly, and then it all comes crashing down.

One second I'm soaking in the warmth of her skin, and the next, I feel nothing. The heaven of her touch is ripped out of reach once again. Coldness seeps back in, and an indescribable distance stretches between us. I try talking to her, yelling her name, touching her, grabbing her, but nothing works. I'm invisible to her once again. And just like that, I'm all alone.

tastes like bad decisions

CHAPTER SIX

Skye

June 6th, 2020 - Two Months and Three Weeks Later

Flick, click, whisp. Flick, click, whisp. Flick, click, whisp.

The soothing ignition of my lighter drowns out my inner thoughts that have latched onto that craving again. They say it just takes one hit to create an addiction, guess they were right. I'm not in love with him or anything, I'm not delusional, but it's hard to find good dick these days, and damn did he know how to fuck. But it was more than that that has him on my mind nearly three months later. What really has me hooked was the way he seemed so in-tune with my needs. It didn't feel like that was our first time together; he understood what my body needed and how to make it happen. Of course, something like that couldn't last; just my luck. Anything that brings me joy is always fleeting.

I learned that hard truth over and over, like when I had my first boyfriend but then found out in front of the entire class that he'd only asked me out as a joke, or when I moved into the dorms and thought it would be a fresh start, but quickly realized I was still the odd one out of the friend group. I didn't let myself get excited anymore. That way, when the downfall came, it hurt so much less, if I felt anything at all. I tried to avoid that at all costs.

The only illumination in the room is my lighter as its flickering flame hovers just shy of my extended tongue. The anticipation of the burn calls to me like a siren to greedy sailors. I crave that physical pain, an exorcism of the frustration that festers within me. That allure of temporary calm wins out over my good sense and I bring it to the tip. I can only bear it for a few seconds and then drop the lighter on my lap as I berate myself for my weakness. *Fucking coward.*

My mouth salivates, the drool pooling in the open cavity as it tries to counteract the burning. Sweat coats my forehead and my heartbeat thumps angrily. I pull in deep breaths as I keep my tongue suspended above my teeth, savoring the burn. As the pain begins to dull, satisfaction swells with the release.

The thing about self-harm is that the relief is fleeting.

As the shock of it settles, my brain picks back up right where it left off. Self-loathing, loneliness, and the eternal misery of the human condition crowd the space of peace I'd temporarily cleared out. Once again, I'm consumed by what a fool I was to allow myself to find that release in someone else. Someone who left without a word. Another person who didn't want me.

    I bite my tongue to reignite the pain. I earn myself several more minutes of peaceful silence before the trick has run its course. With a sigh, I return to my most reliable outlet, music–especially pop punk. Nostalgia and words long memorized redirect my wayward thoughts. Music isn't just a tool, it's my closest companion. I choose to live alone. I'm one of those people who is naturally inclined toward the solitude. Someone who *should* be left alone. I mean, I have people I'm friendly enough with, Ava and I had lived together for a few years after meeting at our internship, and I have Binx–but there is no one I spend time around regularly. I don't have "friends". It's hard enough to get through a single day with the heaviness that weighs me down, that keeps my smile small and my actions quiet. Being around others means pretending and absolutely exhausting myself, or worse, sucking them into my pit of despair. I learned early that misery is contagious, and people will hate you for it while wrapping you in their arms. Nobody wants to say it out loud, but you're supposed to

COME OUT COME OUT

suffer alone. Suffering isn't pretty, it isn't sweet, and it isn't the watered-down sugary shit people drink up by the gallon every damn day. No, thank you. I'll take my suffering straight up.

Sure, I self-medicate sometimes, but at least I have a say in the dosage, control of the desired outcome. As much control as someone can have as they're dragged toward their undeniable end. Depression is greedy and hard to escape like quicksand and I gave up hope a long time ago. I'm just sinking slowly, enjoying the view with my head just a few inches above water.

Once upon a time I tried. I cried out every time I was in pain. But nobody wants to deal with someone who cries but doesn't know how to explain what's wrong. How is a kid supposed to describe the all-encompassing bleakness that takes your mind and heart in a vice grip and controls your every breath and thought?

The thing people get wrong about being depressed is that it's a feeling of emptiness. It doesn't start out that way, though. It empties you over time, a malicious, clawed hand rooting around inside tearing out chunks and breaking pieces of you until numbing yourself is the only way to escape the never-ending ache.

How does anyone explain that as an adult? I never figured it out. Any attempt I made was met with claims of being dramatic or not trying hard enough to find joy—as if I hadn't chased it relentlessly until my legs gave out. Instead of explaining, I isolated myself. It was so much easier this way.

It's fine; I don't want them around. People only know how to move and shift pain throughout the world. You alleviate theirs and it rests heavily on your shoulders. They take on yours, and the burden breeds resentment. It's an endless cycle that's frankly too much to bear for someone as unwell as I am.

To be fair, I did try living with roommates. It was fine, *for them*. For me, it was a constant hell that required way too much energy—energy I didn't have. While most women would probably be horrified if their roommates all decided to jump ship on their lease because they were convinced the house was haunted; for me, it was an answered prayer.

Besides, I hadn't ever witnessed anything scary. Did some of my things end up in different places than where I thought I'd left them? Sure. But nothing sinister, nothing concerning. The others claimed they'd been woken in the middle of the night to feeling a heavy weight shifting in their bed, breathing in their ears while they were standing in the mirror, and about a dozen other stories of creepy things they'd experienced.

It's not that I don't believe them, I do. I was just never subjected to the same treatment. Whatever it is, it hasn't given me a reason to fear it. Is it fucked up that I find it kind of comforting that maybe I'm not completely alone after all? I shiver at the thought, my eyes scan around the room and my ears strain to hear anything out of the ordinary. I wait, but the seconds tick by without disturbance.

I laugh at myself. It's silly really, to think that all of a sudden it's just going to be around because I'm thinking about it. I shake my head as I slide under the covers. As soon as I pick up my e-reader, thoughts of my potentially haunted house are quickly overrun by those of the sapphic vampire queen and her new bride. God, I love some good smut. It's definitely one of my healthier methods of escape, so I revel in it.

I only make it a few pages before the need begins to build between my legs and at the tips of my nipples. My imagination replaces the bride in question with me.

The beautiful vampire's sharp nails dig into my hips as she bends me forward and traces her tongue between my cheeks and eats my ass. To my dismay, when she turns me over on my back to lick my pussy, she's replaced by my mysterious stranger. His lean frame stands over me, palms holding my knees apart and his possessive blue-gray eyes fixated on me.

I sigh. Even in my fantasies, I can't forget about him. *Instead of fighting it, I let him pick up where she left off.*

His hand clenches around my throat, pinning me to the bed before sinking his cock deep inside me. I'm rough as I plunge my fingers in and out of my pussy, trying to mimic the feeling. As I allow myself to delve deeper into the fantasy, it's almost enough. I pinch my nipples and imagine that it's his strong fingers inflicting the delectable pain. I clench the side of my throat, the prick of my nails adding a sharpness to the steady ache of it. With each thrust of my fingers, I'm pushed closer and closer to the edge of my impending orgasm. Seconds later, it all comes crashing down as my bathroom door flies open, effectively killing the mood by scaring the shit out of me.

I jerk upright and stare into the darkness. My muscles spasm and jump at war with the need to move and the urge to stay right where I am. My legs are no longer shaking from pleasure but from adrenaline and the distinct awareness of eyes on me. The hair at the back of my neck prickles ominously.

It would be really fucking unfair if I'm murdered or possessed, or whatever, without getting to come. They couldn't have at least waited?

Without tearing my eyes from the open door, I reach over and grab the solid candle holder from my bedside table. I slide my panties back into place and slowly get off the bed, jumping when the frame makes a creaking sound.

COME OUT COME OUT

Just get it over with. I bully myself as I take reluctant steps forward with the candle holder raised and ready to swing like a bat. When I reach the end of my bed, Binx is sitting there with his head tilted and eyes wide—the picture of innocence. He lets out a meow and walks into the bathroom fearlessly. With a laugh of relief, I flick on the light and follow him in.

Nothing to see here. The cat must have pushed the cracked door open. *Little cockblocker. Or is it fingerblocker? Whatever.* It might have been imaginary, but still. I glare at him as he prances away, jumps on the bed, and curls up in the warm spot I left behind.

When I finally crawl back into bed next to him after brushing my teeth, the reality of my loneliness presses against me. I pull Binx close and tears spring to my eyes. "I love you, Binxie," I whisper into his now-soaked fur that I've snuggled into.

Cats hate being wet, and yet, he lets me cry into him whenever I need. I know I say I don't have friends, but I guess *he* is my best friend. People used to laugh at me when I said animals were my friends, but what's better than someone who loves you unconditionally? *People* say they love you unconditionally, but usually, they don't. There are limits, unspoken terms and conditions. Binx is the only one in my life who hasn't looked for the loopholes; he's the only one who doesn't run from the ugliness. Instead, he comes to me and offers whatever he can. He's been the most consistent presence in my life since I graduated college. Animals might be small, and we might not speak the same language, but they have the biggest hearts. If I'm being honest, he's the biggest thing that keeps me here.

My little wraith

CHAPTER SEVEN

Aiden

September 30th, 2020 – Three Months and Three Weeks Later

Now that I'd had her, it was so much harder to sit idly by and watch her misery fester. I wasn't egotistical enough to think that I was the cause of the uptick in her self-destructive habits. Although, I'd bet money she still thinks of me—if the increased roughness with which she fucks herself is any indication. I even caught her fingering herself on the stairs once. It seemed like she, too, was wishing we could go back to that night.

The relief, the release, everything I experienced quickly fell through my fingers like fine sand. I've become obsessed with trying to find a way back to her, but no matter how much

COME OUT COME OUT

I try to will it into existence, I'm not able to become corporeal again. I never even believed in ghosts or the other side before I died, but the only thing I've been able to come up with is that the veil had thinned for a short period, allowing me through. I can't be sure and honestly, I don't fucking care, I just want it to happen again. But days turned into weeks, which turned into months without incident. It's bullshit, but I lost control of my life long ago.

I'm angry and have stewed over how unfair it was that I'd got to touch her, taste her, fuck her, hold her, and then it was just over. I'm forced to idly watch the object of my obsession take on her inner demons alone.

It's absolute torture as I sit here and watch her from the other side of the room as she cuts thin white lines that disappear one by one up that lightly freckled nose. The worst part is, Skye stares straight through me, utterly unaware of my presence or my pain that is so tangible to me. It's haunting how this empty stare is such a far cry from the fiery challenge I'd seen in those eyes when she threatened to force me to leave her house.

The absence of that spark gnaws at something deep within me. When she moves on to creating those little knicks in her skin—the ones that won't do any lasting harm, just take the edge off—it spreads like a toxin that surges through me in a torrent of primal need. She isn't allowed to harm what's mine.

If I ever get another chance, I'll teach her that I'm the only one who doles out punishments from now on. I want to take ownership of her pain, become the hand that pushes her under the water when she wants to drown in herself and also when it's time for her to breathe again.

But for now, I'm suffering right along with her with no reprieve from the misery she's forcing us both to endure. I helplessly watch as her consciousness finally fades and the sheets stain red with beads of crimson from her ankles resting underneath the covers. I'm always on edge while she sleeps, wondering when the day will finally come when she doesn't wake up.

GONER

October 31st, 2020 - One Month Later

My jealousy mounts until it's thick in the air around me as I watch Skye put on the tiny black skirt with a lacy bodysuit that shows off every inch of her ample cleavage and thick thighs. If I could suffocate from the toxicity billowing around me, I would. I feel as if I'm about to detonate when her phone dings and she races down the stairs. As her skirt bounces, I catch a glimpse of her bare pussy. She's not wearing any fucking underwear.

"Hey, there." Her voice is sickeningly sweet as she opens the door to reveal a man with, wouldn't you know it, dark hair, blue eyes, and tattoos. She really hasn't forgotten about me. Hope ignites in me before jealousy snuffs it out as a petite woman with pink hair comes up behind him. She's fucking me out of her system with not *one* but *two* people? If I wasn't in shock, my ego might have swelled at the thought.

Watching her suffer was torturous, but witnessing her experience pleasure is the seventh circle of hell. I pace as I watch them undress her. When her tits spring free, the woman immediately starts sucking and playing with them, leading her back to the couch.

I halt my steps as an unexpected hunger grows in my stomach when the man sinks to his knees and flips up her skirt to lap at her pussy. I move to stand behind him, getting a view that's easy to imagine myself in. Her pretty pink pussy is on display for me as my replacement plunges his tongue inside her and works her clit.

"Yes, just like that," she whines and douses any satisfaction I was experiencing. I don't care how hot she looks spread out and writhing in pleasure, I don't want anyone else earning those sounds from her.

No thought goes into it, I simply act as I slam my fist against the switch plate and turn the lights on and off in a quick sequence. That gets their attention. I fling the door open so hard it crashes into the wall with a bouncing thud. They all stare in my direction, mouths open in fear instead of pleasure, but nobody moves. I want them the fuck out of here, *now*. I march over to where his shoes are carelessly discarded and throw them onto the porch one after another, then I grab hers. Finally, their lust-addled minds catch up and register the danger.

"What the hell is going on?" The woman backs away as she stares at the open door, shaking in terror.

"I didn't sign up for this shit. I'm getting the hell out of here," the man yells as he grabs his clothes. "Come on, Sasha." He doesn't look back to see if she's following, but she's hot on his heels. Neither of them even checks to make sure Skye is going to be okay. If I could, I would follow them out and make them apologize to my girl, but their tires are already squealing down the dirt path as they haul ass away from the house.

I slam the door and turn my attention back to Skye who hasn't moved. Lips parted and breath shallow, she waits. I consider trying to interact with her again, but it's clear she can't see me as her eyes dart around in fear. Instead, I find a shred of composure and go upstairs to wait for her to recover from what just happened.

As the minutes pass, guilt sinks its claws into me. It's not that I don't want her to be happy, I just can't bare it if it's not with me. I know it's sick, but I'm not the man I used to be. Our circumstances test the limits of my sanity day after day, this pushed me too far. I hate that I've taken away some semblance of safety she felt here, but there's no going back now. As long as she remains in this house—and I intend to do anything in my power to keep her here—she's mine. Mine to watch. Mine to worship. Mine to hurt. She can't escape me. Not now. Not ever.

I don't know how, but I know in my gut that it's true. I'll have to wait and see how our story unfolds. My time in this home, in the in-between of life and death, has taught me one thing: I can be a patient man if I want something bad enough.

All I have is time, after all.

There's nothing more motivating than the hope that I'll have her in my grasp again. And if—no, *when*— I touch her next time, I'll leave my mark, so she can never doubt how much I want her again. She'll learn who she belongs to.

My Binxie boy

CHAPTER EIGHT

Skye

November 1st, 2020 – The Next Day

My eyes are heavy and my mind is more sluggish than usual as I finally turn off the light I left on overnight. I'm not sure if it helped me sleep or made it worse. I did everything I could to avoid drifting off but eventually, exhaustion had won out once the adrenaline waned. The stiffness in my neck and the throbbing in my back are evidence of that.

Despite my discomfort, I find that I can't move. My fingers clench around the covers and my limbs are locked with the aftershocks of terror. Even my lungs are hesitant to expand and contract, as if the slightest movement might summon *it*. I swallow thickly as my temperature rises. The longer I remain still, the higher the tension in my room rises. I wait and wait,

COME OUT COME OUT

but all there is is silence. I don't let my guard down though. The house is holding its breath, caught in a custody battle between the two beings that now occupy it.

God I really have to pee; this is such bullshit.

I squirm in the sheets as I weigh my options. It hasn't bothered me since those two randos I invited over left, but it also might be lying in wait. I really am not in the mood to be possessed or whatever it is this ghost has in mind for me. But I also don't want to die covered in my own urine.

How many times do I have to learn, *dating apps never lead to anything good.* Between the guy who nearly flipped the table when I beat him at Scrabble after a few drinks to the bubbly brunette who wouldn't stop talking about how much she couldn't wait to start a family *on the first date,* I'd never gotten any payout from the effort it took to weed through all the weirdos.

The pressure in my bladder, my emotional hangover, and the absurdity of my situation come to a head and I fling the covers off me. I stomp into my bathroom, slam the door, lock it, and finally, let the relief flood through me. I know a lock probably, scratch that, *definitely* isn't going to keep a ghost out, but it's the best solution I've got.

I stare into the water as I lather and rinse my hands, then force myself to meet my own gaze in the mirror. Dark, swollen bags and a paler-than-usual complexion greet me. The only thing that will make me feel better is a shower, so I risk it. I make it quick though, nearly rubbing my skin raw with the exfoliating net as I scrub my body from head to toe. When I turn the water off and grab my towel from where it hangs over the rod, the hairs on my arms rise; something feels *off*. I don't see anything suspicious through the slight blur of the clear curtain, but I still hesitate for several seconds before pulling it open. I shouldn't have let my guard down.

The word *Mine* is written on the steamy mirror. I've never moved so quickly in my life. My heart is at a gallop as I round the open doorway to the bedroom. *Absolutely, the fuck not, I'm getting the hell out of here.* I immediately start stuffing any clothing in reaching distance in my duffle bag. I grab Binx and run downstairs to pack up his essentials as I shove my phone to my ear. My heart picks up pace with each shrill ring.

"Ava, can I come stay with you for a few days." My voice is tight and being drowned out by the cat's cries, but thankfully she doesn't make me explain. I'm positive she knows why I'm calling her. She lived here, after all.

In under ten minutes, Binx and I are in the car and on our way to her house. It's a struggle to direct the steering wheel between my shaking hands and racing thoughts, but I manage. When the vibrant, manicured lawns and cookie-cutter

COME OUT COME OUT

houses of her suburb come into view, I finally loosen my grip just slightly and take what feels like my first real breath. I stop outside the beige home she now lives in with her girlfriend and take the keys out of the ignition. A knock on my window nearly sends me running out of my skin. When I look over, I'm relieved to see her concerned grimace.

Ava opens the door. "Hey, come on, let's get you inside."

I let her carry Binx while I grab our stuff and follow her inside. "I'm sorry,"

She cuts me off, "Don't be, I understand."

We were never super close, but I can tell she means it when she hands me some spiced cider and offers me a blanket on her couch before setting up Binx's food and water for me. I take a few deep breaths and remind myself that I'm somewhere safe. When I finally look up at her, she's watching me closely.

"Do you want to talk about it?" Ava asks as she twirls a strand of dark purple hair around her manicured finger. Her round face is tense with worry, but I don't see any smugness.

"Are you going to tell me 'I told you so'?" I sigh and look away.

"No." She gives me a small, sympathetic smile and squeezes my knee in reassurance, so I tell her what happened last night. After she adds some dark rum to our next cup of cider, I tell her about the guy who broke in, too. That's what surprises her most out of everything I've told her.

"And he never came back?" she finally asks.

"Nope." I roll my eyes at the disappointment in my voice.

"Damn. But maybe it's for the best?"

"Maybe," I lie to both of us.

"Well, you can stay here for as long as you need. You can sleep in the office." She gestures to the room down the hall.

"I don't want to put you out. I shouldn't have even bothered you with this. I'm sorry. I haven't seen you in months, and this is how I show up . . ." I run a hand through my hair, embarrassed by what an ass I must seem like.

"And I haven't reached out much either; it's okay. But I mean it. Take a few days, get some rest, then see how you feel. You're not putting us out. Cara is on a work trip, anyways. It'll be nice to have the company, really."

Finally, the tension leaves my shoulders. "Okay. Thank you."

Happy

COME OUT COME OUT

November 3rd, 2020 – Two Days Later

Now that I've caught up on sleep and had a few days to process in the comfort of Ava's distinctly *not-haunted* home, I've decided this ghost really has some motherfucking audacity. *Are they paying rent? I think the fuck not.* The house is the first safe space I've had of my own; it's become my sanctuary of solitude that I never had growing up. I won't have it taken from me.

I have coffee and breakfast with Ava—all the while stewing in my mounting frustration—and thank her for her hospitality. It's time for me to go home.

I'm on anger-driven autopilot the entire drive back. My brain its own haunted house. I'm not letting some dead asshole dictate how I live my life. I know I've made the right decision when I pull up to the house and feel a sense of peace. Sure, there might be an undercurrent of fear, but it's not enough to deter me.

With determination, I turn the key in the front door and push it open with my foot as I pick Binx's carrier back up and walk inside. Everything looks just as I'd left it. I don't know what I expected, honestly—pictures knocked off the walls, broken glass, upturned furniture, maybe?

Breathing in deeply, I set Binx down and walk deeper into the house. The door is left open, just in case.

"Where are you, you invisible prick?" I clench my jaw and hands at my side. Nothing happens. "Look, I'm not going anywhere. So, either you leave me the hell alone or I'm bringing someone in here to get rid of your ass."

A few minutes pass and it's just me here making a fool of myself. When no booming voices tell me to get out and nothing goes bump, I take another deep breath and decide to settle back in. If it's not going to make itself known, then I'm going to go about my life. I mean, it's not like I haven't suspected it's been here the whole time. What happened on Halloween was scary as hell, but as I replay the events back in my mind, I reaffirm that it hadn't done anything to me. It threw *their* stuff out, it reacted to *them*. Maybe it wasn't a fan of having strangers in its house. As an introvert, I can relate to that.

Like clockwork, my mind reminds me of the stranger who'd barged through my door almost eight months ago. My eyes flit to the staircase and vivid memories of the blurry stairs looming in front of me as I held on for dear life come back to me.

"Don't let go; we wouldn't want you to snap that pretty neck." The gritted words ghost across my mind and send tingles straight to my pussy. What's wrong with me that I'm turned on when I should be scared out of my mind and load-

ing my shit into a moving truck. Whatever it is, I'm sure it's nothing I haven't heard before.

    I walk upstairs—ignoring the memories of getting gloriously fucked from behind a few inches from where I'm standing now—and reclaim my bedroom. It's going to take time to become at ease with the idea of residing with a ghost that's now made it very known that it's here with me. I walk to my bedside table and pull out a joint I thankfully had the forethought to roll and save. With a flick of the lighter, the paper begins to burn and I inhale deeply. Immediately, tension drains from places I hadn't even realized I was holding it.

tastes like bad decisions

CHAPTER NINE

Skye

November 10th, 2020- One Week Later

Even though I told myself over and over that the ghost hadn't tried to harm *me*, the palpable hostility in the air that night did terrify me. However since I've been back, there haven't been any disturbances. A week later, I'm finally at a point where I feel like this is my home again. I actually slept through the night for the last couple days. I blare my music, put up glowing Christmas lights while naked without a care—yes, in November—and sip on a pumpkin cider.

    The refreshed energy I've been making the most of doesn't last long, though. Like a spiderweb, the threads of anxiety and depression have rebuilt themselves in my mind despite the interruption to their regularly scheduled program-

COME OUT COME OUT

ming. Even though my family has thankfully become even more distant since they scattered across the country, it doesn't stop the creep of holiday pressure and guilt that comes along this time of year. Restlessness slithers under my skin and I want to tear it out with my bare hands. Instead, I run a bath, turning the knob as far to the left as it can go. I want it to be unbearably hot; the sting will be a welcome distraction. I drop eucalyptus and mint bath salts in. As the water rises so does the refreshing scent of the essential oils that release into the air. The hold of the sticky web of my mental illness loosens just enough for it to be manageable.

    I hate when it feels like one small thought latches onto another and then another until all the worst parts of my brain are interconnected and everything else gets caught and devoured by my inner demons. I just want to be blissfully unaware of my own misery for a bit, is that too much to ask? I think not. Returning to my room, I grab the vial of coke along with my credit card and a straw I'd cut in half, then set it on the bathroom counter. I'm so glad I re-upped while I was at Ava's, I'd been out for the last few weeks. Centering myself, I focus on cutting two small lines with slightly shaking hands. I fit the straw to my nostril as I lean down, keeping my eyes on the marbled countertop, and inhale deeply. As I'm brushing my teeth, a rush passes through me like a shock to my brain of sudden relief—my very own pesticide, the thick webs of depression release their grip. I sigh contentedly and shrug out of my clothes. Finally, a moment for joy, artificial as it may be. I lean forward until I'm inches from the mirror, transfixed by the blown pupils that sit beneath my shaggy bangs and the curve of my lips I'm not used to seeing.

There I am. All better. I tell myself the pretty lie without so much as blinking.

Heat travels up my legs and roots me in the moment as I slide into the tub. Water sloshes around the edges, more than I'd like and spills over to soak my bathmat and the tile. A reminder of how fragile my current state is. It taunts me. *The mess will still be there to clean up, even if you numb yourself enough to ignore it.*

I know that, I do. I know that the drugs can't be my safety net forever. They keep me just numb enough to make this existence bearable. But I know there will come a time when I'll have to make a choice: give myself over to their control completely, or face the real world. I'm not sure which is worse.

With that cheerful thought, I realize I left the rest of my coke out of reach. I'll need more than the one line if I hope to effectively escape my reality. I weigh the pros and cons of standing up and dealing with the discomfort of the biting chill

COME OUT COME OUT

that's seeped through the house on this autumn night. I'm wavering, but then my eye catches the razor sitting at the other end of the tub. It'll take the edge off just fine. I grab it and disconnect the blade from the handle. It's no straight razor but it's sharp.

I'm not trying to do any real damage, I just want a little release, that's all. I bring it to the side of my wrist, metal kissing the heated skin and sigh, as I drag its teeth against me. I repeat the motion a few times until I feel that satisfaction course through me at the sight of those tiny lines of red and puckered flesh.

Satiated, I dip my head back and enjoy the sensation of disappearing beneath the water. The first pricks of discomfort tease me as the heat permeates the sensitive skin on my face. I force myself to endure it for a few seconds, but when I try to lift my head, I'm unable to. My eyes snap open and immediately the heat is too much, but I can't afford to close them. Eyes burning, I frantically scan the surface above me. There's nothing. I don't understand what's happening to me, but my instincts take over. I clutch the sides of the tub and push myself forward with all my strength. I remain submerged. I kick my legs violently. Still, I remain submerged.

My muscles are rigid, my lungs are clenching, and my heart is about to burst from its cage in my chest. I continue to kick, and push, and struggle. Yet, I remain submerged. Panic overrides survival and my lips part on a scream. Bitter, minty bath water rushes into the open cavity, choking me until my cries are nothing but a dull drum. My body puts up a struggle, but my mind is ready to take a break as consciousness slips into the background and I'm just flailing limbs, tense muscles, and searching eyes. A few more seconds pass and I'm none of those things. I'm nothing. I'm disappearing. I don't fear whatever's happening anymore. Is this the peace I've been looking for?

I finally submit to what this is. I'm so tired, I deserve some rest. Warmth surrounds me and I fade into darkness. *This is nice.*

The slowing, soft beat of my heart is a lullaby that puts me to sleep.

The now-tranquil water swaddles me.

I bask in it.

A throb of pain echoes through my chest, then my limbs, and then my head. Suddenly, everything is freezing cold. On a sharp, gasping inhale, I launch myself upright and choke up bathwater. Blinking through the skull-aching pain, I look up to find the shower pouring frigid water down upon me. Shaking wracks my body as I try to focus enough to take in my surroundings.

COME OUT COME OUT

I'm alive. I'm alone. I'm home.

The peace never lasts.

I slump back into the nearly empty tub and close my eyes, ignoring Binx's cries at the door. Seconds, minutes, maybe even an hour pass and I simply remain there. Nothing and everything runs through my mind at once. Mostly, I wonder what the fuck just happened.

When my shoulders and back begin to ache from the hard tub pressing into me, I finally sit up and haul myself out. Stopping in front of the mirror, I stare into my reflection, as if I'll find the answers in my haunted gaze. I don't see anything. I only feel the resistance of whatever forced me to remain underneath water.

The ghost. Chills erupt across my skin at the reminder that there's something here with me. We'd been getting along so well, though. It had left me alone. My fear banks and it's replaced with curiosity and questioning. If the ghost truly wanted me gone, why didn't it just finish the job? I'd been so close, could feel the sweet, icy kiss of the Grim Reaper's lips.

Only I was still here, so there must be a reason.

My little wraith

CHAPTER TEN

Aiden

November 10th, 2020 – The Same Day

I couldn't save my sister, but I will save Skye. If she wants to live like a wraith, I'll become her grim reaper. I'll give her a taste of death until she can no longer stomach the idea. Until she was afraid of it. *Until she wanted to live.*

I set the wheels in motion today.

I had every intention of staying away from her, I couldn't bear how on edge she'd been since Halloween. I want her to feel safe again. When she'd left, I'd sunken into a dark, desolate place that was far worse than the time I'd spent here before she moved in.

Of course, I knew what I'd done was wrong—and so unlike me—or, I suppose, who I was in life. I'd been someone

COME OUT COME OUT

who minded my own business and respected people's boundaries. I'd live and let live. I would never pry or push. I let the people I cared about be who they wanted to be, I'd never taken it upon myself to decide what's best for them. But now, I can't seem to help myself. Maybe it's because I have nothing else to fixate on, or maybe it's because the stakes are so high. Regardless, I don't really know who I am anymore. In death, I'm becoming someone I don't recognize most of the time. When everything is ripped away from you, what's left? Without societal norms, a long life to consider, and all the things anchoring me to the world I'd once known, I'm finding that what's left is something far more primal. I'm hungry for affection. I'm desperate not to be alone anymore. I'm in need of companionship. My identity has boiled down to my most baser desires.

My decision to kill them was the catalyst for change, but from the moment my sister died, all of that bullshit, like what people *should and shouldn't do,* ceased to matter. And when that knife punctured my body and the last of my mortality sank into the wood of this very house, the axis of my reality shifted from life to afterlife.

Through that bloodshed, a new Aiden has emerged. I'm embracing him, I have no other choice, but more often than not, I'm faced with a stranger, one whose whole world orbits around Skye. She is the sun and I am the earth that relies on her.

    I'd never been a possessive partner, never saw the reason in it. But now, I'm relentlessly protective of her—*jealous, greedy*—my conscience corrected. *Could anyone blame me?* How could I not become obsessed with her when she is the only escape I have from the grief that haunts me. Eight months, hundreds of days, and thousands of hours all spent getting to know her. And I do. *Know her.* Better than she knows herself, even.

    It might be wrong, in any other circumstance, the way I watch her, but there is no going back. I haven't gotten the chance to ask her all the things I'm eager to learn and she doesn't have the luxury of unveiling just the parts of herself she was comfortable with. And yet, here we are.

    I know the most basic things, like the fact that her favorite color is black. But it's not just any black. It's the black of smoke and gauzy curtains. It's the hazy kind of black that's half-in, half-out. Just like her. Hair black, lips black, nails black, even her panties are black. The color suits her in every way.

    I also know the most intimate things, like the fact that she's severely depressed in a way that tells me she could end up just like my sister. She thinks she hides it well, but there's no hiding from me. She relies on the usual coping mechanisms: self-harm, drugs, and alcohol to dull the agony. Her impending self-destruction isn't something I revel in watching, but I can never tear my eyes away for fear that I'll blink and she'll be gone. Despite the darkness that bears down upon her like a heavy shadow, she does have some light in her life. She loves web and graphic design, so she can easily get lost in front of the screen for an entire day. My favorite parts of days like these are when she finally gets it just right and sits back to admire her work, the blue light glowing against her smiling, rounded cheeks. Pride looks beautiful on her, even if she'd never share these moments with anyone willingly.

Then there's her other love, her books. It's so peaceful to sit here in silence with her as she loses herself in new worlds. She's read so many since she's been here that I can tell what types of scenes she's reading just by her reaction. When her favorite characters are in danger, her brows furrow and she bites at her long, pointed nail. When she's reading something scary, she pulls her shirt up to cover her mouth, as if it will hold in the gasp she eventually lets out every time. And when she's reading one of her romance books, well, that's obvious because she can't help but touch herself. I'll admit, I'm partial to those kinds of books. If I'm feeling especially lonely, sometimes I'll move one into her line of sight when she's not looking in hopes that she'll pick it up. She usually does.

One of the things I appreciate most is her taste in music. She's one of those people whose entire soul transcends when she hears a song that she connects with. She can't live without it, and neither can I—and in death, its absence was especially notable for those first few lonely weeks. When she moved in, it changed everything for me. Part of myself that had been lost started to revive. This shared passion of ours has given me back so much—memories of my father and I singing along to Green Day when he'd pick me up from school, getting stoned with friends listening to Nirvana, driving with the windows down next to my sister with blink 182 blasting and the wind in our hair. It's one of the few things that can shake the heaviness of this existence I've fallen into, it even makes this empty house feel more alive.

When she isn't doing the things she loves, though, there's a deep melancholy that plagues her and she doesn't have anyone to share the burden with. Skye can tell herself she doesn't need anyone, that she doesn't want anyone, but I hear the words she leaves unspoken when she cries into her pillow. She's desperate to be loved just the way she is, but she'll never ask it of anyone.

The thing is, she doesn't need to ask, I'm right here and I'm well on my way to falling head over heels for her despite everything that makes it totally impossible.

COME OUT COME OUT

My girl exists in a bubble of sadness and I know one day, that despair that builds within it will smother her. She'll leave me here without a second thought, not even knowing someone can mourn her the way I will after all these months of watching her.

She doesn't understand how badly I yearn for her, but I'm determined to make her see. My need for her is a tightening collar around my throat that grows more possessive each day. Sometimes the linked chain pulls so taut, there's no room for me to breathe. And because the other end is attached to her, *my little wraith*, I don't even miss the air. It might be pathetic that I've nicknamed a woman who doesn't even know my name and can never be with me, but I don't fucking care. I left my pride and all sense behind when I died.

Lighter, scissors, drugs, alcohol—they were all a means to an end and they'd served her well. They kept her here, waiting for me, didn't they? But her time fending for herself is over. I'm here now and I can do so much better. What she needs is someone who understands her pain and the release she craves. *I* understand it.

She needs a reprieve from the endless energy it takes to make herself pay for her mere existence and perceived failures. She needs to exorcise the deep ache caused by her mere existence. I can do that for her, I *want* to take on that burden.

I'm ready to take ownership of that chaos.

Now that I've found her, I'm never going to let her go. I need to play my hand carefully. But first, I need to show her that I'm here and that I'm not going anywhere.

I will make my presence known one way or another. As I stand at the end of her bed watching her sleep, I plot how I'm going to make it happen. My thoughts are disrupted by the movement of her mattress as my little wraith battles her inner demons. Skye's legs kick in distress, pushing her blankets off. She mumbles incoherently and her eyelids flutter as she fights for freedom from the nightmare that holds her hostage. All I want is to soothe her.

Giving into temptation, I reach out; the stroke across her forehead is just a whisper shy of a real touch. I can't feel the warmth beneath her skin, but there's an undeniable magnetism between us. She doesn't react, once again confirming that I can't comfort her like this.

I turn my attention to her bedside table. The tiny powder particles are nearly imperceptible, but they catch in the moonlight drifting in from her billowing curtains. A spark of bitterness sweeps through me. It's cruel that I have to watch her continuously return to this when I'm right here, eager to comfort her, even if it's not the real escape she craves. It won't keep her satiated long. This kind of angel only gives you

COME OUT COME OUT

wings for a few minutes, however my girl seeks a far longer departure.

The sobering reminder brings me back to the urgency of solving this problem. I step back and return to my place at the foot of her bed. The distance between us leaves me achingly empty. But I'll have Skye any way I can for now, even like this.

My Binxie boy

Chapter Eleven

Skye

November 13th, 2020 – Two Days Later

After what feels like endlessly scrolling through rental listings in the area, I finally find one that wouldn't require me to live with a bunch of people. The last thing I want to do is deal with the hassle of packing up all my shit and moving, but I don't really have much of a choice. It's either get out or get terrorized by this goddamn ghost that seems to have finally decided to turn its attention on me.

Nothing has happened since my near-drowning, but I'm not really one to fuck around and find out. I just need to make it the remaining few weeks until my new lease starts. For now, I have plenty of packing to do. I've been at it for a few hours already and I only have three boxes packed. At least my donate and trash piles are looking pretty healthy; that's progress.

I flick through my hanging clothes, starting with my extensive band-tee collection. A staple in my wardrobe, but there may be such thing as having too much of a good thing. Reluctantly, I find one to donate, but I can't bear to part with any others. The hangers click together as I continue perusing my wardrobe. I'm admiring my favorite sweatshirt, pausing when I hear the tell-tale creak of the stairs. Each step wheezes under the weight of someone's steps. When I hear the distinct, *clunk–clunk* of them reaching the top step, my throat dries and my fingers stiffen around the neck of the hanger. *Move.* I urge myself to unglue my feet from the floor where my toes dig into the carpet, but I'm rigid as I listen closely for the next sound.

With each passing second, it becomes more difficult to hear as the pounding of my pulse becomes louder. Unease oozes from my pores, coating me in slick, cold sweat. An internal war over what to do next churns the dread in my stomach and I have to forcibly swallow down my mounting fear.

Just when I think I can't stand the agonizing anticipation any longer, a familiar voice comes from the hallway causing me to jump in surprise. "Thirty, twenty-nine..."

No hello. After eight months of *nothing*, he not only breaks into my house *again*, but he just starts counting? *That twisted asshole.*

I'm in awe of his audacity, but my body responds to the teasing threat in his voice. Unable to resist the alluring promise of what this game has in store, I quietly creep toward the bathroom and ever-so-slightly open the side of the shower curtain. I step in with one foot, then the other. The porcelain bottom is slippery because of the thick thigh-high socks I have on, but I manage to get in without knocking anything over or falling.

"Sixteen, fifteen, fourteen . . ." His voice is closer now and I can hear the arrogant satisfaction as he draws out each number in a sultry taunt.

Panting breaths sneak past my lips despite my best efforts to hold them in. The clunking of his boots sends chills across my skin. He's just outside my bedroom door. I swear I nearly pass out from anticipation as the long whine of the door announces his arrival before he does. "Come out, come out wherever you are," he whispers.

My pussy flutters at the raspiness of it. Eager to draw this out for as long as possible, I carefully tuck myself back farther into the shower. The tension of this game is the ultimate foreplay. I'm soaked, my boy shorts cling to me and my nipples are straining against the fabric of my oversized sweatshirt I'm wearing as a hot flush of need runs through me.

COME OUT COME OUT

Every inch of my body is primed for action and my brain is on high alert. This feeling is addicting and he's the only one who can deliver it into my system. I can't stop myself from slipping my fingers below the waistband of my panties and circling my clit. I need to take the edge off just a little while I wait for him to find me.

Clunk.

Clunk.

Clunk.

Clunk.

His steps reverberate like the sounds of a hunter loading their gun as they close in on their target. Unlike a deer in a meadow, I'm willing prey. *God, do I want him to catch me and rearrange my insides.*

A long pause doubles my rapid heartbeat to a punishing pace. It's so loud and disorienting that I can barely hear his steps turning in the other direction. He whips my closet open, the sliding door slamming against the wall and causing me to gasp in surprise.

A barely-audible chuckle leaves him. *Fuck.*

"I haven't been able to stop thinking about you," he says as he closes the closet. I watch through the open edge of the curtain as he turns his attention to the bed. "I've been waiting so long to see you again. It's been agony. Have you missed me?" He drops down and flips up the bed skirt. An impatient laugh leaves him.

I roll my thumb in fast circles over my clit and a moan slips past my lips just as his words cut off. I hold my breath. Measured steps headed straight into the bathroom confirm he heard me. They stop just outside the half-open door. From where I'm standing, I can see him leaning against it, listening. His hand grips the handle in a strangling hold.

"Little wraith, is that you?" The antagonistic tapping of his long, lean fingers on the hollow wood intensifies my need to have them between my legs. "If I come in there, am I going to find you wet and panting for me, like the needy little slut we both know you are?"

I should have dried up instantly, any other man who would ever call me that would get a fist to the face, but those words from his lips only make me want him more. My thighs clench around my hand and my jaw tightens as I force myself to remain quiet and hidden here instead of throwing myself in his arms.

Mercifully, he doesn't make me wait any longer. The shower curtain tears open, metal and plastic echoing chaotically in the tiny space. I pull my fingers away from my pussy, but he catches my wrist before I can hide the evidence.

Icy hot desire flares back at me in those gray-blue eyes.

COME OUT COME OUT

I'm speechless as he grabs my wrist and pushes my fingers past his lips. My breath catches in my throat as he swirls his pink tongue around them until all of my juices have been wiped clean. A moan finally breaks through the awestricken silence.

"You just couldn't wait, could you?" He releases my hand roughly and steps into the tub with me—combat boots still on and all—forcing me to bump into the wall and knock over several bottles. The hard planes of his stomach and hip bones jut into my soft stomach as he crowds my space.

"Are you going to hurt me?" My voice drips with lust instead of apprehension.

"I'll give you exactly what you need, don't worry, love." His gaze searches mine intently for several intense seconds. Thankfully, he's satisfied with whatever he finds there. "Are you ready for me to make you feel good?"

The tension floods from my body at his promise. I continue to hold his gaze and eagerly agree to unspoken terms and conditions of what's at play.

A wicked smirk curves his lips. "Very good, but you'll have to work for it. You ruined my game. You were supposed to make it hard for me to find you."

"I didn't know you were coming," I combat, "a head's up would have been—" My stranger's inked hand wraps around my throat, halting my words. The chill of his silver rings pressing into my sweaty skin makes me shiver. I take advantage of our proximity to admire him. He looks exactly the same as I remember–devastatingly good looking with his intentionally messy hair, chiseled cheekbones, and pouty lips, wrapped in the perfectly understated package of black denim and a cut-off tee. I realize it's the same one with the hand and rose, but I didn't note the upside down words before, 'violent delights have violent ends'. He *would* love Shakespeare. I file that tidbit away as he leans his head down to recapture my attention. His eyes are rolling storm clouds now.

"What kind of punishment does my little wraith deserve for her poor choice of hiding spot?" He uses his palm to add pressure to the front of my throat. Panic flares within me and my hands snap around his, but when his eyes remain steady on mine, I force my heart to slow and release my grip. I don't know him, *but I know our game*. I know he'll respect whatever rules I set.

"That's my girl." The pressure lessens and I take a greedy breath. "How about we try again. And this time, you find a real hiding spot."

Excited to continue, I move to leave the shower but his fingers tighten. "Did I say 'ready, set, go'?" His jaw flexes.

"No." I shiver under the punishing glare he gives me.

God, this is so fucking hot. This is everything I never knew I needed. I wait impatiently for his instructions.

"For not following the rules, I'm going to make you suffer." The final word is a purr and the glint in my eye tells me just how well he understands what it does to me to hear him say that. "Bend over and face the wall." He finally releases my throat.

Facing the wall, I plant my hands firmly on the tile and bend at the waist. I keep my gaze straight, waiting for his next instruction. Seconds pass without a word from him and I'm shaking with the need to see what he's doing. Partially out of curiosity, but also out of fear that he's disappeared again. I resist the urge.

"Look at how desperate you are." A low laugh skates up the area of my thigh that's exposed above my tall socks and I have to curl my toes not to jump at his proximity. He's as silent as the dead when he wants to be. "Now, let's see, is this pussy wet for me?" His thumb slips under the barely-there mesh fabric of my boy shorts.

"No, it's for the other guy who's teasing the ever-loving-fuck out of me." I sass, trying to provoke him. I need to be touched. I want his brand of punishment.

"Mmmm, mmmm, mmmm," he sighs, "I love that smart-ass mouth, but it's like you're eager for me to teach you a lesson." *I am.* He tucks my hair behind my ear as he brings his mouth an inch away. "Are you going to beg for me, little wraith?"

I nod in response and arch my back, so my ass rubs against his hard cock that's still unfortunately tucked away in his jeans.

"You're going to have to do better than that. I asked you a question, and I want an answer."

"Please." My whine echoes around the shower. "Please, please, please." I'll beg for it. Fuck, I'll pray to him if that's what he wants. I'll get on my knees, I'll bruise them, bloody them, I'll sit here all night if that's what it takes. He's the only who can give me what I need. It's an insatiable itch that's been torturing me for months. I *need* him to scratch it or I'll lose my mind entirely.

"What a pretty song. But sluts don't get rewards." A sharp slap on my pussy makes me cry out. "Here's what's going to happen, I'm going to bring you to the edge,"

I whine in protest, interrupting him, and he lands another slap in the same spot.

"I'm going to bring you to the edge," he repeats through gritted teeth, "and then you're going to go hide and think about what happens when you don't play along. When I find you, maybe I'll let you come."

Come Out Come Out

A whimpering sigh escapes me but it quickly turns into a moan when he pulls my boy shorts aside and slips his fingers between my pussy lips. His fingers pump deep inside me at a quickening pace.

For a minute it's quiet except for the obscenely wet sounds of his fingers working inside me, accented by my gasps and moans. The thought of those chipped, painted nails glistening with my wetness does something to me and I feel myself clench around him tightly.

"Your pussy is already weeping for me." His voice is pure grit as he forces the words out. "Do you think I can make you cry real tears for me before I give into you?" He pinches my clit, punctuating his taunt. "I think you will, and I'm going to drink them all like a man left in the desert because that's what I am without you, insatiably parched."

"Oh fuck," I groan at the acute pleasure and his taunting words. This man should be an actor because this role-playing is next level and I'm fucking eating it up.

"I know. It feels so good to let me take over and ease those beautiful, sick thoughts in that mind of yours, doesn't it?" He strokes my clit in soft, teasing circles with his thumb as his pointer finger enters me. "Mmm, you have such a perfect cunt."

My legs shake at the unexpected praise. He adds another finger and my toes curl. His digits are relentless as they pump, stretch, and fill me over and over again. He urges my foot up on the edge of the tub, opening me further.

"Oh my god, don't stop." My breath speeds up, my pussy tightens, and my eyes squeeze shut. Right when I'm on the edge, he pulls his fingers out of me, just like he promised. "No, no, no, no. Please."

My stranger's strong fist wraps around my hair and he yanks my head back. "I know you're excited, but it's not the time for begging yet." He forces his hand back between my clenched thighs and pulls my panties back into place. I shudder at the brush of his rings that are cruelly cold on my overheated skin. With his other hand, he pulls me back so I'm leaning against his chest and whispers in my ear, "Take off the sweatshirt."

"But it's freezing in here," I argue.

"Trust me, you won't be cold for long." He inhales deeply along the curve of my neck. "Now. Take. It. Off." The tension in my scalp increases briefly before he releases me completely.

I feel naked already at the loss of him, but I do as he says and take off my sweatshirt. My breasts flop as I pull it over my head with effort. When it's finally off, I turn to face him. He lifts his fingers tentatively, then gently brushes my bangs to the side. The gleam in his eyes is almost wistful, but within seconds, the light that shines there is snuffed out and his gaze darkens as it trails down my near-naked body.

Without tearing his eyes away, he rubs a thumb across my lower lip and starts counting, "sixty, fifty-nine, fifty-eight . . ." His voice is an impatient growl.

My heart rate rockets and I'm moving as soon as he drops his hand. When I get to the stairs, I stall. I need to find a good hiding spot, for I want to make him happy. On quiet feet, I take the stairs one at a time, even though I'm running out of time.

"Twenty, nineteen, eighteen . . ." he drawls from the shower.

I'm half-running to the kitchen when I stop in my tracks, remembering the creepy, dingy basement that I've avoided the entire time I've lived here. My heart thumps as my mind races with indecision. It's the perfect hiding place, but there's also the risk that I could run into the ghost down there in the dark.

"Ten, nine, eight . . ."

His counting makes it difficult to think, so I just act. Hoping I don't regret it, I backtrack a few feet and slip into the darkness just as he reaches *one*. My breathing is jagged as fear wins out over anticipation. Dampness sits heavy in my lungs, and the smell of old cardboard clogs my nose. I stand frozen at the top of the stairs, just listening for a few seconds. When nothing grabs me from below, I begin my descent. Each step is agonizingly slow as I cling to the wood railing and stick a toe out to test each step in front of me. A sliver of light from the gap under the door just barely breaks up the blackness. If I squint hard enough, I can make out the rough outline of the shape of boxes.

    I reach the bottom and freeze again, listening for any clues as to where he is. My stranger's rushed steps tell me he's decided he's finished his sweep of the top floor. He doesn't even try to hide his movements. For a moment, I envy him. I have to force my limbs to move as I cautiously navigate the darkness I've plunged myself in. I slip into a corner that's out of reach of the sliver of light.

    Standing here half-naked in the darkness, time passes so slowly. My denied orgasm, mixed with the adrenaline, has me shivering almost violently. I inhale and exhale deeply, in part to relax myself, but also to give my mind something else to focus on besides the panic that waits just below the surface. Another few minutes pass and I start to worry he won't find me.

    The light coming from under the door flickers. The shadow of two feet stretches forward. I slap my hand over my

COME OUT COME OUT

mouth just in time to muffle the gasp that escapes my lips. I shouldn't have doubted him.

"Come out, come out, wherever you are." He rattles the rusty handle. "I wonder what's behind this door?" A sinister chuckle bellows against the wood. "Are you down there quivering in the dark, little wraith? Mmm, I bet that fear dripping down your thighs tastes delicious"

My feet rock forward and I grip the ledge of what I assume is a workbench behind me. A battle ensues between my body and mind as my desire for him to find me and fuck me, and the instinct to hide fight for dominance. No winner is declared because he opens the door, flooding the stairs in a yellow light, and starts down the stairs with zero hesitation for his own safety. "Ready or not, here I come."

I try to flatten myself against the work bench behind me, but the second I shift, he sees me and stops mid-step. With a wicked glint in his eye, my stranger tilts his head and his smile stretches wide. "There she is." He jumps down the remaining stairs with a heavy thump that makes me yelp.

The chase is on as my feet take the lead and carry me through the darkness. I don't make it far, tripping over one of the boxes that must have been left behind. "Shit," I growl as I get up on my hands and knees that are throbbing from impact. My ears perk up, straining over my heavy breathing to listen for him. When I turn back around, a flashlight flicks on and illuminates his sharp, beautiful features. I can't contain the shrill scream that pierces the silent night. He found me first.

Come out, come out, wherever you are

CHAPTER TWELVE

Aiden

November 13th, 2020 – Same Day

"Too slow, baby." I clamp my free hand around Skye's ankle to hold her in place. I'm momentarily captivated by the pleasure of feeling her pulse jumping beneath my fingertips. It's beating so fast I can feel it beneath the adorable thigh high socks she wears. Snapping out of my lustful daze, I slowly shift the flashlight I'd found on the workbench away from my face and onto Skye. The fear in her eyes has my dick aching to be free. I drink it in for a few seconds before continuing the light's descent, lingering on the way her breasts sit on the delicious curve of her stomach, her nipples hardening under my attention. Satisfied, I continue, halting once I get to those damned boy shorts that softly grip her thighs.

COME OUT COME OUT

I swallow harshly, my mouth suddenly overwhelmed with saliva. I'm fucking famished for her. "Spread your legs."

Her sultry brown eyes never leave mine as she shifts them apart excruciatingly slowly. Frustration and desire stir within me. The jiggle of her thighs when she stops sends another swell of saliva to coat my tongue.

"Pull your panties to the side, love." The light quivers in my hand as I restrain myself. "Now, open up for me." Obediently, her long, black nails press against her pussy lips and part them like petals of a blooming flower glistening with morning dew. She's so wet. "You like our game, little wraith."

It's a statement, but she answers anyway. "Yes, but I wish they weren't so few and far between." Her voice is breathy. I don't miss how her fingers twitch with need as she holds herself open for my viewing pleasure.

"I know, and I'm going to make all the anticipation worth it." I place my hands on her knees, lean forward and spit. A small gasp leaves her lips and it elicits a groan from deep within me.

"Do you like when I treat you like a slut?" I know the answer, but I need to hear her say it. Skye's eyes flare wider for a fraction of a second and then they're rolling back in her head when my fingers start spreading my saliva methodically. "Say it. Tell me how much you love it."

"I love being treated like a slut—*your* slut." Her correction makes my chest swell with satisfaction.

"What else?" My voice is a reverent whisper.

"I . . . I love having your spit on me, inside of me." She lifts her hips when my fingers near her entrance. "Do it again . . . please?"

"How can I say no when you ask so sweetly?" I lean forward, cock my head back, and give her what she wants. I run my finger over her slick pussy, gathering the mixture of my spit and her wetness, then spread it across her lips. "Have a taste."

Her tongue darts out and caresses her black lipstick, leaving her lips glossy. I can't wait another second.

"Sit on my face. I want a taste, too."

"Right here?"

"Yes, right now." I pass her the flashlight then lay on my back on the dust and grime-covered floor and pull her toward my face, my arms wrapping around her thighs. When she relaxes her legs and finally sinks against me, I revel in the full weight of her. Her body anchors me in the moment. For the first time in too long, I'm no ghost untethered. God, I never want to get up. I could stay in this moment forever.

She gasps and drops the flashlight as my tongue swipes through her. I stop abruptly, clucking my tongue.

COME OUT COME OUT

"That won't do. Pick it back up. I want you to hold on tight and let me see every moment of pleasure on that gorgeous face while I eat my fill."

With shaking hands, she brings the flashlight in front of her and grips it tightly. I squeeze her thighs to remind her to relax while I start circling her clit with my tongue. My mouth, chin, and nose are already soaked, covered in her.

For my first meal as a dead man, I couldn't have asked for better. I can't get enough. I swipe my tongue between her lips and spear it inside her, causing her to writhe above me. I open my eyes to capture the glorious moment of her slowly riding my face and I'm not disappointed by the view. The soft glow kisses her features in waves of light, illuminating her perfect furrowed brows, the sweep of her lashes as her eyes flutter with pleasure, and her teeth sunk into her bottom lip like it's the only thing that's tethering her control. We can't have that; I want to see her lost to the feeling of me between her legs.

I reach up and slip my wet thumb between the seam of her lips, forcing her teeth free. "Stop holding it in, I want to hear everything." Her moan in response vibrates against my finger. "That's my girl."

Pleased, I refocus my efforts, flicking and rubbing my tongue against her cunt. I flatten my tongue and give her a pointed lick that ends with a nip at her clit. She throws her head back and yelps.

"Such sweet sounds, but I want you to use your words. Tell me how good you feel."

"It feels so fucking good when you do that right there—ah," she sucks in a breath as I work my tongue inside her. "Yeah, just like that." Her palms massage her breasts and I reach up to guide her fingers to pinch her nipples sharply. She whimpers in response. "I love it when you make it hurt."

"I know. I can make it hurt so good. Don't worry; I'm going to give it to you just how you need it." I suck at her clit, then nip at it again. "I love watching you play with those amazing fucking tits. Don't stop touching yourself."

She nods, biting her lip again.

I fist the back of her hair with one hand and wrap the other around her thigh, forcing her open wider. "What did I say about holding it in?"

"I'm sorry." She whines.

"Don't be sorry, just listen to instructions." I double my efforts, sucking and licking and playing with her pussy until she's quickly rolling her hips and desperately fucking my face.

"I'm coming, I-"

"Aiden. My name's Aiden." I need to hear her say it, needed her to know something more about me.

COME OUT COME OUT

"Fuck, Aiden, I'm coming."

Hearing my name roll off her tongue with a husky moan is almost as good as coming myself. I lap at her pussy, groaning with satisfaction creating vibrations against her. I don't stop until I can feel her pulling to get away from me as she comes down. Finally, I let her scoot back so she's straddling my chest.

"You taste like heaven."

"I know," she responds and I nearly melt at the playful smile that graces her lips. She shifts back further, settling her weight on my legs as she unclasps my belt. Skye's eyes never leave mine as she pulls my cock out and begins to stroke it with a strong grip. Her tongue darts out and sweeps over the head teasingly making my hips buck up off the floor.

"Does that feel good, Aiden?" She stops to look up at me and I nod in response. "Use your words," she taunts as she tightens her fist.

"Careful, little wraith," I warn with an arched brow.

In challenge, she sucks the head of my cock into her mouth, then pulls it out with a loud pop. Her hand shifts up and down my shaft as she watches me closely, planning her next move. Little does she know I have my own plans for that mouth.

"Yes, it feels so good." I give her an inch. "Now wrap

your smart mouth around my dick and don't stop sucking until I fill it with my cum." I fist her hair and guide her lips back down, reminding her who's in charge here. I thrust my hips up and shove my cock to the back of her throat. She gags and I moan. "Just like that, baby. I love hearing you choke on my dick." I use her hair to pull her back to the tip and she follows my lead, swirling her tongue around the head and licking at the pre-cum that waits there. Pleased, my hold loosens just slightly and I give her back a little control.

    Skye's hand and mouth work in tandem sucking, tugging, and licking in perfect harmony that has me struggling to keep my hips on the ground. A few more seconds of her slurping with hollowed cheeks and I can't take it anymore. "Put your hands behind your back." She does and my fist tightens in her hair once more as I snap my hips up and slam into the back of her throat. She gags so prettily around me that it almost sends me over the edge, but I'm not ready for it to end. I slowly pull back out, then repeat the motion. My lips pull into a smile as something like pride blooms in my chest while she quivers with the effort required to remain in this position. I watch more of her drool pour down my cock for a moment longer before I release her. "Come here." I pull her forward onto my lap.

    I drink in the mess I've made of her lipstick as Skye

wipes away the saliva around her mouth. *My beautiful disaster.*

With her hands on my chest, she looks down at me and just smiles. Time stands still for me. It's such a simple thing, but it makes me want to treasure every second I have with her. Words are lost on me for a moment, so I clear my throat.

"Sit on my cock and don't move. I've waited so long to be inside you, it's only fair I get to bask in it. Every time you squirm, it's another minute I make you wait to come."

Her brow furrows and challenge heats her dark eyes. "You've waited–", she starts to argue, but I cut her off when I sit up quickly and capture her lips with mine. I bring my knees up to support her ass and the movement allows me to sink even farther inside her. I'm in fucking heaven.

Her cunt tightens around me in response and I groan as she pants into my mouth. I swallow those deprived breaths like if I took enough of them they could somehow bring me back to life. I can taste the faintest hint of lemon and it reminds me of the hope of summer and the stands Becca and I used to run in our driveway. The reminder is bittersweet as I caress Skye's tongue with mine. I could stay like this forever with her body wrapped around me and my cock buried so gloriously deep inside of her.

She's sitting so pretty for me too, not even trying to move her hips to get the friction I can tell she so desperately needs by the way her thighs clench and shake around my waist. This moment is all for me and I love that she's handing it over so selflessly. I should reward her. I wrap my hand around the back of her neck and kiss her deeply for another minute, inhaling every last sip of her that I can, then I release her and lean back, stroking my fingers down her arms and sides before I lay down. With my knees still propped up behind her, I dig my heels into the dirty concrete floor and start to fuck into her without warning.

"Aiden," Skye moans out as her hands hungrily grab at her breasts. "Oh, fuck! Your cock fits so perfectly in my pussy–ah–the way you stretch and fill me." She slides her hand between us to play with her clit and I claim her free nipple with my mouth, teasing it with my tongue. Her breathing accelerates with the added stimulation and I match my thrusts in time with it.

"You're taking me so well," I grunt out as I hit deep inside her at a punishing pace. "I never want to come so I can stay buried deep inside this sweet little cunt." I'm truly not ready for this to be over, so I slow my hips until I can convince my body to stop completely even though it feels so fucking good. "Stand up."

"What?" She whines as she rolls her hips.

"Stand. Up." The second she lifts off me, I miss her

warmth, but I need her harder, faster. I take the opportunity to finish undressing fully.

"Where do you want me?" The flashlight on the floor illuminates half her face as she watches me.

I latch my hand around her wrist and lead her through the dimly lit basement, back over to that work bench. It's littered with tools and my gaze homes in on the saw. I move us so we're directly in front of it.

"Aiden . . ." she says hesitantly, her voice shaking with uncertainty, but she doesn't even try to pull away.

I continue with my plan, propping it up against the back wall where other tools hang, then place a heavy toolbox in front of the blade so it doesn't fall forward. I kiss her temple, breathing in the musky scent of her sweat. "Do you trust me?"

Several seconds pass between us but eventually, she nods. "I don't know why, but I do," Skye admits with a breathless laugh.

With that confirmation, I take one of her hands and slip her fingers through the handle, closing them in a fist. Despite the tension in her muscles, she allows me to place her other hand against an open space lower on the wall. "Stay just like that, baby." I lean back and shift her hips so her ass is higher in the air.

"Do you know how fucking beautiful you are?" My fingers trace the curved dip of her arched back and follow the straight line down until I slide them through her dripping cunt. "I've never met anyone so perfect for me." I circle her clit and she presses back against me. "Are you ready for me, Skye?"

"Yes." She whines as she looks over her shoulder at me. "I've been ready."

I laugh, pleased by her eagerness. "You've been so good; I'm going to let you come again. But until then, I'm going to need you to let me take over. Do you understand?"

She bites her lip and assesses me for a second too long for my liking. I pull my fingers away from her needy pussy, causing her to gasp, and shove them in her mouth to force it open. "Do you understand? Yes, or no?"

She attempts to talk around my fingers, so the affirmation is slurred, but I'm satisfied. Before I remove them from her mouth, her tongue circles the two digits and my cock hardens further at the placation. "So good for me." I praise and slide my hand down so my thumb and pointer finger hold her jaw tightly. "Now, remember, don't move. As long as you let me have control, you'll be okay."

Skye's gaze slides to the propped-up saw briefly but she meets my eyes again and nods. "You're in control." Her features relax.

With her full consent, I take her life into my hands, *exactly where it belongs*. I work two fingers into her, plunging in and out so easily with how soaked she is. I take some of her natural lubricant and stroke it up and down my cock, moaning at the tease of what's to come. Carefully, I notch the tip at her center and slip it in just a fraction. We both groan as she stretches around me. It's the final frontier of her trust I needed to claim. I lean back as much as I can without relinquishing my secure hold on her jaw and watch myself sink into her another inch.

My greedy girl tries to shift herself back onto me to swallow me deeper inside her, but I grab onto her hip roughly with my free hand and she yelps. "Who's in control, Skye?"

A distressed whimper leaves her lips but I hold her still with my grip until she gives in. "You are."

"Right, so you only get as much of this cock as I say. You'll have me fully seated inside you when I'm good and ready, and not a second sooner." I apply a fraction more force to my hold against her face before I slide my dick back out to just the very tip. Skye's muscles flex with her restraint under me and the hold I have on her is the most satisfying thing I've ever experienced. When I have her like this, it's the only thing I have any sway over in my existence anymore and I'll milk every second of it. A glimpse of the wetness dripping down her thigh makes me weak, and I shift another inch inside of her. A few seconds more and I slip in a bit farther, then one more pause and I'm all the way in. We both sigh gratefully, but the peace doesn't last long before I slam into her and force her neck closer to the jagged blade of the saw.

Skye's gasp is one of terror and pleasure as she clenches around me. I don't slow down, pumping into her continuously as her head hovers over the viciously sharp tool. With each pass, she shudders beneath me. My hold on her remains firm, keeping her throat angled upward and steadily positioned several inches above it. Just enough space to make the threat to her life appear real to her, but far enough away that I know I can keep her safe. The illusion is fun for me, but I hope the perceived risk is another testament to Skye that she still wants to live.

God she's so slick as I shift in and out of her, the sounds of my cock shoving into her are obscene when they punctuate the moans and cries that fall from her lips when I continuously hit that spot deep inside her. "Are you ready to come, little wraith?" I remove my hand from her hip and press against her clit with purpose. I'm hanging on by a thread, but I want to make sure she's satisfied first.

"Yes, fuck, make me come." I don't let up as I circle her

clit and push her over the edge. "Oh, god, Aiden." My name on her lips is all it takes to send me right along with her while she's clenching around me so goddamn tightly. I can barely think straight, but I do have the sense to draw her back against me and take several steps back so she doesn't plunge forward onto the teeth of the saw.

We both stand there in complete stillness except for the heavy rise and fall of our chests. Once our breathing steadies, I slide out of her and bend down to grab my clothes, it just so happens to be perfect timing to see my cum seeping out of her, down her thighs, and into her now-uneven thigh-highs. I take a mental image that I know will be burned in my brain forever, then drag my tongue up the inside of her left leg, catching some in my mouth. We taste so perfect together, her sweetness with my saltiness.

"I need clothes," Skye says as she rubs her hands up and down her arms. I nod and buckle my belt quickly, then pull my shirt back over my head–thank God I died in my favorite one since I have to wear this thing all the fucking time.

Once my boots are laced up, I follow Skye up the basement stairs and into the kitchen without a word; my stomach is in knots that any minute this could end. But I'm not the only one who's distracted. Skye fills two glasses with water and ice and silently hands the other to me. Clinking ice and our eager swallows are loud as we stand there.

"I'll be right back," she announces.

I want to object, I'm not ready to be without her, but I don't. Instead, I sit at the kitchen table and am quickly joined by her cat, Binx, who rubs against me fondly. Over the last few months, I've grown attached to him. He's the only one who sees me. Sometimes it's the most comforting thing to see him slow-blink at me while I sit there pining after Skye as she sleeps, none-the-wiser to my presence. I'm lost in the moment, not hearing when Skye sits down across from me, now wearing a pair of black joggers and a black crop top with a pink heart outlined in barbed wire. Her hair is in a messy bun that I want to grab onto. The rest of that thought scatters as I take note of the time and date on her phone. 11:30 p.m. Friday, November 13th, just a month shy of a year dead. *Has it really been that long?* The impending anniversary creates a weight of guilt that sinks into the pit of my stomach. I can't imagine how my poor parents must feel right now with the holidays coming up and no kids to celebrate with. I don't regret it, but I do wish my decision hadn't led to more pain for them.

"Aiden?" She sounds nervous. "Aiden," she calls my name again. When my attention returns to her, she continues. "Are you good? Do you need something to eat?"

The concern in her eyes is everything, even though I

know it's just her showing basic human decency, it's more than anyone has expressed toward me in so long. "Sorry, I—" I school my face into a smile. "No, thanks. I'm okay, I just got distracted for a second."

"Okay . . ." Her eyes scan over me as if she doesn't believe me. "So, what now?" There's something like hurt in her eyes and I wish I could ensure that I would never see that look from her again. "Are you going to disappear into the night for another eight months?"

"Skye," I start, but she cuts me off.

"Look, it's cool. This can be just a casual thing, no need for labels or anything. I like the games we play; I do. It's just . . . I never know when to expect you."

"Isn't that just part of the game?" I try to play it off, skirting around the real question, 'When will I see you again?' I don't want this to be a casual thing. I want to tell her that I can be here as much as she wants, that I'll be back again soon, but I don't know that, and I can't lie to her. I might relish in bringing her the punishing release she craves, but I don't want to do her any real harm.

Skye rolls her eyes and gives me a fake laugh, effectively ridding her gaze of the vulnerability that was burning there as she stands and walks to the fridge. No matter how much she doesn't want to admit it, she's lonely. But not in a way that most people can fulfill. She finds my company calming in a way she can't explain; it's because I know exactly what she needs and I intend to keep showing up for her when I can, which I desperately hope is more often.

"Another game?" She slides an open beer across the table.

"What'll it be?" I ask before taking a long sip.

Skye pulls out a deck of cards from her back pocket. "How about war? But whoever loses each round has to tell a truth about themselves."

"No dares?"

"Maybe later." That spark of lust between us reignites.

I pull the deck toward me and start shuffling. "Can't have you stacking the deck against me, can we?"

"If anyone's the cheater, it's you." Her hand flattens over mine, halting my shuffling, and her warmth seeps through me. It's something so simple yet comforting that I relinquish the cards with no hesitation.

Skye deals and starts the game, "Three, two, one, war!" She shouts excitedly. We both flip over our cards and I can't even be disappointed about losing, seeing this side of her feels so good.

"Time for a truth." Skye tilts her head, assessing me. "What's with the tattoo." She points to the one on my neck that says 'GONER'.

"Umm . . ." I rub my fingers across it. "I got it when I turned eighteen. It was kind of a fuck-you to the kids who used to bully me back in school. They'd always tell me I was a goner, so I decided to own it."

Her brow furrows as she studies me. "You were bullied? For what?"

"Well, for one, I wasn't really the athletic type. I always preferred drawing and painting, which of course made me distinctly not *'one of the guys'*. And then there was the disdain people held for how open I was about being into well, everyone, just as much as I was into girls, even in elementary school. People weren't as accepting back then–I guess they aren't so much now, either." I run a hand through my disheveled hair. I'd never felt a lot of pressure to hide my identity, but even less so now. There were no social stigmas in death. "Plus, I was always kind of an outcast. I was always doing my own thing. That was a hard pill to swallow for people who hinge their self-worth on being accepted," I shrug off the memories of my youth that feel so distant now.

A fond smile tells me she can relate. She doesn't press for more. "Three, two, one, war."

This time, I win the round with a ten owning her four. "Are you going home to visit family for the holidays?"

"No."

I arch a brow, letting her know I expect more.

"I'm from The Bay, but my family doesn't live up here anymore. They've scattered all over the country. My parents divorced when I was young–it was a good thing, they were always fighting–and our relationship kind of deteriorated from there. It was a messy divorce and they both were too caught up in their own shit to notice how much I needed them. So, I decided not to need them anymore. I have an older sibling, we're not close, though, and she moved to Maine. I went to visit her for the holidays last year. We couldn't get along, she said my 'shitty attitude and picky eating took the fun out of it all'. Same old story of why most of my relationships of any kind haven't worked out, I'm too difficult for her."

Needing to comfort her, I reach my hand across the table. "You're not too difficult. Fuck her."

A sad smile tips her matte-black lips that have been restored to perfection. "You don't know me."

"I understand you better than you think, Skye. Anyone who tells you that you're too much doesn't deserve you."

Her eyes blur with unshed tears but her jaw is tight with discomfort. She really doesn't want to cry in front of me. She doesn't know how many times I've witnessed just that and how much I'd never judge her for it. Since I can't explain that to her, I add the cards I won to my pile, then pick up where we left off. "Three, two, one, war."

She flips over a queen and I flip over a nine. My stomach twists with nerves. "So, is your family as shitty as mine?"

The question plunges into my heart like a knife and it takes me a minute to recover. I try to cover up the shock with a long swig of the beer. When the tension ebbs from my throat, I finally answer, "I'm not super close with my family anymore, but I do get along with them. I have a sister—*had* a twin sister—we didn't have much in common, but we did have a lot of great memories." My brain conjures up the heartbreaking image of Becca's lifeless body that still haunts me to this day. My stomach rolls and I think I might be sick. "I'll be right back." I don't wait for her response as I take off toward the bathroom. A cold sweat coats my skin.

Needing to chase away the clammy feeling, I turn on the sink, but the frigid metal doesn't bite into my skin, I barely feel it at all as I twist it on. I cup my hands and bring water to my face; it's not as refreshing as I expect. I do it again, it splashes onto the floor behind me.

God dammit. No, it can't be over so soon.

tastes like bad decisions

CHAPTER THIRTEEN

Skye

November 14th, 2020 - A Few Minutes After Midnight Strikes

I don't want to make things weird, but I'm growing restless waiting for Aiden to come back. I check my phone, 12:04 a.m. Saturday, November 14th. It's been like ten minutes, that feels like a long time.

"Aiden, you okay?" I call out, cringing.

Two more minutes go by, nothing. The chair screeches against the floor as I get up to investigate. I knock softly on the bathroom door. "Aiden, you in there?" Again, nothing. I turn the handle and I'm greeted by an empty bathroom. "What the fuck?" I ask the question out loud, confused. "Is this another part of your game?"

COME OUT COME OUT

Excitement replaces concern. I walk the ground floor, looking for him. I go to check the porch, but the door is locked. You can only do that from the inside. I start to walk away, but then I realize that I haven't unlocked or locked that door since yesterday. So, how the hell did he get in here? I check the back door that I never use, it's locked like always. *Weird.*

Now, I'm even more determined to find him. "Aiden, come out, come out, wherever you are." I call playfully as I search my bedroom. The other rooms are empty too. Did he up and leave again without saying goodbye? I'm annoyed but disappointment quickly overrides it. My cheeks burn with embarrassment that I'm actually upset that he left. *This isn't anything. He's just a fun fuck.* I try to remind myself. *It didn't feel like just casual sex.* My subconscious unhelpfully supplies, making me feel even more like shit.

I toss our unfinished beers and go upstairs to get ready for bed. I don't fall asleep though. Instead, I turn the night over in my mind, dissecting the things I do know about him. His name is Aiden, his sister passed, and he's interested in me—or fucking me, at least. He came back for a reason. But why did he stay away for so long? I swear I'll be so pissed if he's married. But there's no ring and no tan line from one. I've seen those fingers in close detail, prayed to them, worshipped at their altar. I'm confident that's not it. Still, I jump up and rifle under my bathroom counter to find my emergency contraceptive—suddenly reminded just how much I don't want kids, especially not with a random stranger.

    Curious, I look at my phone's calendar to see when the last time I took it was. I scroll back up to March and look for one of the few dots on my very empty schedule. There it is: Friday, March 13th. Interesting. I go back to my lock screen and realize he's once again come to see me on a Friday the 13th. That's a *really* weird coincidence. My stomach tightens with unease as I google Friday the 13th's significance. I know people are superstitious about it being bad luck, but nothing else I read grabs my attention in any meaningful way. I have the fleeting thought that I hope this isn't some ritualistic murder thing. I circle back to my original worries from when he first entered my house all those months ago. I can't seem to get that fear to stick, though. There's something about him that feels safe and comfortable. Part of me doesn't even think it would be a stretch to say he cares for me—it's in the way he *looks* at me, even the way he *touches* me. But I dismiss that thought; I can't afford to become attached to someone, especially not someone like him. Who knows if I'll ever see him again? I feel a prick behind my eyes but I refuse to acknowledge it.

    Thankfully, a notification pings on my phone in that obnoxious bell tone. My traitor of a heart jumps at the thought

COME OUT COME OUT

that it might be him. But we never exchanged numbers. Still, it has me picking it up and looking anyways. Of course, it's not him. It is, however, a nice text from Ava checking on me. I type out a quick response.

Switching my phone ringer off, I lay back down in bed and pull the covers around me. I swallow thickly when I notice Binx standing still and staring at the doorway intently.

"Binxie, please don't be creepy," I whine. I don't have the energy to deal with ghost shit right now. After another moment, he crawls up and curls up next to me. I stroke his side absentmindedly as I try to distract myself with social media. Quickly bored of my uneventful feed, I pick up my e-reader and disappear into my current read. *All I want is my own morally grey love interest, is that so much to ask?* I barely make it a few pages before my eyes are heavy and the words start to blur.

Happy

Between school and getting ready for Ava's birthday, I don't have time to devote to unraveling the Aiden mystery. I do, however, find myself thinking about him more and more as I sit at this party surrounded by couples. I can't help but think he'd be the life of a party. He says he used to get bullied, but whatever nerdiness or shyness he may have previously suffered from, he's all sure confidence now—and sexy as hell. He's hot in the way that the charming actor who always plays the attractive best friend is. I can imagine him pulling me out of my chair in the corner and forcing me to dance with him. Everyone would watch us and comment on how we look at each other like we can't possibly wait until we get home to tear each other's clothes off. Mercifully, Elle approaches me to pull me out of my embarrassing fantasy about a guy I barely know.

"Hey, Skye. How are you?" Elle pulls me into a hug and I try my best not to tense against her. It's a reminder of how little we actually got to know each other even though we'd lived together for almost two years in multiple places.

"Oh, you know, staying busy." I skirt around the truth. I'm terrible at small talk, I don't understand why we need to exchange niceties with people we aren't friends with, or why people ask how you are when they know you're likely not well. Again, it confirms she never really knew me even though we lived together and we aren't friends. It frustrates me, but I force myself to keep up the charade. "How are you, Elle? You look beautiful. Green is definitely your color." There, polite, complimentary, completely void of meaning. Nailed it.

"I'm great! Sarah and I are living closer to the main part of town now. It's so much more convenient. Have you considered moving?" Her tone drops lower with the last sentence.

"Yeah, actually. I'm in the process of moving. My new place just isn't ready yet. I should be out by the end of the month, though."

"I'm so glad to hear it." Her smile is tight. "Well, it was good seeing you, Skye." Elle gives a small wave, then seeks out Sarah. Those two are the definition of co-dependent. I've never had a best friend like that; I imagine it's nice.

When I finally meet my two-hour, self-imposed event social requirement, I say goodbye to Ava and get the hell out of there. I have to sit in my car for several minutes to decompress. My head is pounding and my thoughts are racing. I mostly kept to myself, because, beyond the depression, I simply couldn't keep up with the mental marathon that was pretending I wasn't one overstimulating action away from unraveling entirely. My entire life I've been called irritable, dramatic, and bitchy for it. Do I feel guilty? Yes. But it's hard not to snap when you're using every ounce of energy to not fracture into a million pieces in public. Soul-sucking lights. Loud, sloppy chewing. Dozens of voices overlapping. Shrill laughing. Thudding music. That stomach-churning, awful mix of smells of too many people simply existing in one room. No matter what I do, it's always way too fucking much. A personal hell all for me and nobody else notices.

I learned a long time ago that most people would never understand and nobody in my life would sympathize. So, I was always the asshole when I'd snap on occasion. It's laughable really, the cruelty of which those around me ignored the suffering so clearly written on my face. But that would be inconvenient. Would ruin their fun, wouldn't it? It's better for everyone if I stick to short outings and spend most of my time alone. I'm happier and they're happier. It's a win-win, I guess. I've spent my entire life telling myself I'm happier alone because the alternative would break me into a million pieces. Accepting that everyone I've ever opened up to decided I was too hard to love would break me in a way I could not recover from. Instead, I tell myself I'm happier this way—alone and out of the way.

When I finally get home and take off my short, platform heels, I let out a heavy sigh of relief. The bottoms of my feet burn as I trudge up the stairs completely drained, and I couldn't be more grateful to be home. After a hot shower, I've managed to stabilize enough to feel calm as I lay my head on the pillow.

My relaxed state doesn't last long, though. Movement out of the corner of my eye catches my attention. I want to believe the shifting of the mattress was caused by Binx, but he's nowhere to be seen. There's a slight indent, like someone

COME OUT COME OUT

is sitting at the bottom of my bed. The sinking pit in my stomach tells me someone is there. I feel eyes on me. Chills erupt over my skin and my throat dries. I stare at the spot, terrified to blink, and find that it's moved. Me and what I'm assuming is my persistent ghost both sit there frozen.

After another minute without movement goes by, I find my courage. "What the fuck do you want? Please just leave me alone. I'm so tired." And just like that, any composure I'd gathered under the steam of the hot shower is out the window. I'm sobbing now and there's no stopping it. The ghost must take pity on me, or maybe I'm just too overwhelmed to care because that's the last I think of it.

My little wraith

CHAPTER FOURTEEN

Aiden

November 28th, 2020 – Two Weeks Later

"Skye, please don't leave me."

"I can't do this."

"Skye, I'm begging you. I'll do anything."

I plead at the foot of her bed where my entire life lies. She stares into her phone absolutely oblivious to my suffering.

"Don't leave me here alone."

"Skye . . ."

I'm unraveling. It's as if I can feel the phantom heavy breaths and rapid pulse of past breakdowns but without the comfort of knowing they'll recede eventually. Mentally and emotionally, I've untethered from the sense of peace and control I've found since Skye's arrival. *She's leaving.* She's leaving, and there's nothing I can do about it. I want to rage, I want to scream, I want to get on my knees and beg her to stay, but I can't.

Like a lost puppy, I follow her back and forth from the bedroom to the bathroom as she gets ready for the day. I'm terrified to take my eyes off of her; I can't afford to lose a single moment with her. This is so cruel, it's so unfair. It's unfathomable that she was brought into my life, and now she's walking out and has no idea what she's leaving behind.

She starts placing her items in the hall and I follow her again, watching her as my mind scatters in a million directions despite how hard I'm trying to hold it together. I fight the urge to kick the stack of boxes waiting at the top of the stairs. It wouldn't do any good. Plus, I don't want her last memory here to be a bad one. Losing control and scaring her is the whole reason I'm in this mess.

Instead, I stand helplessly as she takes boxes down two at a time and sets them by the door. Flashbacks of those lonely weeks I spent in this barren house sink their fangs into me and inject their venom into my spiraling thoughts. What am I supposed to do without her? I can't possibly go back to the way things were. *I'm not* going back. I have two days to figure something out. I need to give her a reason to stay. I grab that hope with a strangling grip and try to force myself to focus on the only thing that matters. I resign myself to sitting against the far wall where I can still watch Skye work but feel slightly less chaotic out of the fray of it all.

Unfortunately, two hours later, I still have no plausible ideas. I need to understand how I've been able to become corporeal those two previous times; that's the key to making this work. I need her to *see* me. I need her to *hear* me. If she knew . . . if she knew, maybe she'd stay.

Finally, Skye calls it a day. Her cheeks are red and sweat coats her brow as she surveys the progress she's made. She did a lot. *Too much.* There's so much empty space, now. The house feels as hollow as I do.

My eyes are glued to her as she strips off her dirty clothes. I memorize every inch of her body—each freckle, the dips and curves, the faded scars on her ankles and wrists. My heart twists at the possibility that one day, I might forget all the little reasons I fell for her and all I'll have is the ghost of our memories to keep me company. I want her to be more than that. I want us to have more than that. What I wouldn't give to trade a lifetime of pointless fucks and puppy love for a chance with her.

The spray of water on the tile breaks me from my thoughts and I move to the bathroom. I perch on the countertop and lean against the medicine cabinet for the best vantage point. Her shoulders sag with tiredness from the exhausting effort of going up and down the stairs all day. My fingers flex with the urge to rub the knots out of her skin. They clench around empty air as always.

Stepping out of the shower, Skye wraps herself in a towel as she approaches the counter, and stops right next to me. I can almost convince myself that I can feel the heat radiating off her skin. I slide off the counter and stand behind her, capturing this mental image of us standing together, the one she could never see. I lean around her, bringing my finger to the fogged glass and write the word I want to scream.

Her eyes flick up to the mirror as she stops mid-lotion when I get to "y." I can hear her swallow thickly and I don't miss the chills that erupt over her exposed flesh. I stop, standing absolutely still and leaving the letter incomplete. The tail is short, but there's no mistaking that it says *"Stay."*

Skye stands frozen as she trembles. Her gaze shifts slowly to just above her right shoulder, exactly where my own reflection would be if she could see it. Neither of us does anything for several seconds.

"What—" Her uneven voice is barely above a whisper, but I'm close enough to hear. "What do you want?" A single tear slips free, and she clutches her tucked towel to her chest.

Everything. I respond, but despite our proximity, she

can't hear me. Instead of waiting for a reply, I write the same word again. She shakes her head and it might as well be a physical blow. I move over to the right, where there's still undisturbed steam on the mirror. I move my finger quickly across the wet glass and write the word *"Please"*.

An uneasy laugh leaves her lips and she slaps her palm over her mouth in surprise. Her breath echoes in the cup of her hand as she tries to suffocate the mounting fear that's clear in her eyes. Still, she doesn't move.

This is my chance.

I bring my finger to the mirror again and write, *"I won't hurt you."* I pause then add, *"I'm sorry."*

Skye's large brown eyes widen in disbelief, but her hand slowly falls from her mouth, revealing reddened lips she's clearly been biting to hold back her terror. Her gaze searches the mirror and stops several inches above her shoulder, as if she can detect me in the empty reflection. If I had a beating heart, it would have stopped. The breath would have stilled in my chest. Instead, I become rigid and try to keep the hope at bay.

"Please, please, please, please . . ." I chant in my head.

When she starts to scan the mirror, her eyes shifting quickly, it's obvious she doesn't see me. I try not to deflate completely. I know she *feels* me. I'm as present as she is right now.

Several moments pass and I worry she'll run, but she takes a slow, deep breath and then lifts her hand. The letters she draws on the mirror below mine are uneven. *"Why?"*

"Because I want you to" is what I really want to say; it won't do. Instead, I appeal to something I know she'll relate to. I write back, *"I'm lonely"*.

There's a moment where I worry it was the wrong thing, but then her shoulders drop. She sees herself reflected in those words even if she'll never admit it out loud. Her pink tongue swipes across her down-turned lips. Her lashes soften with tears as she shakes her head. "I'm sorry. I can't do this." The words are a whisper, but it doesn't lessen the blow.

I knew and yet, I hoped.

It's over. She's made her choice. I should let her go. I *have* to let her go.

That's what you do when you love something, isn't it? Everything within me bucks against the notion, but I don't know what else I can do. For months, I've taken every opportunity I can to make this work. I'll admit, some of the moments were not my best, but I did, *try*. Was I really so delusional in this space between life and death that I thought maybe things would work out? It's like they say, I guess, lonely people are desperate.

As the reality of our situation sinks in, the bleakness weighs me down, and for the first time since she arrived, I feel genuinely hopeless. Succumbing to the truth, I remove myself from the situation. I can't watch her go. *I won't.*

Instead of inflicting more torture, I resign myself to the basement, the only place I know I can go in this cursed house where I won't see her. With one last look over my shoulder, I soak in the tragic beauty that is my little wraith.

My Binxie boy

Chapter Fifteen

Skye

November 29th, 2020 – The Next Morning

As I follow the moving truck out of the driveway, I can't help but watch the house in the rearview mirror until it's out of view. It feels like I'm leaving a piece of myself back there and I can't explain why, only that there's a tether pulled taught that's going to snap. And when it does, it'll rip out a chunk of me that it'll keep there forever.

I remind myself that this is for the best, that the house wasn't safe to live in anymore. A wayward thought in the back of my mind chimes in, saying that we misjudged that house and the spirit that came with it. The words *"I won't hurt you"* in foggy silhouette play on a loop.

I want to convince myself that it was just manipulating

me, but I know that's not the truth. It defies all reason, but I just *know*. It might be totally irrational, though it wouldn't be the first time I've been accused of that and it won't be the last. The confines of what's normal and acceptable never had much bearing on me. With a disdain for most other humans, I had always wished there was more and never shied away from the idea of embracing whatever else was out there. I'd gone down enough rabbit holes online over the years that my mind was pretty wide open to the possibilities of all sorts of paranormal phenomena. How could people really believe that it was just us here? No lingering souls, no beings from other dimensions, or no species outside of humans? That seems *irrational*–and frankly, narrow-minded–to me.

As the miles pass and I get some distance, the house's hold loosens on me ever so slightly and I remember what I'm doing here. My decision has been made. What's done is done. I should put all thoughts of what transpired there in the past and look to the future.

It, thankfully, only takes about ten minutes to get to my new home, the freshly painted light blue exterior coming into view as I take a wide turn into the neighborhood. It's much more suburban than anywhere I've lived in a long time. I thought it'd make me feel safe, but looking around at the neighbors and the similar houses, it feels suffocating. I'm sure

I'll adjust; *I hope.*

    The movers reverse into the driveway and I push the garage door opener as I parallel park on the street to stay out of their way. While they prep, I unlock the door and bring a very confused, yet relieved, Binx inside. Neither of us enjoyed the drive with him meowing his displeasure about being stuffed in his carrier and on the road against his will. He especially hated the jaunt down the freeway.

    Ironically, the house feels dead inside. The bare, intensely white walls glare back at me. The new tile floor echoes my footsteps back at me intimidatingly. Everything is cold and devoid of all personality. *Anyone* could live here. There's nothing special or unique about it. I fight the urge to recoil as I make my way to my new bedroom. It's just going to take some adjusting. Sure, the old house had a lot of character, but it also had a ghost. One that did try to drown me. *But didn't.* My subconscious tacks on.

    I stop in the bathroom to let Binx out. Once I unload all his necessities, I go back out to the living space to start unpacking. The plan lasts about five minutes. As soon as my bed is unloaded, I leave the half-unpacked box of dishes on the counter and grab my laptop instead. I'm unable to focus on the website redesign I'm supposed to be working on, though. Everything feels *wrong*—and it's not just because the bare

COME OUT COME OUT

mattress is itching the shit out of my legs—but I push myself to focus since I have a looming deadline.

Disappearing into my work always helps. After another hour, the movers finish up and I'm officially alone in my new home. A low rumble from my stomach reminds me that I didn't get a chance to eat today. I'm suddenly ravenous, like I'm about to tear into the first thing I see, hungry. I inhale a string of cheese to stave off the edge while I make something more filling. That's when I realize I don't have anything unpacked other than the few fridge things I brought over in the little cooler. Taking inventory is quick—just a few apples, string cheese, and some Greek yogurt. I eye the nearly empty box of cereal on the counter and my stomach rumbles louder in protest at the idea. Yeah, that's absolutely not going to cut it.

I shut the fridge disappointedly and go find my phone. I pull up my go-to food delivery app and scroll through the options. I know I'm hungry, but for what, I have no clue. *Some dick.* My brain supplies unhelpfully. For a second I consider opening one of my dating apps, but then I remember how it ended the last time and immediately shut that down. Just food it is, then. Finally, I decide on pizza, with a side salad and cannoli, of course.

I have about forty-five minutes until it arrives, so I decide to take a shower. Thankfully, I know myself and have a towel, clean sheets, my pajamas, and toiletries packed in a duffle bag for easy access. Once the water is hot, I step into the shower, closing the door behind me. It's kind of tight quarters—apparently even new builders don't consider fat people when building houses, typical. At least there's enough room for me to raise my arms and wash my hair, but it's going to be kind of a bitch to shave my legs. *A problem for future Skye.*

    I scrub my hair, rubbing my scalp to ease some of the tension that's been haunting me since I got here. I use my favorite watermelon-mint soap and by the time I turn off the water, I feel so much lighter, fresh even. I slide on a pair of soft shorts and a cropped tank top of the same breathable material and throw my hair up in a towel. When I check my phone, the delivery app tells me my driver is fifteen minutes out. That's the perfect amount of time to open that bottle of wine I'd set aside and enjoy a glass while I put some sheets on the bed.

    As I toss the last of my arguably too many throw pillows on top of my duvet, the doorbell rings. I grit my teeth as the shrill sound reverberates off the walls. Once it stops, I gulp down the rest of my wine and grab my phone as I head for the door, careful not to trip over Binx as he excitedly weaves between my feet. I pass the mirror and give myself a quick once-over. The bags under my eyes are pretty bad from all the lost sleep over the last few months, but who cares. It kind of

COME OUT COME OUT

works with my grungy aesthetic anyways.

When I open the door, I'm shocked to find a hot blond with perky tits that I want in my mouth immediately. I must be staring openly because she lets out a soft laugh that's music to my ears. She clears her throat drawing my attention to hazel eyes that shine with flirtation.

I wrestle with the urge to invite her in but decide against it. "Thank you, I already tipped in the app, so we're good."

She doesn't turn to go. "I know. A generous one, too. I think that merits some extra assistance." When I don't immediately object, she smiles brightly and steps closer.

Fuck, she smells like the perfect blend of spice and florals. I'm barely able to resist the temptation. "I appreciate the offer, I do, I just . . ." *Can't get a fucking stranger I'll probably never see again out of my head.*

"I get it, no pressure. If you're ever, umm, up for a *special* delivery, look me up. Name's Melissa Pierce."

I sigh and shut the door behind me; disappointed with how he's got me so wrapped up over *nothing*. I head to the kitchen and sit down to eat, but my mind isn't on my food. Instead, it cooks up a nice little fantasy—one where I didn't turn her away.

She follows without hesitation and shuts the door behind her.

Melissa even removes her shoes and leaves them by the door. I like her already.

"You have this place all to yourself?" Curiosity and suggestiveness color her words.

"I do." I set the bag on the counter. When I turn back toward her. She doesn't waste any time. Melissa presses me against the fridge while her fingers travel down my sides exposed by the crop top. Her nails dig into me just slightly as she feathers kisses along my jaw and up to the corner of my lips.

"Get up on the counter," she whispers seductively.

My ass barely makes contact with the marble before she's tugging at the waistband of my shorts. I lift my hips in response and revel in delight as her pupils blow wide at the sight of my bare cunt.

Soft as rose petals, her dainty fingers part my thighs. "Is this okay?" Her hot breath tickles the sensitive skin as she leans closer. Green eyes shine up at me with desire that has my muscles clenching.

"Fuck, yes." I pant as her pouty lips place a kiss on my clit. My hips roll against her mouth of their own volition. She responds by flicking her tongue up and down my center, teasing and massaging eagerly as I become increasingly wetter. "Mmm, yeah, just like that." I grip her shiny ponytail in my fist and pull her head back. She smirks up at me with glossy lips and I haul her up to taste myself on her lips. Our tongues tangle in a fiery kiss. Hungry for more, I pull her tube top down to expose her small, silver-tipped breasts. I slide off the counter, desperate to have them in my mouth. The moan she lets out when my hot tongue meets her rosy, pierced nipple sends a flood of arousal gushing out of me.

As if she can sense it, she slides a hand between us and rolls her fingers over my clit in taunting circles. "Bedroom?"

I nod and break away, leading her down the hall quickly. I sit on the bed and watch her finish undressing, removing a pair of lacy panties and jeans that hug her ass so perfectly.

The fantasy glitches and suddenly, Aiden is standing behind her, a jealous scowl on his face. With some effort, I redirect my thoughts and pick up where I left off.

Melissa marches up to me and slides her hands under my shirt, rushing it over my head, then pushing me back against the mattress. My hands find her ass and squeeze; when I do, her slick pussy grinds against my stomach. I slide a hand between us, thankful I removed my nails before moving, and tease her clit. She grinds down on my hand, and I'm mesmerized watching her tits jiggle above me.

With an eager moan, she pulls away. "Scoot up on the bed, I want to ride your face."

As soon as she hovers above my face, I wrap my arms around her plush thighs and anchor her to my mouth. I suck her clit, loving how she rolls her hips in response. My tongue moves eagerly between her lips and teases her entrance, making her whine in a way that has me clenching my legs together. When I spear my tongue into her, she does it again. I eat her pussy like I would the dinner that's going cold on my counter—I couldn't care less.

"Oh my god, that feels so fucking good." Her movements become jerkier as she fights her orgasm, but I'm not stopping yet. I double my efforts and am rewarded when she spasms around my tongue and writhes above me. Finally, she dismounts my face.

"You're amazing at that," she says before licking the lingering wetness from around my mouth and down my chin. I move to sit up, but her hand on my chest forces me back down. "I'm not done with you yet; you haven't even come. What kind of service would that be?" Her brow furrows in mock concern before she brings her mouth to my nipple and sucks and nips at it. I arch into her and she shifts her attention to the other peak, that skilled tongue making me pant and moan.

I slide my fingers down my stomach and start to play with myself while she teases my sensitive breasts, but she's not having it. Melissa kisses her way down my stomach before she runs her finger through my center.

"So needy," she mocks. It would be hot, but my mind once again conjures up Aiden, who says the same. He hovers over me, pumping his fist up and down his cock. I force him out of the fantasy; he won't ruin this too.

"Yeah, and?" I brush it off then shove her head down and bring my hips up to meet her lips, trying to silence her so I can enjoy this a little longer. I can fuck him out of my memory if I try hard enough, right? I'm determined to test the theory.

Melissa licks me slowly at first, testing my patience. I want to be struggling to think straight, but all I can picture is Aiden telling me what a needy slut I am before punishing me. A hard suck on my clit has my back bowing. I cry out, but she doesn't give me a chance to catch my breath before she does it again. That's better. But it's not enough.

"'Yes, right there." I groan as she works her fingers inside me.

She strokes my inner walls and teases my clit a bit more before she finally obliges. She leans back on her side and lifts my leg and fits herself between my thick thighs, then uses one for leverage as she slides her dripping wet pussy against mine. I moan as she grinds on me. That combined with her sexy whimpers and the way her body flexes around mine, is enough to distract me from my wayward thoughts.

I grab my breasts and pinch and tug my nipples, driving myself toward an orgasm.

"Not so fast, little wraith. Nobody else gets to make you come." The memory of Aiden's voice in my head shatters the illusion altogether. That incessant fucking asshole.

ALEXIA ONYX

I sigh down at my barely touched food that's gone cold. So, this is how it's going to be?

tastes like bad decisions

Chapter Sixteen

Skye

December 1st, 2020 – Two Days Later

Sun creeps through the vertical blinds that are the bane of my existence. Their clacking woke me up half an hour ago and I haven't summoned the energy to get up and either turn off the ceiling fan or open them a bit more so they stop making that god-forsaken noise. I exhale a long sigh, drag my hand over my face, and finally force myself to get out of bed. It's nothing new for me to be low-energy, but the thought of having to unpack all this shit for the second time within less than a year is absolutely draining.

Once again, I find myself wishing I hadn't moved.

The house is fine; the plumbing works, the neighborhood is quiet, and there aren't any ghosts—I should be

COME OUT COME OUT

especially thrilled about that last one. But still, I drag my feet across the floor with zero enthusiasm at the prospect of finally getting settled.

I regretfully twist the wand a few times to open the blinds and squint against the bright sun. *Another glorious morning...*

Binx meows at me from the doorway, letting me know he's ready to be fed. Of course, I follow him. Once my boy is fed, I grab a Greek yogurt and pour some dry cereal into it, mixing it for the perfect crunchy texture, so I can actually tolerate it. As I eat, I can feel the boxes stacked high in the living room looming over me, silently judging me.

I really, really do not want to deal with this shit. Resigned to my fate, I run out to the car to grab my speaker and then queue up some My Chemical Romance, System of a Down, and Radiohead then get started on the first box.

Hours fly by and I finish unpacking everything for the kitchen, so I decide to take a break. I grab my e-reader from my bag and fling myself down on the couch. I really should shower first; I've been sweating, but I can already feel my back and arms protesting from spending all that time alternating between over-extending to reach the top cabinets or crouching down like a shrimp to put stuff away in the lower cabinets. Forcing the thought of my sweat soaking into the fabric from my mind, I scroll through my library and pick back up on one of the paranormal romances I temporarily dnf'd months ago.

I blink my eyes open as my groggy mind catches up with the fact that I fell asleep. Between the accidental nap and the still-unfamiliar space, I'm especially disoriented. A yawn escapes me as stretch my legs, but I freeze when I notice the box of books I had on the floor has spilled over.

Those are way too heavy for Binx to knock over himself. "Binxie, come here, honey," I call out in as even of a tone as I can muster. He doesn't come.

My heartbeat picks up, drowning out my ability to hear. I rely on my tired eyes instead, scanning the area. Nothing else seems out of place in the living room, *odd*. I go to stand, but moonlight gleaming on a faint sliver of skin stops me in my tracks. Excitement lights in me when Aiden comes to mind, but it's extinguished quickly when I remember that there's no way he'd know where I was. I never even told him I was moving, didn't have the chance. Reality sets in that this time, there's a stranger in my house, and they're not welcome.

Bile rises in my throat and tears prick my eyes. I fight the urge to slide my flattened palm slowly toward my phone that I know is under my pillow. After all, there's no point in calling the cops, they wouldn't get here in time to stop the inevitable and I'd rather not endanger my neighbors, they can write gruesome details on a notepad later.

With a rough swallow, I stand as calmly as I can. *I need to find a weapon.* On second thought, I grab my phone. With its heavy ass case, it'll do a little damage if I whack someone in the head with it. I hope.

I stand, keeping my head tilted down inconspicuously but making sure that hand is kept in my peripherals at all times. My racing thoughts are almost dizzying as I piece together my next moves. Is it better to confront them or put distance between us? I genuinely don't know. The funny thing is, I've thought about this scenario, but in reality, it's so much different.

Remembering the self-defense kit on my keychain my dad gave me before he moved away, I force myself to walk to the key holder near the door. With a deep breath, I unlock the mace, flick on the light, run toward the hallway, and spray like my life depends on it. It's not the best plan, but it's what my barely awake brain came up with.

The man in my house cries out throwing his hands up to protect his eyes. I'm impressed with the spraying distance and effectiveness of this little thing; *five stars*. He falls to the ground and I take the opportunity to stomp on his groin several times. I spray a shit ton of the mace in his face again for good measure.

"Wait, stop, I'm your landlord," the man says between shuddering breaths.

My foot freezes midair as I process those words. "What the fuck? What are you doing here?" I take a step back. "Wait, how do I know you're not lying?" I study his face, trying to recall the features of the man I've only seen in online pictures of on the rental website.

"My ID is in my pocket." His voice is shrill with pain.

Reluctantly, I reach into his shorts pocket and grab his wallet. When I take out the ID the name Mike Randolphe is right there next to his picture. The name matches the signature on the lease. "Again, why the fuck are you here?"

"I wanted to see if everything was to your liking since you'd only seen it through the virtual tour before." He hasn't even tried to get off the ground.

"And you just decided to let yourself in?" I don't give him a chance to respond. "Why would you hide in the hallway then?" When he attempts to lean up on his elbows, I hold the mace up. He slumps back down to the floor.

"I …" he draws the word out, raising my suspicions, "used to just walk in with the old tenant, I didn't really think about it. Then I tripped on the box and didn't want to scare you."

"Yeah, because lurking in the hallway in the dark isn't

COME OUT COME OUT

scary. I'm calling bullshit." I pull out my phone and press record. When his mouth pops open, I raise a brow and shake the little canister in my hand. "It was dark in here, so why would you come into a house when it looked empty?"

I look him over again, looking for any clue that he might be here for something practical. But there aren't any tools sticking out his pockets and there isn't mail or paperwork scattered on the ground. To my utter horror, what I do finally notice is that his pants are unzipped.

Disgust overrides fear. *How did I actually end up with a creepy ass landlord?* That cam fantasy I'd conjured up before is feeling a little too real and way less sexy than I'd imagined. "You know what I think?" I squat down, mace still extended. "I think that you're a sick fuck who likes to watch your tenants without their knowledge. Thought you'd crank one out while I was sleeping?" I tilt my head, waiting for whatever lies are about to come out of his mouth.

He shakes his head back and forth, mouth gaping uselessly like a dying fish, so I raise my foot like I'm going to kick him again.

"Shit, okay, look, I'm sorry. What do I have to do for us to pretend like this never happened? Free rent for a month?" His red, tear-stained face is tight with worry.

I laugh at his audacity. "A free month of rent? You have

got to be kidding me. I'm not fucking staying here."

"You signed a lease," he protests.

"A lease that you're going to nullify with zero complaints."

"Come on—"

I cut him off; there's no fucking way I'm living here. "You're going to nullify the lease and you're going to pay for my movers to get me out of here." I stand. "Get the fuck out of my house."

I back up to put some space between us as he picks himself off the floor.

"Can't we work something out?" The desperation in his voice only disgusts me more.

"We already did. If you don't do what I asked, I will make sure everyone knows what a sad, pathetic pervert you are."

He looks like he wants to strangle me, but instead, he turns to leave.

"And Mike," I wait for him to look over his shoulder, "You're not going to rent this house to any single people again. I will be keeping tabs on this place."

"Fucking bitch," he mumbles under his breath. I choose to ignore it because I have far bigger things to worry about, like what I'm supposed to do now.

COME OUT COME OUT

As soon as he's out the door, I lock it behind him. Poor Binx slinks out from under the couch, wide-eyed and crouched down. "It's okay, baby. You're safe now." I stroke his silky fur; the soothing motion is just as much for me as it is for him. I swear, I can't catch a damn break. When Binx pushes against my chest to jump down, I let him go and walk back to my room to grab my computer. For a moment, I consider staying back here, but I want to make sure that asshole doesn't come back.

Once my computer fires up, I bring back up the listings I'd previously viewed. Of course, nothing is available anymore, that's California rentals for you. With a heavy sigh, I go back to the search and add all my filters. Surprisingly, the old house pops up on the first page of listings. Even more shocking is the sense of fondness that washes over me when I look at the photos of the worn exterior and antique interior. Looking at the exterior shots, I squint to see if there's any sign of spirits lingering in windows. It's silly, but I'm a bit disappointed when I don't see anything out of the ordinary.

I chew at my nails. This entire situation has really made the whole haunted house thing seem like a walk in the park. I would rather deal with a ghost than a living and breathing creep. The surreal conversation we scrawled across that steamy mirror comes to mind again. The ghost apologized. Maybe they really were just lonely. Maybe they were as desperate as I was for someone who could stand being around them. Indecision gnaws at my insides.

After several anxiety-ridden minutes of staring at my screen, I decide to add it to my love list and keep moving. I continue to scroll through the available listings, but there's not much to choose from, especially in my price range. It was hard enough to find this place; most people aren't moving during the busy holiday season. I could move farther, I guess, but this area has become my comfort zone. I know all the streets, I have my regular food places and the grocery store with the tolerable overhead lights, everything is just a few minutes apart. Moving somewhere else would totally disrupt my life. It takes me so long to adjust and I'm already struggling to meet the bare-minimum demands of my existence.

With only four plausible options—if you can call a haunted house that—I close my laptop and decide to sleep on it. I messaged the other three places. If they respond overnight, I'll schedule a viewing.

I walk to the kitchen, double-check the slider lock, and then grab one of the short barstools I'd bought specifically to fit this house and wedge it under the front door. Once the windows are all closed and locked, I head back to my room. Even with the house all locked up, I find unease slithering under my skin. Everything in me is screaming at me to drown it out, but I know better than to drink or use anything tonight. Who knows if this fucking weirdo is going to try anything. So, instead, I sit with the discomfort, the fear, and the indecision. I don't get any sleep, but I do knock out some projects I've been neglecting because of the moving process. At least that will help my bank account, which is majorly suffering.

At sunrise, I get up and feed Binx, then check my email. I have one response. Apparently, it's already spoken for, they just forgot to take the listing down. *Great.* I'm determined to at least wait for a response on one of the others before making my decision, but I do go ahead and email my previous landlord about the house to see if he'd be willing to re-rent it to me. I get a response back within minutes, he's confused, but he agrees. I leave it unanswered, just in case another one of the rentals comes through. For now, I busy myself with re-packing the kitchen. Suddenly, I'm relieved I'd put off getting settled. It would have been such a bitch to have to box up everything again. I was still sore from all the lifting, crouching, and moving I'd done already.

By lunchtime, the kitchen is as empty as it was just a few days ago. I grab an orange soda, string cheese, and my laptop and head to my room for a break with Binx at my heels. When I reload my email, I have a response saying the studio apartment in town is available. Unfortunately, they don't allow pets. Wish they'd had that in their listing, but that's why I'd asked. Two down, one more to go.

I also have a short email from Mike. I grimace and open it.

Attached is the nullified lease as discussed. – Mike

Temporarily satisfied, I decide to call the movers so I can respond with an invoice. Unfortunately, they don't have availability for tomorrow but I took the first appointment for the next day. I respond back to Mike and am pleased to find that the five hundred dollars shows up in my bank account within ten minutes.

Just two more sleepless nights to go.

Come out, come out, wherever you are

CHAPTER SEVENTEEN

Aiden

December 4th, 2020 – Two Days Later

Five, going on six, endless days without Skye. I would think it's been an eternity if it weren't for the clock on the stove. I wonder when they'll turn the power out and I'll be plunged back into darkness. Not that it matters, the floors and walls could fall away into an empty abyss and it wouldn't feel any different. I'm trapped in a meaningless existence, dead like the trees that were broken down and reshaped into the planks that hold this house together.

Skye reshaped me. Watching her was like a life raft that pulled me in from being adrift at sea. Loving her gave me purpose, made me *someone* again.

Without her, I'm no one. Floating aimlessly.

COME OUT COME OUT

I wonder if this is why spirits have their reputation for being angry and hostile; is it the loneliness that does it? Drifting into darkness and isolation without a say, always left behind, cast off, and easily forgotten. Never seen. What other option was there? Sunken into the seams of the world, where nobody can see us. It wasn't a choice at all to become a swirling mass of loss and loathing, I could feel myself becoming it.

In these moments, when I feel so lost, I can't help but think of Becca. I hope there was something better waiting for her in death. The complete and utter isolation had gnawed through all that I was in life—and I was someone who'd embraced my fate of being on the outside of everything. For Becca, someone who'd been social and a high achiever, this existence would have destroyed whatever was left of her when she passed.

From my perspective, she was the kind of person who was so full of joy and vibrancy. Sometimes I wonder if she was hiding her own darkness beneath that hopeful exterior. Maybe she was like Skye, someone who battled their inner demons on their own. I'm ashamed to consider that maybe I allowed her to suffer in silence. After all, I never would have believed there was any possibility of her taking her own life. *Could I have possibly failed her in so many ways?* God, I hope not.

The last year had felt like an eternity; I can't even

imagine what the hell six years would be like. I want to believe that she's somewhere better, that she's found peace from the things that tormented her in life. But if she is here, in this world still as much as I am, I hope my parents stay in that home despite the painful memories that haunt those halls like me as I pace through this large house.

I stroll past where I killed Rob; the point of no return for my descent into madness. I stop in the kitchen and lean against the counter opposite of where I first fucked Skye. Despite how many times I've thought back on that memory fondly, it isn't the tight grip of her pussy that I'm thinking about or the way she whimpered and begged me to fuck her. No. It's the feeling of my hands on her soft skin, the thrumming of her heart pressed against my chest, and the trust shining in her eyes when she let me make her come that holds me here in this spot for God knows how long.

I grip the countertop and my finger brushes against something. There's a lone piece of paper. This must be her forwarding address left for her landlord. Knowing the information won't do me any good, I still pick it up and trace my fingers over the rough scribble of someone who's spent the vast majority of their life typing and now can barely write a thing.

I've never been there, but I recognize the town. I almost

wish I didn't. She's only a few miles from me but just as out of reach as she would be if she was on an entirely different continent. At least when she ran errands or went out on the very rare occasion, I knew she'd be back. I knew that even though I'd spend far too much time staring at that front door, she'd walk back through it and everything would be right again.

For the hundredth time, I curse my circumstances of being tethered to this house. I march out to the front porch, a small reprieve from the walls that start to press in around me. I latch on to the signs of life around me, the rustle of the wind through the trees, the birds that fly freely in the grey sky above me, and the squirrels that race around tree trunks. It's easy to forget that there's still a world out here, beyond the glass windows that cage me in. I step back off the porch and look up at my prison. The paint has chipped and peeled in so many places, some of the decorative shutters are missing a few of their slats, and dirt and debris coat random sections of the exterior, but even still, it's a beautiful house. I can at least appreciate that.

My reverence for the old structure is broken by gravel crunching under tires. A moving truck is coming up the driveway. *That was fast.* I want to feel relieved that I'm no longer alone—people watching is better than complete silence—but disappointment weighs me down. The excitement I felt when

Skye and her roommates moved in is nowhere to be found. Even before I knew her, she'd brought me joy.

With nothing better to do, I take a seat on one of the weather-beaten, white Adirondack chairs that decorate the porch and watch the movers get to work. They start with the furniture and the bedframe grabs my attention. There's something familiar about it—and not in the way that all black furniture looks the same, but how distinct the scratches and knicks in the paint are. More tires over the dirt and gravel draw my attention back to the driveway and even though I recognize the car, I tamp down the hope that's building inside me like a volcano about to erupt.

I don't realize I'm leaning forward, getting the best view I can without getting up, until one of the movers says, "Did you see that?" He and the mover who's helping him bring the bed frame up to the door stop and stare. For a minute, I'm sure they can see me. "Did you see it move? See the legs lifting off the ground?" he asks his friend.

"Yeah . . ." the other man responds, his eyes fixed on the back legs that I promptly slam back down just to fuck with them. There's such a rare opportunity to make myself laugh these days; I can't pass it up. As I expected, he jumps and drops his end of the bed frame. We all collectively flinch. *Oops.*

I don't hear the rest of their conversation because all of

my attention is zeroed in on the black-haired beauty who gets out of the car in the driveway. She stops mid-step and stares up at the house. *Is she looking for me? Could she have missed me?* I find I don't care what the answers are, I'm just grateful that she's back. I don't know how, and I don't know why, but I'm more sure than ever that our paths crossing is fate. What other explanation could there be? My temporary elation is darkened when I catch the end of the conversation beside me. "Let's just focus and get through this job as soon as this bitch comes to unlock the door. What the hell is taking her so long?" I slowly turn my head, identifying the speaker as the man who'd dropped the bedframe. I would celebrate Skye's return later, but for now, I'd make it my mission to scare the shit out of this asshole the rest of the time he's here. No one talks about my girl that way.

    Before Skye makes it up the short set of steps, I move around the men and open the door to the house, in part to welcome her back but mostly to make them uncomfortable. I almost miss the slight upturn of Skye's lips while reveling in the hard swallow and wide eyes of the man who was previously shit-talking her. I can't even guess what would drive her back here, but her relief about being back at the house, *at home*, is palpable. I bask in it a moment longer before following them inside.

While Skye busies herself with setting things up as they're being unpacked, I focus my full attention on terrorizing the mover who thought it was a good idea to insult her. I trail him closely up the stairs and into Skye's room. On his second trip back up, I shift the small stack of boxes he set down, so when he turns back around, he trips, checking his shoulder hard against the wall. Child's play, but I don't want him running out of here when she still needs help. When he places a few boxes in the bathroom, I nudge the door open, encouraging it to creak ominously on its hinges. His face goes slack and his eyes dart side to side. A genuine smile finds its way onto my face as he speed walks back to the staircase and goes down as quickly as he can without breaking an ankle.

"You good?" One of the other movers asks. He doesn't respond, just nods briskly.

This is the most fun I've had in a long time. I take the opportunity to rearrange things, crowd his space, and otherwise disorient him as he urges his team to pick up the pace so they can wrap up the job quickly.

"One more trip and then we're finished. I want to get out of here, this place gives me the creeps."

A full laugh leaves my chest. For my grand finale, I intend to truly scare the shit out of him. The perfect opportunity presents itself when he places her nightstand on the wrong side of the room, so naturally, I give it a hard shove sending it sliding across the floor. His mouth drops open, lips quivering as he backs his way out of the room, nearly tripping over his feet as he turns the corner. I follow, nearly skipping down the steps, to make sure he doesn't give Skye any more shit.

"We're all finished," the man says from outside the open front door.

"Be right there," Skye calls back from the kitchen. Her brows are furrowed as she enters the room. "That was fast."

His eyes are shifty as he glances around the room. "We're really hungry. Had to have my men work double-time."

"Oh, okay." She laughs awkwardly. "Well, I already paid online, so I guess that's it. Thanks for the help."

With a single nod, he books it to the truck without a look back. *Good riddance.*

Feeling weightless compared to the last few days, I head downstairs to see what Skye is up to. I stop in my tracks as I take in the sight of her sitting at the kitchen table eating dinner, the picture of perfection.

Skye's return was the birth of stars in the dark of night, illuminating all that I'd lost sight of. Mere hours ago, I was ready to succumb to the bleak reality of life without her, and now, now I was certain that she was mine to keep. She'd come back. *She'd come back to me.*

That is everything. It's more than I dared to hope for. I'll show her how right the choice was. She'll see that she belongs here, *with me.* But for now, I'm content to sit back and bide my time. She needs to feel safe, to readjust; she needs to come to me. I'll wait as long as it takes.

My Binxie boy

CHAPTER EIGHTEEN

Skye

January 1st, 2021 - One Month Later

It's a new year, and not much has changed. I've been buried in work non-stop for weeks—everyone wants to start the new year off with a bang, which means updated websites, new logos; the works, for a lot of them. I'm grateful for the steady income, I am, but now I'm completely mentally depleted. I've hardly had a minute to think, let alone get re-settled in the house. I've officially put up my 'out of office' message for the next two weeks and intend to give myself the break I desperately need. There's stuff everywhere that needs to be organized, especially since this chaos is putting me on edge, but I've earned some rest first.

I decide to spend this first day off in bed. I'm indulging

myself in a movie marathon. More specifically, a horror movie marathon. With the food I had delivered earlier, I had them make a second stop at the liquor store for some mimosa ingredients as well as a candy and chip haul. *You can't have a movie marathon without snacks.*

Binx is pleased with my plans for the day as he curls up at my feet and I turn on the first movie of the day, *Jennifer's Body*, the bisexual spooky girl essential. I first fell for Megan Fox when she was in *Holiday In the Sun* and there was really no going back. I take a sip of my mimosa before lighting up a joint. I inhale deeply, letting the smoke nearly drown me before blowing out. I lick my lips, reveling in its misty kiss. Within a few minutes, I'm ready to crack open the Cool Ranch Doritos. *Fucking delicious, as always.* Satisfied with my choices, I lean back into my mountain of throw pillows and pull my blanket tightly around me.

At some point during the second movie, *From Hell*, I drifted off to sleep and I'm greeted by the credits scrolling on the screen when I wake. I sit up, crunching the chip bag noisily under my side. I groan, shrugging off the heavy weight of sleep and sore muscles. I debate whether to stay in bed and restart the movie or rinse off. The shower wins out. I grab my phone and the warmer-than-preferred bottle of sparkling wine. *Shower wine is good for relaxation, okay.*

The hot water beating against my bare skin is almost erotic in the way it releases the tension from my body. I sigh and take a long swig from the bottle. I stand under the spray way longer than I intend to while I finish off my drink and enjoy not having a worry in the world for the first time in a long time. When my feet start to prune, I finally get out. I pull the twin towels over the top of the shower curtain, wrap one around me, then use the other to scrunch the water out of my hair before throwing it back over the rod. I cringe slightly when the metallic rings slide noisily over the rod as I step out. I remind myself for the thousandth time that I need to switch to plastic rings.

The fluffy, absorbent rug is soft under my feet as I stop in front of the mirror. I lean forward to swipe my hand across it but freeze mid-way. Instead, I press a finger to the steamy surface and write, *Hello.*

I start to feel foolish, but then the beginning of letters start to form under mine.

Hi.

"Can you hear me?" I ask out loud.

Several seconds pass, then *Yes* appears.

Okay, well . . . now what? I really hadn't thought that through. Maybe the whole 'you shouldn't drink and text' thing should apply here too. After a minute or two, the awkward silence causes me to blurt out one of the questions I haven't been able to get out of my mind.

"Have you been watching me this whole time?" The thought makes my pussy clench. I want to feel absurd, but I can't find the shame.

My heart is thumping in my ears as the *Y* appears, followed by an *E* and an *S*.

I take a steadying breath. "Have you watched me . . . touch myself?"

Again, *Yes* appears.

I swallow as a thousand thoughts compete for my attention, only one stands out. "Do you like it, watching me touch myself?"

I'll admit I'm relieved when they write *Yes* again.

I'm burning hotter than I did under the hot stream of the shower. I shift my legs against each other as my pussy becomes slick. Staring straight into the blurry mirror, I untuck my towel and let it drop to the floor. A few beats of silence pass. I don't know what I expected to happen—maybe for the ghost to touch me—but while I can feel a heavy gaze roaming my body, the only hands on me are my own.

With a tentative lick of my lips, I step backward, running my hands down my chest and cup under my breasts. The next step, I stop breathless when a coldness envelopes me for a split second. My heart speeds up, about to pummel its way out.

"Was—" my voice is weak, so I clear my throat, "was that you?"

It takes them a few seconds to respond. *It was.*

I have trouble wrapping my mind around that. I walked through them. *We touched.* Another flood of wetness between my thighs. I'm so turned on and I know I shouldn't be, but I can't seem to care. Instead of covering myself in shame, my thumbs roll over my nipples and I resume walking backward until I'm supported by the wall, my eyes never leaving the mirror. With a smirk, I turn away and bend forward, raising my ass in the air and spreading my legs slightly. Feathering my hands up the insides of my thighs, I take my time exploring the sensitive skin. When I finally touch myself, I'm in awe of how wet I am. Angling up on my tiptoes, I give them the perfect view of me teasing my clit in torturously slow circles. I groan; I need more. Turning back around, I arch against the wall, then run my fingers down my stomach, slide one hand between my thighs, and cup my pussy as I pinch my nipple with the other hand. My teeth sink harshly into my lip to hold back a moan.

I'm about to finger myself over a ghost. *For a ghost.*

There's no reservation as I let my legs butterfly open.

COME OUT COME OUT

I make eye contact with myself in the mirror then let my gaze trail over my naked body. Fuck, I look so hot like this, still flushed from the shower and panting with desire. Hypnotized by my own reflection, I trace between my pussy lips then bring my slick fingers over my clit and rub in languid circles. I tug at my nipple again and my back bows almost painfully. A gasp escapes me when I apply more pressure.

"Do you want to see me fuck myself?" I ask, my voice breathy with need.

I expect another yes, but they surprise me. *Roughly.* One word and it's more than enough. The air leaves my lungs at the command. I'm so fucking wet as I sink a finger inside. I tease the opening with another, then slide that one in too. I pump slowly at first to adjust, but I'm so wet, they glide in and out easily. Speeding up the pace, my fingers move fast and hard while my other hand attentively teases my clit. A gasp and shudder rocks through me when I raise my hips and thrust against myself.

I force my eyes open against the pleasure and find a message waiting for me. *Another.*

A laugh of disbelief leaves me, but I comply. My toes curl at the stretch of the third finger. It's been a minute since I've been this full. *Since Aiden.* My pussy grips my fingers tightly at the thought of him, pulling a reluctant moan out of me. I continue the punishing pace as my legs start to shake with tremors of my impending orgasm. I build on the fantasy, imagining that they're leering over me. Just close enough to see every bead of sweat and hear every whimper but refusing to touch me. I clench my eyes closed, trying to create an image of what they could possibly look like in my mind—it ends up being Aiden's face that comes to me. I can see him so clearly, his clenched fist against the wall just above my head, the other intently stroking that beautiful cock, the eye of his tattoo staring up at me in challenge. I can almost hear him say, *'You better come, little wraith'*. Fuck, I'm so close. I drop down into a squat and open my mouth, letting my tongue sit heavily on my lower lip like I'm about to welcome his warm, salty cum into my throat. God, I want to drink it all down. I'm shaking violently now, desperate for release. I'm only able to hold it together for a few more seconds. I press harshly on my clit as I pump relentlessly and gyrate my hips, wholly lost to the heady desire I've created for both of my mysterious strangers.

    I collapse onto my knees, breathing heavily. My limbs are loose; I could fall asleep any second. I tilt my head up so I can see the mirror, but I'm disappointed to find that it's fully cleared of steam over the last few minutes. *Well, that was fucking weird. But it was so fucking good.*

My little wraith

CHAPTER NINETEEN

Aiden

January 8th, 2021 – One Week Later

This past week, Skye has towed the line of flirtation and driven me up the wall with the need to sink my cock into her. Her teasing after the shower has been more fulfilling than I'd expect, given that I can't really participate, not the way I want to. But the real satisfaction comes from her finally acknowledging me—and not in a fearful or bitter way, in acceptance. She's happy I'm here.

I sit on one end of the bathroom counter while she sits at the other end, closest to the shower that's currently running hot. Steam billows around, dramatizing her dark hair and pajamas—if you can call the tiny scraps of fabric that. Her right leg is tucked under her left that swings over the edge giving me a clear view of the old silvery scars on her inner thigh. I ache to run my fingers over them and soothe the old hurt that's buried there. My attention is drawn to the fogged mirror as she writes *Color?*

Green. And I follow it with, *Urs is black.* I chuckle to myself, the more convenient shorthand reminding me of my preteen years.

"Observant," she says under her breath, but I hear her clearly in the small, echo-y space. I don't miss the blush that colors her cheeks pink, either.

The hope I try so hard to keep close to my chest almost slips its leash, but I reign it in. *She doesn't know it's you, Aiden. Right now, you're just a ghost. You don't mean anything to her.* I tell myself sternly, even though I can taste the bitterness of the lie as I stare into her smiling face.

"Band?" she continues the conversation, the moment passed us.

Ever? I write in response.

She laughs and nods.

Cruel. I write quickly before pausing to think about it. That's a universally tough question, no one has just one favorite band. Finally, I respond. *Queen.* A few seconds later I add, *Green Day.* About ten other names fly through my mind immediately—Def Leppard, The White Stripes, Nirvana, blink

182, The Rolling Stones, the list is endless.

"So, you have good taste, then," she quips, "good to know I'm not driving you out of your mind with my music choices."

Never. Then I add: *Thank u.* I can't exactly express how much her love of music has meant to me in this otherwise isolated existence, but that will have to do, for now. If I ever get a chance to see her again, when I'm whole and solid and visible, I plan to tell her everything.

Another hour goes by with us exchanging fun facts about ourselves, passing the time easily, but then she's yawning and watching the mirror through drooping eyes.

Goodnight. I force my finger to form the letters. I could stay here with her for an eternity, but I remind myself that Skye is still very much alive, meaning she needs sleep. Desperately so. She's haunted even when her eyes are closed and her body's at rest.

"Night," she mumbles sleepily before turning off the light, plunging me in the darkness once again. With nothing else to do, I turn over the memories of the last week. Spending time with her, being seen by her, is the closest I've felt to being alive in months.

It's more than I realistically should have ever hoped for. And yet, it'll never be enough. I could never be satisfied with anything less than everything with her. That's the price I'll pay for my sins; never knowing true fulfillment, remaining just shy of happiness. I'd kill those three bastards again without a second thought to suffer like this. To know how it feels to yearn for her like this.

I thank the fates in one breath and curse my luck in the next.

Unable to stay away from her now that I have her back, I follow her into the bedroom. To my surprise, she's already asleep. Binx stops mid-cleaning his paw and watches me from his perch on her bed. We exchange a slow blink and he goes about his business. I love that damn cat, too. He's always been welcoming, but now that Skye's fear has subsided and the energy in the house is more at ease, he's gradually becoming a companion of sorts. One I could surely use. I'm grateful for him, *for them*.

Mixed in with the relief I feel about having them back is the guilt. There's a growing pit in my stomach over the thought that she doesn't know who I am. A lie of omission is still a lie. But I don't know how to explain my circumstances. I don't even understand them myself. I wish she'd ask me. But then again, it's probably a discovery made best in person. I wonder if she'll be mad that I didn't tell her who I am. Maybe she won't care. She doesn't even really know me except for my name anyway. I mean, she knows my body and I know hers, but Skye hasn't had the opportunity to observe me, *obsess* over me, the way I have with her.

Crossing the room, I stand beside the bed, looking down at my girl. Over the last year, I fell for her. I've never felt this way about anyone, always too scared to truly let my guard down. But this, *her*, I can't hide from it. I don't want to.

Skye is stunning with the moonlight draped across her. A lone star in the eternal night I've been cast into. The silver light catches the faded scars on her forearm and my fingers flex with the need to touch them. Curiosity burns within me, and I wonder at what point the agony became too much to contain. When did her soul start planning its escape to somewhere better?

Did nobody notice that she was bursting at the seams? They must have, they just refused to look. Rage snakes through me and I swear I taste the bitterness of it on my tongue. I hate whoever made her feel like she could never share the burden.

I never understood why people refused to look depression in the face. It was the childhood boogeyman of mental health issues. Don't talk about it, don't look at it, and maybe it won't get you. It isn't real if you don't acknowledge it. Meanwhile, the other person is left shivering beneath the covers as it circles their bed, tugs at their feet, and eventually pulls them underneath with it.

It isn't fair.

I won't turn away from her. I'm crawling beneath that bed, cool wood pressed beneath my palm, dust tickling my nose, breaths stilted from the small space we've crowded into. I'll wedge myself between her and her boogeyman, take the worst of its gnashing teeth and claws while my fingers remain interlocked with hers. She'll never be alone again as long as I'm here.

Giving into the aching need, I run the back of my hand down her cheek. Disappointingly, she doesn't nuzzle into it. I recall the heat of her soaking into my skin and my breath catches at the thought of never experiencing it again, stirring something needy and desperate within me. I need to hold her again, *soon*.

tastes like bad decisions

CHAPTER TWENTY

Skye

February 26th, 2021 – One and a Half Months Later

If someone had told me a few months ago that I'd be willingly spending my free time hanging out with the ghost who terrorized me and my friends—something we probably should've talked about but doesn't seem to matter anymore—I would have laughed in their face. But it's true. Here I am laying in bed with something that feels like anticipation lighting me up from the inside. I *never* wake up excited to start the day. However, lately I'm smiling and laughing so much more. It's so novel to have someone so engaged, so eager to learn about me, and vice versa. We seem to have a lot in common, like how we believe animals should be treated like family and the fact that we passionately agree that art is critical to the human experience. It's not just surface-level things, like our taste in music, but the things that are important, too, like our agreement that women deserve bodily autonomy — yes, I needed to know so I could banish him from my house if need be.

My stomach does a flip and I suppress the smirk that threatens to reveal that I'm not still asleep. I'm not quite ready to start the day. I have so much work to get through. But then again, the workdays aren't as long anymore. I've been so much more efficient now that I'm determined to spend way fewer hours hunched over my computer and more trading flirty messages in the bathroom mirror.

It's bizarre to think that he's probably watching me right now, that he could always be watching me. Thrilling, is another word for it. Sometimes, it's even comforting. I used to think that would be creepy. It just feels like home. I always felt connected to this space, reasonably safe within these walls. Was it because of him? I think so.

What does it say about me that I find it easier to talk to a ghost than ninety percent of the people I've met in my lifetime? I suppose it validates many of the assessments people have made about me over the years—unusual, mentally unstable, bad at conversation. But for the first time, none of it feels true. More importantly, it doesn't matter.

Despite everything, this feels normal. Well, other than

the fact that I don't know his name or where he came from, and you know, the whole being dead thing. What did that matter though, when we had so much in common, when he made me feel safe, when he made me feel like I wasn't completely and utterly alone for the first time in my life?

If he is always watching, that means he sees me—every dark secret, the things I've always tried to hide, all my worst days. And still, he wants to be around me.

I mean, sure, he doesn't have much of a choice about being here—I assume as a ghost, that he's trapped here—but still, he doesn't have to make himself known. I choose to believe that he *wants* to be around me. He said he likes watching me. I'll take his words at face value, that's what I always wish others would do.

I try to tell myself I wouldn't care either way. I want to deny that I've grown attached to the spirit in my house. Both would be lies.

He's become a steady presence in my life. One that doesn't require me to change. He's quite possibly the first . . . person . . . I don't have to tiptoe around. What a novel concept, to not feel like a burden to someone.

That motivates me to finally open my eyes. Only a soft glow of sunlight greets me, the brunt of the brightness thankfully contained by blackout curtains. I could kiss whoever invented them. I stroke Binx's tiny head and am rewarded with soft vibrations of affection. When I turn to my other side, I open the drawer of my bedside table and reach for a joint out of habit but freeze when my fingers touch the rolling paper. It's been days since I've turned to any of my usual vices. I haven't felt the urge to run away.

It won't last, it never does, but I know the pattern well. *Fuck.* I think I'm catching feelings for a ghost. Suddenly, my saliva is as thick as syrup as I try to swallow down my shame and shock. It's absolutely ridiculous. I don't even know his name. The pace of my heartbeat quickens as a thousand loud thoughts run through my mind. The quietest voice stands out, though. It's the one saying that yes, it's silly and fruitless, but I should hold on tight to this rare source of joy until it inevitably fizzles out.

Nothing can come of it, after all. I'm anything but a traditionalist, but even I'm not delusional enough to believe that I can have a relationship with a ghost. *I don't even know his name.* I remind myself for the tenth time. And more to the point, I know it won't last because it never does. People—alive and dead, I would imagine—fall in love with the idea of me. The reality, not so much.

The idea of Skye is sexy and mysterious. Then the mystery unravels and they find out that what's been hiding is a fun little treasure chest filled with anxiety, irritability, a medley of little peculiarities that are anything but charming if you look too closely, and of course, the incessant depression. It doesn't matter how big my tits are or how eager I am to ride them, nobody, not even the typically more open-minded people I've dated can stick it out. So, I guess there's no danger in letting this absurd crush last a little longer. Soon, I'll be on my own again and he'll be a distant memory. He'll avoid me like they always do. I'll get the hint and stop looking for him. We'll go back to being two ships passing in the night. And I'll be stranded once again.

And there my brain goes killing that rare light of excitement once again.

With a long sigh, I finally get out of bed. I brush my teeth in silence, avoiding my own reflection, unable to look at myself and the misery I know I'll see reflected in my eyes that I've inflicted on myself. But even if I don't look at it head-on, I can't ignore it; the voices that confirm all my doubts grow louder and louder. To drown them out, I reach for that little vial that's been sitting idly on my counter for the last few days, tidy up a line, grab the rolled dollar bill, and inhale, initiating chemical warfare against my inner demons. *Much better.*

By the time I step into the shower, I'm humming one of my favorite songs and basking in the refreshing scent of my

COME OUT COME OUT

eucalyptus and lemon body wash. *A breath of fresh air.* Massaging the shampoo into my hair feels like heaven as I knead the little scrubber against my scalp. After I finish washing my hair, and shaving myself silky smooth just because, I finally turn off the water.

My toes curl around the soft fibers of my rug and a little zip of satisfaction tingles through my loose limbs, but it's immediately overrun by a hot flare of anger when I see that the vial has spilled over into the still-wet sink. *Fucking hell. How?* I run back through the minutes before I got into the shower. I didn't close it, but I also don't remember spilling it. I would have *definitely* remembered; it's not easy for me to get more of.

"Binx," I hiss, stomping through the doorway and back into my room. His head pops up from under his paws as he startles awake with an irritated little meow. I was only in there for about ten minutes. Was it really plausible that he got up, jumped on the counter, knocked it over, and then came back in here to the *exact same spot* and fell back asleep? All without meowing his displeasure that I was in the shower . . . possible, but not likely. Slowly, I turn back toward the bathroom. My face is pinched in a squinting glare as I stomp my ass back in there.

"Did you do this?" My voice echoes in an angry growl

that I barely recognize. Just when I think the coward might ignore me, letters begin to form on the mirror in front of me. *Yes.* My rage intensifies. "Who the fuck do you think you are?"

Several seconds pass. *You're hurting yourself.* First, the jealous fit when I had that couple over, and now this. "It's none of your business. You're not my boyfriend and you certainly aren't my keeper."

I stand there, nearly crushing the tiny container in my grip. I bite my cheek to try to get a hold on my anger but when there's no further explanation and no apology, that goes out the window. "Go fuck yourself." I slam the door behind me. Logically, I know it won't do anything, but emotionally it feels like it creates the space I need from him right now.

I don't know when the hell I gave him the idea that he had any kind of say over my life, but I'm going to make sure it's crystal clear that what I did was none of his business. He wouldn't, *couldn't*, stop me from doing what I want. I'm a grown-ass woman. And as any rational grown woman would do, I turn on some of my most repetitive, synthy, bubblegum pop music that I hope will annoy the shit out of him, crank the volume all the way up, and proceed to indulge myself in the remaining coke I still have.

That'll show him.

Come out, come out, wherever you are

Chapter Twenty One

Aiden

March 10th – 2021 – Two Weeks Later

I made a mistake when I'd thought Skye's anger would blow over and she'd see my side of things—a side I didn't get the chance to explain but had hoped she'd see. It's been weeks now and she's still ignoring me. Her initial pettiness was understandable, but the anger that she still holds for me is shocking. It is like a physical force pushing me away from her. I intended to respect her boundaries, but it is also almost like I don't have much of a choice. When I step too close to her, I can feel the air around her protest. A sensation that appears to be unpleasant for both of us if the visible tension in Skye's body is any indicator.

I don't regret what I did, but maybe I would have

gone about it differently if I had known the cost of my actions. Hindsight is twenty-twenty and all that. I'm annoyed with myself for once again being reactionary to seeing her harm herself. In that moment, I'd been so taken aback that she'd turned back to her coping mechanisms when things had been going so well. It was arrogant of me to think that my company would be enough.

It wasn't fair of me to even expect that, and yet...

I'm torn between feeling like I've completely fucked things up and justified in my actions. I just want what's best for her. I just want to take care of her. But I can admit that wasn't the right way to go about it. I don't know how to fix things. If only I could talk to her face-to-face, really talk, not what we've been doing. But even if I could, would it really help anything? Would she even find me worth listening to at this point?

It's easy to forget the disparity between what I feel for her and what she might feel for me. I'm trying to keep my expectations of her low. I'm trying to be patient, but it's so goddamn hard.

I've never been more confused by a relationship dynamic in my life. I'm in the worst possible position. Not quite friend, not quite fuck buddy, definitely not a boyfriend—as Skye so kindly reminded me. I mean, I get it, I'm a ghost for fuck's sake. Skye has been surprisingly open-minded about me, but I don't think even she would be up for that. I might be a selfish bastard for even getting involved with her as much as I have, but I would never ask her to make that kind of compromise for me. What kind of life would that be for her? I'm no longer the man I used to be—a son, a brother, or a friend. She is everything to me and I'm just a small piece of the tapestry of her life. I know this in the most rational part of my mind, but the longer I'm dead and the longer the greatest temptation of my life is dangled in front of me, the quieter it becomes.

For better or worse, I'm no longer defined by the limitations of a human life. I'm not in denial of what I am, but accepting that I'm dead, that I can't offer her the depth of a human life, that is something I conveniently avoid thinking about. Referring to myself as a ghost feels so much less . . . final. And being around Skye makes it so easy to forget that I'm not really *here*. I'm not really *with* her. That truth sinks in my gut like an anchor that drags me back to the day I realized I was here, all alone. The day I realized that I was dead.

I look at my reflection—the one that only I can see—in the mirror and it strikes me how much things have changed. Two years ago, I was standing in this very bathroom jacking Nate off with a hand around his gasping throat, showing him who dominated who after all those years of taunting and un-

COME OUT COME OUT

fair power dynamics. Arousal, disgust, anger, and grief whip through me in quick succession. Now we were both dead. *And my sister,* my subconscious brutally reminds me. What would she think if she could see me now?

She would be horrified at the way I've unraveled. I may have been a bit rebellious growing up, but I'd always been calm and collected. I don't know where that Aiden went. I haven't seen him since I got in my old car and drove to this house. I never realized how delicate that balance was. I wish I could get ahold of the threads of fate just to see what moment sealed my damnation. Was it the decision to get revenge for Becca? Had it been the relief I felt when Nate took his last breath? I'll never know. The only answer I have is the fucked-up reality of my sentence—I'm in love with a woman who wants to die and I'm desperately trying to keep her alive.

I know I've fucked up, I don't know how to do this, but I know I can make her happy. I tried to respect her boundaries, but this is too much distance, and for too long. I need to convince her to give me another chance. The more time and space I allow her to put between us, the more likely it is that I'll never get her back. That isn't a possibility I'm willing to entertain.

I try to get her attention while she cooks herself dinner, opening and closing the cabinets while she cooks. Instead of acknowledging me, she grabs her headphones and puts them on. It's infuriating. I'm tired of the cold shoulder treatment. When she goes back up to her room and turns on the shower, I rush in there and write *I'm sorry* in the barely formed layer of steam on the mirror. I don't regret pouring out the poison she uses to numb herself, but I do regret how deeply I've upset her.

She stops, her face screwing up into a twisted grimace of hurt and anger. "It doesn't matter; I can't do this anymore. I've been living in some twisted fucking fairytale." Skye sucks in a ragged breath. "I don't understand how I got so swept up in this, but it's wrong."

Skye, please. I write back because there's no way for me to communicate what I really want to say to her. Helplessness keeps me silent.

"This has been fun, but I can't let myself get wrapped up in you. You don't even respect my choices. You aren't who I wanted you to be." Her voice wobbles as tears gather in her lashes.

I'm watching her as she builds back up all the walls around her, sealing herself off from me brick by brick. The defiance in her eyes stems from her own self-loathing and I know that if I don't do something right now, I'm going to lose her forever. Skye isn't the kind of woman who gives people chance after chance to keep disappointing her. Pride swells within me before my own panic drowns it.

Before I register the decision, my finger is scribbling across the mirror. *It's me, Aiden.* There's no going back now.

Her big, brown eyes scan from left to right several times before understanding dawns on her. My own travel to the tips of her fingers that have begun to shake, I trace the trail of goosebumps that break out over her soft skin, and finally meet her gaze. Despite the aching silence between us, she's saying so much. I find disbelief, fear, and betrayal staring back at me. It's as if I can see her trying to put together the puzzle pieces that don't fit quite right. This is why I wanted to tell her in person.

I lean forward to write something else but she lashes out, disrupting the smooth, frosted surface and eliminating any space I would have had to continue this conversation. Sweat coats her brow and her chest lifts up and down frantically as she processes the perceived deceit.

"I want," she grits out hesitantly as tears begin to trail down her cheeks, "you to leave me alone. You're not welcome in this space anymore. I want you to stay away from me."

She may as well have slapped me. I resist the urge to swipe everything off the countertop in protest. The last thing I want is for her to be terrified of me, but I feel absolutely powerless. That chasm she'd formed between us is growing by the second and I'm scrambling for a way to pull us back together.

She works her jaw as she stares into the mirror. "You're not welcome here. This is a safe space. You're not welcome in this room anymore, I'm reclaiming this space." She repeats similar phrases over and over again and I feel the power of them. Tension brackets through my body and I'm pulled back by some force far greater than me. It tugs me from my core, leaving me helpless to resist. No matter how hard I fight, the space between us grows until I'm on the other side of her bedroom doorway. As soon as I'm capable of movement, I try to take a step forward, but I find myself blocked by an invisible wall. I push, I ram, I kick and beat my fists, but still, I can't go in. I watch helplessly as she shuts her bathroom door, cutting me off from her entirely. Panic seizes me as I pace just outside the barrier she's manifested into existence. A sick feeling washes over me as my thoughts scramble. I want her to feel safe although having me out of the picture is not the way.

"Skye," I whisper uselessly. "I was just trying to protect you. Can't you see that I'm here for you? I just want to take care of you." I sink to my knees, the fight fading out of me as the conviction of her words washes over me. There's no doubting just how badly she wanted to be rid of me at that moment. It's tangible. I slam my fist against the door once more, and her gasp is another stab to my chest. "I just don't want you to end up like her." The admission that only I can hear is a twist of the knife that Skye's already embedded within my heart.

It always comes back to Becca. How could it not?

The weight of the loss of my sister and now Skye anchors me to the floor. Is that all I'll have left of them now; my memories, my grief?

My Binxie boy

Chapter Twenty Two

Skye

March 10th, 2021 – The Same Day

I close the bathroom door and slide down the smooth surface until my thighs touch the tile. The contact sends me over the edge and the tears I've been holding back break through the dam. I don't know what I'm feeling, it's all too much. I catch fleeting wisps of what I think is anger, followed by embarrassment, rounded out by fear. I don't know what conclusion is more terrifying: that I've been fucking a ghost or that he's lying and just using Aiden to manipulate me. How can you tell if a spirit is lying to you? There's no way you can. It's been months since I've seen Aiden, and maybe I won't ever again.

A sob escapes my lips and I clamp a hand over them.

The act is futile, he could be standing right here watching me fall apart. The potential humiliation is unbearable. I cover my face to at least guard that part of myself. I try to sort through the muddy puddle of shock, disgust, and betrayal, but sifting through the mess for any clarity is useless when my thoughts are flitting around like a disturbed hive of bees.

In an effort to collect myself, I stand. My fingers wrap tentatively around the doorknob. I take a few breaths then crack it open an inch. Pressing my face against the frame, I peer out with one eye, surveying the state of my room. Everything looks just as I left it. I crack the door another inch, flinching at the creaking hinges. When nothing happens, I open it the rest of the way and step into my room, then quickly cross the floor to shut my bedroom door and lock it. I know that a piece of wood isn't going to keep him out, but the definitive separation of my space from the rest of the house brings me the smallest bit of comfort and I cling to it.

I'm not aware of the plans firing off in my mind, as my feet move to the computer on their own. I turn on my monitor and watch the cursor blink expectantly in the search bar then type in Aiden's name and drop my fingers from the keys. It becomes glaringly clear how little I know about him. I add in the county name and finally "dead." My pointer finger hovers ominously over the enter key; my muscles are frozen in indecision. Once I click this button, there's no returning to the blissful ignorance of the fun I've been having. My teeth dig into my lip as I contemplate whether I'm ready to take on the weight of the truth of the disappointment of a fruitless search. My eyes find the welcoming sight of my bed piled high with pillows and my sleeping cat. It would be so easy to drink until I can't think straight then pull my covers over my head.

With a twitch, I press enter.

My eyes widen as the search results populate.

Local Aiden Murphy dead at twenty-eight after slaying several people in their home.

Aiden Murphy killer stabbed by one of his victims. Both dead on the scene.

SCHS community rocked by the gruesome murder of beloved alumni football stars.

I struggle to swallow against the dryness of my throat. I'd never heard about any of this. I guess it shouldn't be surprising, people die all the time where I'm from, and without watching the news you'd never know. With a shaking hand, I drag the mouse over to the first link and click. A news article swimming with pop-up ads assaults my eyes, though I still try to focus on the text.

On Friday, December 13th, 2019, local Aiden Murphy was pronounced dead at the scene after stabbing several young men in

COME OUT COME OUT

their home. After further investigation, the police found the link between the killer and his victims. Murphy and one of the deceased, Nate Peters, were found to have a long history, dating as far back as childhood. The two were known to have their disagreements through high school, a classic case of outsider versus the quarterback, but they seemed to have reconciled in recent years, being spotted at the same parties without issue. A source close to the victim reports that she'd seen them in friendly conversation several times. No one is sure what the catalyst was for the attack.

Nestled within the text is a full-color image of Aiden. My Aiden. Beneath that is a picture of the house I currently live in in all its charmingly disheveled glory, down to the Adirondack chairs and peeling shutters.

I lean back, trying to process what I just read. *Aiden is a murderer? The ghost might really be Aiden? If that's true, I've not only been fucking a ghost, I've been fucking a killer?* I lurch out of my seat and throw the toilet lid open just in time to vomit into the bowl. Empty heaving pulses through my body until it finally accepts that there's nothing else coming up. I flush and brush my teeth, my body sagging against the gravity that threatens to pull me to the ground. My stumbling heartbeat is painful as I shuffle back to my room. I stop several feet shy of my computer, staring into the glowing screen as I debate whether I can handle learning more right now. My churning stomach makes the decision for me.

With unsteady hands, I pull back the covers on my bed and slide beneath them. Absentmindedly, I stroke a bewildered Binx's head as I pull apart each piece of information I read in the article. But there's no question, the man in the image was the same man I found sitting in my kitchen uninvited, the same man I let fuck me, the same man I trusted not to hurt me.

The only question now is if the asshole spirit in my house is actually Aiden or if he's lying. I don't know if I'm ready for the answer.

tastes like bad decisions

CHAPTER TWENTY THREE

Skye

April 30th, 2021 – One and a Half Months Later

Between the falling out with my ghost . . . friend . . . and the information I'd learned about Aiden, it's been too much. The last month and a half has been a blur of so many days shutting the world out in my bed and a haze of liquor and weed and blow that's rivaled even my hardest nights of partying. I had to let myself fully shut down. Shit had gotten way too real way too quickly. Thank God I'm my own boss, or I definitely would have been fired by now.

Even Ava, who I rarely hear from, stopped by out of concern based on the text response I sent her that apparently had her mother-bear senses tingling. I let her bring me food and help me clean up a bit, but it'd all gone back to shit within a few days.

The truth was, no matter how hard I tried to put it out of my mind. Ever since I read those news articles, I can barely think of anything else unless I'm gone out of my mind. I'm falling behind on work, I can't finish a book to save my life, and I can't even escape the need for an answer when I sleep. All my subconscious thinks about is Aiden, too. The nightmares I was having at first were terrifying, with him covered in blood and faceless dead bodies on the floor, and an ominous ghostly presence following him around. But that nightmare version of him, that's not the Aiden I know. That's the version of him I get in my dreams now; the one who sees straight into my soul with that haunting blue gaze. Last night, I dreamed that he was trapped inside the house while it was burning down and I was trying desperately to let him out. I woke up and my face was covered in tears. That was my final push to go after the answers I so clearly needed. I just want to know who he really was.

I tell myself it's for safety reasons, that if he and the ghost are one and the same, I should know who I'm living with. The more honest part of me knows that my hesitation is due to the inexplicable attachment I feel to him. Any rational person would simply have a ghost–especially one who was most likely the spirit of a homicidal man–cleared out by a professional immediately.

Instead of reading more articles that were likely going to sensationalize all the details, I decide to go straight to the source. It's scary how easy it is to find someone's home address. A quick search for Aiden Murphy provides an address just a few miles up the freeway. A more recent one comes up in New York, but hopefully his parents still own the local house. Guess I'll just have to go over there and find out.

The lump in my throat is hard to breathe around as I walk up the steps of the little green house and knock. Every muscle in my body is tense and ready to run away as soon as they don't open the door, but just as I'm about to leave, a woman with Aiden's dark hair and stormy eyes opens the door. There's no going back now.

"Can I help you?" Aiden's mother asks kindly. Her voice is light, but I see the deep sorrow set in the dark bags under her eyes and the hollow of her cheeks.

I clear my throat. "Yes, umm . . . I'm so sorry to bother you, but I was friends with your son before he passed. I'm visiting the area on a work trip, and I was hoping I could speak to you about him."

Her brow furrows and her lips tremble, but she regains composure quickly. "Ah, yes, you must be someone he met in New York. What's your name?"

"Skye," I answer, holding her gaze, trying to assure her that she can trust me.

"Hello, Skye, I'm Erin. Please, come in." She opens the door and steps aside. "Take a seat on the couch. I'll be right there."

When she rounds the corner to what I assume is the kitchen, I step closer to the gallery of family photos on the wall. I can't imagine how hard it must be to look at these every day. One of the oldest photos shows what I assume is Aiden's sister tackling him to the ground, birthday hats askew. Frosting covers both their smiling faces; it's obvious they're twins, barely indistinguishable at that age, except for her slightly softer features and the party dress she wears juxtaposed by his jeans and tee. Some things never change, I suppose.

The clink of glass catches my attention and I quickly seat myself on the couch just before she re-enters the room.

"I hope you like lemonade." Aiden's mother extends a glass toward me with a frail, shaking hand, and I take it appreciatively.

"Yes, thank you so much." I clear my throat again, trying to force the awkward conversation out. "I hope it's okay that I'm here. I'm so sorry for your loss, I just… I became close to Aiden in the short time I knew him, and I couldn't help but think of him while I was in town. He's quite unforgettable." I force myself to make eye contact with her.

"He was special, they both were," she says fondly, her eyes watering. "I don't know—", she takes a shaky breath, "I'm sorry, what is it that you want to know, dear? I'll try to answer anything I can."

With her permission, I trudge forward. "I guess, what I've heard about how he passed, it doesn't sound like the Aiden I know. I don't mean to be crass, but I just wanted to know, was Aiden always . . . violent?"

Her blue-gray eyes flare momentarily, but she considers my question carefully. "Were you his girlfriend?"

"No," I answer quickly and my stomach lurches. She gives me a curious look but doesn't pry.

"You'll have to forgive me, Aiden pulled away so much after he moved. More and more so as the years went on. He didn't tell us much about his new life, if we could even keep him on the phone long enough to ask." She lets out a long sigh that feels heavy with regret and longing. "But to answer your question, no, he wasn't. We were completely shocked by his actions. But we'd never seen Aiden as devastated as he was after Becca's death. Even five years later, he was still a shell of who he used to be. The two weren't especially close at the time she passed, but they say losing a twin is an excruciating experience that no one outside of that bond can really understand."

She takes a long sip of her lemonade, the clinking ice filling the otherwise awkward silence. "The police said that they found screenshots on Aiden's phone, evidence of cyberbullying, that they believe prompted him to . . . do what he did."

Murder them. I remind myself. "Cyber-bullying him?" That surprises me; he doesn't seem like the type to give two shits what someone else thinks of him.

"No, Becca. Apparently, these boys—no, these men— they were harassing her almost non-stop for several months before her death. We believe it's what drove Becca to . . . do what she did." Erin sounds exhausted, like each word carries the weight of the world.

I feel for her, I do, but I also have to continue to pry. I'm the one who's very likely living with him, with a murderer, and I won't know what to do until I have more information—more than what the tight-lipped or speculative media can provide. "Are you saying he killed them because they bullied her to death? Because he couldn't bear to let it go?"

Lost in memory, Aiden's mother stares into her glass for what feels like forever. "It's what helps me sleep at night. But yes, I do believe that. That sounds like my Aiden—always the protective brother. He was a sensitive boy and never shied away from it. He favored music and art over sports and cars and parties. He was proud to express himself doing whatever felt right to him. Often painted his nails and colored his hair on a whim as well." She traces the wedding band on her finger. "When his sister died, he even took up wearing some of her favorite rings. I always appreciated how sentimental he was."

Going out of my comfort zone, I reach over and press a hand to her knee. "I'm so sorry to trudge this all up." And I am, but I'm too selfish to stand up and leave just yet.

"Despite everything, it's nice to be able to talk about them with someone who isn't trying to find an angle to write a story or podcast episode." She shakes her head. "I know what he did was wrong, and I grieve for the other families, I do. But between you and me, they took Becca from us first. They were grown men and they harassed her to the point that it broke her. I know I should condemn him, but I can't hate Aiden for what he did. God, I wish he hadn't done it. I wish we could have helped him grieve, got him counseling, something less violent. But what happened, happened, and I might be damned, but I understand why he did it." A choked sob escapes her and it's the least I can do to move to sit next to her and comfort her while she cries on my shoulder.

When her tears run dry, she offers to let me see Aiden's room, and I jump at the chance. This is my opportunity to get to know him outside of what he chooses to project, to see a peek behind the curtain of what makes him tick.

She stands in the hallway and points at the door. "It's just in there. Feel free to look around. Please just let me know if you decide to take something." Her eyes shift warily to the door just a few feet further down the hall. When I follow her gaze, I can swear the strand of butterfly crystals hanging from its knob sways ever so slightly. A chill creeps down my back and I shake it off. "There have been some odd happenings around here, things going missing and whatnot. I just want to keep track of what little I have left of them." With that weird comment, she finally breaks her stare and heads back to the living room.

I wrap my hand around the contrastingly plain knob of Aiden's door and push inside. The walls are a deep navy blue that's nearly the same color as the chipped polish he wears. One is covered in vintage band posters and vinyls on display, while the others are mostly bare. The desk in the corner catches my eye and I go over to it.

There's not a speck of dust, but there are a few random items sitting in a tidy pile on the corner. Two drumsticks sit near the edge, there's a pair of headphones that are surely dead, and beneath it, a portfolio. Carefully, I pick it up and walk over to the bed covered in a charcoal duvet and sit. With cautious fingers, I open the portfolio and stare at the drippy black and white paintings that take up page after page. These *feel* like him. Despite the grief and sorrow spilling from each piece, there's something so rebellious, so powerfully *present* about the imagery. I stop at one that looks exactly like the tattoo on his arm with the lips and tongue, and run my fingers over the textured paper, tracing the artfully messy lines. They're eerily beautiful; I fight the urge to take one.

Instead, I lay back on his bed and close my eyes, taking in the essence of him that remains here. The smell of him clings to the comforter and the familiarity of the citrus and earthy notes soothes the uncertainty I'd walked into this house with. Taking a deep, shuddering breath, I stand and return the portfolio to where I found it. With one last glance around the room, I shut the door silently behind me. His mother is waiting on the couch, her stare distant.

"Thank you so much for your hospitality, this has been so healing." I'm not sure if healing is the right word, but I don't know what else to say.

"Of course, sweetheart. Thank you for letting me speak honestly, I hope that I can trust you won't share our conversation with anyone."

"You have my word." I give her a genuine smile and walk to the door Erin holds open. With a nod, I step back out and down the stairs. My feet carry me to my car and I make the drive home with barely any awareness, still consumed by the conversation I had with his mother.

Is Aiden the cold-blooded murderer the news stories depict, or is he the sensitive, loving son his mom remembers? I honestly don't know if who he was in life, even in those last few hours, really matters. To me, he is something different altogether. But I need time to figure out what that is.

My little wraith

CHAPTER TWENTY FOUR

Aiden

April 30th, 2021 - The Same Day

When Skye returns home, her energy has shifted. There's still a purposeful wall between us, but the force of it has lessened. For the last month and a half, the protection she placed around herself was powered by anger and betrayal. It felt as if the barrier pounded against me any time I tried to get near her, intent on keeping me as far away as possible. But now, while the barrier is still intact, it's a much milder presence.

Change is progress. A tiny seed of hope plants itself inside my non-beating heart, but I know we have so far to go, and I'm completely at the mercy of her forgiveness.

COME OUT COME OUT

GONER

May 31st, 2021 – One Month Later

It's another day watching Skye bury herself in work all day and reading until she can't keep her eyes open at night. She's been running from something, spending the last two months doing anything to keep herself from thinking about me. *About us.* I correct myself, because I'm not giving up on the idea that there will be an us. She's in self-preservation mode, I understand that. But for me, there's nothing to fight for *but her*. Without her, nothing else matters. So once again, I push the limits of my existence to test the boundary of the veil between us that she's stubbornly erected. I don't care if I'm scattered into a million pieces, I just need to make it through. I need her to see me again. If the last thing I see is recognition in her eyes before the final fibers of my being fall to rest at her feet, well then, it was all worth it. I was always a goner anyways. My fingers press upon the blackout tattoo that wraps around the front of my throat and trace the white letters that serve as a reminder.

My futile efforts are interrupted by her grocery delivery. I follow her downstairs and watch her put away the copious amounts of alcohol I know she'll go through far too quickly. It worries me, how much she's still consuming. But I can't intervene. Even with the weakening of the barrier between us as she becomes intoxicated, I can only get closer to her. I can feel it becoming more malleable, the border softening just slightly, when my little wraith thinks of me when her conviction that she needs to stay away from me wavers.

    Binx paces in front of me, his little chirping meows grabbing both Skye's and my attention. Her eyes flick from him to the space I reside in, just in front of the cat. She stops mid-sip of the cocktail she's made as realization washes over her. Chewing on her cheek, she considers it, smirks, then takes another swig and resumes cooking dinner.

    My blood boils faster than her pasta water. She must know the excruciating torture she's put me through these last few months. She thinks I deserve it, and maybe I do. But at this point, it's cruel what she's doing. Especially when she wears next to nothing like she is right now. She looks like a damn vampire, ready to drain the little life that's left in me. And yet, I eagerly allow myself to be lured in and sucked dry, my eyes devouring every voluptuous inch of her in the luxurious red and black lingerie. Fucking hell, I'm depraved. It's been too goddamn long. I want to peel down the garter belt and those lacy thigh-highs with my teeth, then pull those panties to the side and edge her over and over until she's trembling and sweating and sobbing as she begs for release. Having her so close yet still out of reach is maddening. I want her to taste that same desperation. But I'm utterly and wholly powerless to do so. The reality of our circumstances wraps its shackles around me, tethering me here while she's all the way over there. I thrash, I yell, I push and push, but nothing I do is enough to set me free.

◆ **GONER** ◆

August 12th, 2021 – Two and a Half Months Later

My feet dangle over the side of the empty tub that I lay in. It's the only place where my frustration and despair feel contained enough for me to exist with any sense of peace. I would give anything to numb my own pain, to drown my sorrows just like her. I know it's wrong, but it's almost punishing the way she can easily find ways to maintain her distance from me and yet I have no escape from my all-consuming obsession. For a minute, it was kind of cute when she toyed with me as payback as her anger dissipated, but I thought things would return to the way they used to be by now.

But now, I'm a man who's been deprived of his necessities for too long. I cannot continue to exist without her. *All of her.* I've never been one to want or need others. I was fine with solitude, always the problem child, then the weird kid, then the rebel once I grew into my features. Being the outcast suited me even. You'd think it would make me the perfect ghost. But now, a chasm in her shape and size has opened up within me and everything that I am has been vacuumed into the all-consuming black hole. All I think about is caging her against me and absorbing her into my skin, my tissue, my marrow, to fill it.

There's no me without her.

Each day, more and more of myself, of my sanity, gets dragged into those depths. I fear that soon I might wither away from malnourishment without the taste of her that I need to sustain me. I might not have a body that's in danger of deteriorating from the loss of her, but my mind is unraveling far more quickly than I could have anticipated.

The starvation is requiring my brain to run on an endless loop of trying to get to her.

Finally, I grow tired of the fruitless contemplation and force myself out of the empty tub. I toe the cracked bathroom door wider as I exit, the creaking whine causing Skye to look up from her laptop. I catch the briefest glimpse of longing in her gaze illuminated by the screen before she pointedly returns to her work. The illuminated clock on her desk that says it's 11:55 pm snags my attention.

COME OUT COME OUT

Welp, that's another day apart out of God knows how many more to go.

I slam my hand above her doorframe on my way out of her room. Binx calls out with an irritable meow, and I feel Skye glaring a hole in my back. I know I should be grateful that her walls have even come down enough to allow me to be so close to her, but it's still absolute hell being around and not having free reign. I miss how it was before when I could watch her and touch her at my leisure to soothe the unrelenting need that gnaws away at me from within. But that's unfortunately not possible right now.

Seeking a reprieve from my suffocating dark mood, I continue my pointless walk into the blackness of the unlit downstairs and out the front door, slamming it behind me. I consider one of the chairs, but I have too much frustration building within me; I need to move. I pace the long porch under the faint orange light that barely reaches one end to the other, trying to expel some of the energy. The aggressive steps only heighten my state of discontentment as I walk with nowhere to go.

I slump into the singular rocking chair that randomly sits at the end of all the other chairs. I teeter it forward and backward, the reassuring clunk of it on the side of the house giving me something monotonous to focus on while I try to calm myself. I enjoy the peace for less than a minute before the upstairs window slams open. I freeze.

"I swear if you hit that rocker against the wall one more time, I'm going to lose my shit!" Skye yells from above, the promise of violence in her voice. But it's not her anger that takes me aback and sends my heart racing, it's the fact that she's finally acknowledged my existence.

The bright smile that splits my face transforms into a mischievous smirk as I haul myself back against the wall again, and again, and again. An infuriated huff is her only response. I'll gladly take her attitude over her indifference. I continue my rocking, more vigorously even, the banging loud enough to start annoying me, but I don't care. I'm giddy now, knowing she *can't* ignore me.

The door flings open, the loud crack of it hitting the interior wall causing me to jolt and come to a stop. Out steps my girl, irritation like hot lava bubbling in her eyes and fury tensing her body as she stomps in my direction. Her angry gaze roams over the general area, trying to determine where exactly I am. I laugh, but she can't hear.

"Where the fuck are you, asshole?"

I stand, sending the chair rocking back with a hard thud that makes Skye flinch. Her shoulders are nearly touching her ears as she stands perfectly still, waiting for me to do something, I suppose. Unfortunately, I can't do anything to her, no matter how much I want to grab her by the throat, throw her over my knee, and spank that deliciously thick ass for all the torment she's put me through. Instead, I simply take the opportunity to admire her. The energy around her is more open than it has been in a long time, almost as if she wants me near her. *Has my little wraith missed me, too? Is she ready to play nice?*

Something in me softens at the thought.

Fists clenched at her sides and her lip between her teeth, Skye remains frozen glaring at the chair. Her breaths come in harsh pants, her chest shifting up and down quickly. I circle her–taking advantage of the opportunity to be so close–and step behind her. I inhale deeply, desperate for the scent of her that I've only caught distant whiffs of for so long. My eyes nearly roll into the back of my head with satisfaction, but she surprises me by stepping forward and sliding her legs between the arms of the chair.

"Is this what you wanted?" she grits out between her teeth.

My brow quirks, and my cock stirs as I take in her position. Yes, it's what I want. I'm envious of the non-existent version of myself that she thinks is sitting in that chair right now. Skye slams her hand against the wood and wraps her fingers around the top, right next to where my head should be. She uses the leverage to lift and roll her hips. Between the shadows, I catch sight of the bitter smile that curves her lips illuminated in the dim orange light.

"You have my fucking attention. Now, what are you going to do about it?" she taunts viciously as she rolls her hips again. "Nothing."

I can't help but laugh at how hot my little wraith is when she shows her devious side.

Her head whips around, eyes round like saucers as her mouth pops open. The quick movement makes her slide backwards off the chair, but in my subconscious need to protect her, I throw my arms out to catch her. My entire body comes alive when I feel her soft skin beneath my fingertips. I sink to my knees, still bearing her weight since her feet are caught between the arms of the chair.

"Holy fucking shit," she gasps out.

"Hello, little wraith." I smile down at her, my greedy eyes taking in the blush of her cheeks and recognition in her eyes. I hold her gaze even though her heaving breasts are calling for my attention in the lacy camisole she's wearing. It's freezing out here. I want to lick away all the goosebumps that I know cover her flesh.

"What was that you were saying? Oh yeah, what am I

going to do about you teasing me? How about I show you?" I gently release her so her head is sitting in my lap. She squirms, trying to free her feet from where they're still stuck, but it only serves to massage my aching cock. "Oh, fuck," I groan as the sensation of her inadvertent touch lights me up inside. "Months. It's been fucking months of torture. Do you have any idea what that does to a man? The kind of depraved beast he becomes when he can't have the one thing he needs?" I manage to pop the button of my jeans open and pull down my zipper. My hands shake with the shock of our sudden reunion, but I'm not wasting a single second. "Well, you're about to find out. Open up, baby." I wrap my hand around her throat and press under her chin, triggering a reflex that makes her open her mouth a fraction. I slip the tip of my dick between her lips, sliding it back and forth across the plump, moist flesh until she opens further. "Suck me off and show me how sorry you are for putting me through fucking hell. Use that talented tongue to show me how much you've missed me." She's shooting daggers at me, but she doesn't try to stop me.

Hesitantly, Skye circles her pink tongue around the tip and I groan in relief. It's been way too fucking long since I've had her lips wrapped around my dick. "That's it, just like that. God those lips are so pretty when I'm in between them like this. I can't decide if I want to fuck or kiss them more."

I spread my knees apart just slightly, allowing her head to tip back further until it's nearly upside down. The elongated column of her throat makes me want to see my cock bulging inside it. I thrust into it viciously, taking advantage of the new angle to hit the back of her throat. I want her to feel the memory of my dick inside her every time she breathes. A few days of discomfort is a small price to pay for the months she's made me suffer. She chokes and I revel in the sounds of my pleasure and her punishment. My thighs are burning as I ram into her from this angle, but I can't stop, not when I'm *finally* getting what I need, it's too fucking good.

"You're going to hold on and take everything I give you. Can you do that for me?" Skye's hands find my pants and she fists the fabric for dear life as I fuck her throat with every ounce of frustration that's built inside me finally finding a way out. Her watery eyes plead with me to come, but I'm not going easy on her. I want to see her cry over me. After all, she asked for this. She's the one who came down here to toy with me, I'm only giving her a taste of her own medicine.

Only that's not enough. I want more. I want her cries of satisfaction too. I want to know that she likes it when I destroy her and make her pay for the torment I've gone through. I slow for a second, "Can you touch yourself?"

She nods, causing my dick to slide up and down the

back of her throat, making me shiver with pleasure. Skye clumsily slides a hand down her stretchy pajama shorts. I allow her a few more seconds to find her rhythm before I start thrusting into her again. "Such a good little slut. Don't you ever fucking push me away again. Do you hear me?" She nods vehemently. In my appreciation, I caress my thumb along the column of her neck, reveling in the working muscles that suck and swallow me eagerly. Skye writhes beneath me as she plays with herself, her hips trying to undulate against her own hand but failing to get the friction she needs with her legs tangled up in the chair. *Good.*

I smile down at her mockingly and nearly come at the sight of the tears running toward me from her wide, leaking eyes that peer up at me in desperation.

"You want to come?" She nods as much as she can with me holding her and my cock stuffed as deep as possible. "Beg for it, baby. Tell me how sorry you are. Give me a reason to forgive you. Use that smart fucking mouth to say those pretty little words I want to hear. It's so easy, I know you can do it." I gently brush the sweaty bangs away from her forehead as her eyes shrink to slits of disdain.

I laugh and start fucking into her mouth more vigorously, driving myself toward the edge. I'm coming with or without her; she can be stubborn all she wants. I don't give her a chance to protest as my hips stutter and I empty every ounce of what I have to give to her. She coughs and cum sputters on my pelvis and her face.

"Suck as much as you can down and then I'll let you get up." I swipe the excess that escaped off of her lips and chin, then shove it back inside her mouth. The feeling of my own finger gliding along the edge of my dick makes it twitch. When she sucks and licks the rest off, I finally pull out of her mouth. "See, baby, that wasn't so hard, was it?"

Her relieved gasp settles something in me and I release her. When she frees herself from the chair and stands, she stares down at me for a long moment. "You're a fucking asshole," she says between deep breaths. Instead of the bitterness I've grown used to, there's an undertone of fondness that gives me hope.

My Binxie boy

CHAPTER TWENTY FIVE

Skye

August 13th, 2021 – After Midnight Strikes (12:15 AM)

Everything is still and quiet under the heavy cloak of midnight as we stare at each other—I shoot him daggers. He's just looking at me like he won the biggest gamble of his life. I guess he did.

My cheeks are scarlet and hot, but not with the shame I should feel. I'm so fucking turned on right now, and I hate it. I should be disgusted by him, I shouldn't let him touch me, and yet, all I want is his strong hands wrapped around my throat and deep inside me. The pent-up frustration and need that I've felt bouncing around between us for the last few months catches up with me all at once.

Rushing forward, I slam my hands into his chest so

COME OUT COME OUT

hard that he stumbles back into the dirty exterior wall. The crack of his head on the wood would have turned my stomach if he wasn't already dead. Titling his head down, Aiden assesses me through his thick lashes, his smile sharpening to a wolfish smirk. "Has my little wraith not had enough?"

The words I was ready to throw at him are stuck in my dry throat. I swear all the moisture in my body is concentrated in the wetness that's gathering between my thighs as he looks at me like that—like a man starved, like a man who's gone feral and could feed until he's gorged himself on my insides and picked my bones clean. I take a few cautious steps back from him as adrenaline pumps through me for a dizzying high. I'm ready to run; I expect him to chase me, but instead, he sits back in the chair and pats his thigh.

"Why don't you show me what you had in mind when you came down here?" Aiden cocks his brow. "You wanted to fuck a ghost, now's your chance."

"I—"

I want to deny it, but I can't, not after the way I just let him abuse my throat. So instead, I slip my thumbs beneath my waistband, roll my shorts and panties down my legs, step out of them, and approach him. I only break eye contact to cast a purposeful gaze down to his black jeans–the same ones he was wearing the last two times– that are still unbuckled and hanging loosely off his hips. Once they're out of the way, I carefully slide one leg then the other through the arms of the rocking chair and hover over his hardening dick. I swallow thickly as I wrestle with my doubts. I know that this isn't normal, I know I should still be angry with him, I know this can't end well, and yet, I want him so fucking badly. My pussy clamps on the humid summer air, egging me on.

My palm smacks on the wall as I quickly lean forward, shocking Aiden so much that he stops stroking his cock. "Yes, I do want to fuck you." I grip his length tightly and pump my hand slowly up and down his shaft.

Aiden's fist twists the hair at the nape of my neck, forcing our faces closer together. "Then stop playing and show me." There's a ferocity in his eyes I've never seen before tonight.

I roll my finger over the head of his cock. "I thought you like games?" My voice is laced with innocence but is anything but sweet. His lips quirk, while his gaze narrows in challenge.

"You had your chance to hide, but you decided to forfeit. Now I want to claim my prize." Without warning, he grabs my shoulder, the knowing eye of his hand tattoo staring into my soul as he forces me down on his cock, plunging the entirety of it into me in one go. A shocked gasp escapes me on impact, and I dig my nails into his shoulders as I steady myself. The sharp sting dulls to an acute and exquisite pain, and I become liquid as I relax onto his lap.

This is perfection. *This* is what I've been looking for.

Moving my hips in slow circles, I adjust to him inside me, focusing on my comfort and pleasure. Aiden groans and the sound awakens something within me that's been neglected all these months.

"That's it, use my cock." His fingers appreciatively dig into my love handles.

Using his lean yet sculpted shoulders as leverage, I ride his cock and rock us in the chair. It's almost like riding a mechanical bull yet so much better as I gaze down into Aiden's eyes that remind me of the kind of storm you don't want to encounter at sea.

"Take what you need, Skye. No more of that cold shoulder bullshit. Show me how you really feel." He goads me, searching my face for what, I don't know.

My hand snaps around his throat, right over the large black and white tattoo I want to lick every time I see it. "I want you to shut the fuck up for two minutes." He laughs at that but bites down on his lip and nods his agreement. I want to fuck that cocky look off his face. I want to hear *him* beg for *me* this time.

Readjusting, I shift my feet forward to gain a more secure footing, then use my thighs and the stability of his strong shoulders to slam myself up and down his cock. Aiden's groaned "Oh, fuck," goes straight to my pussy at the same time his finger presses against my clit and I buck forward with the spasm of pleasure.

"That's it, take what you came for," he commands as I move my hips up and down, back and forth, in deep rolls that have the back of the chair clattering loudly against the house. With frenzied fingers, I rip down the thin strap on my shoulder and tug my top below my breast, then grip the back of Aiden's head and bring his lips around my nipple. Without hesitation, he flicks his tongue and sucks the sensitive bud in the same rhythm his fingers play with my pussy. I dig my nails into the back of his short brown hair as I clench around him and crash headfirst into an orgasm.

I'm still coming when Aiden grabs my ass with both hands and starts fucking up into me from below. His harsh thrusts nearly make me lose my balance and I'm forced to press my palms to the wall to steady us. He doesn't let up his punishing pace until he unloads into me. As soon as he's finished, my hand finds his throat again and I force his head back so he's looking up at me.

"No more fucking lies. You're going to answer all of

my questions."

His eyes bore into mine as he nods his head and strokes a finger down my spine. The intimate moment has me eagerly pulling my legs free and putting distance between us. Without another word, I grab my discarded clothes off the floor and march back into the house. By the time Aiden follows me in, I've managed to clean myself up in the bathroom and have poured us each a shot of whiskey.

"Talk." I yank out one of the chairs from the kitchen table and plant my ass expectantly.

Come out, come out, wherever you are

CHAPTER TWENTY SIX

Aiden

August 13th, 2021 – 1:00 AM

I sit across from Skye at the table and am immediately transported to the first night I was able to touch her. *How much things have changed.* I could never have imagined a reality where she'd know I was the ghost who haunted her house or one where she'd willingly fuck me knowing that. A flame of hope burns brightly, but with the possibility that our time may be limited, I know I need to give her everything she wants. *I need her to trust me.* This is my last chance. I can't, I won't, fuck it up.

"What do you want to know?"

Her brows raise, and she tips her head pointedly at the shot in answer.

COME OUT COME OUT

The fiery liquor coats my throat and pulls the words out of me like truth serum. "So, you know who I am now. I wasn't trying to hide it from you. It's just not something you bring up in casual conversation."

Skye huffs bitterly. And somehow, it's reassuring; I love that she's a woman who takes no shit.

"You deserve an explanation, and I know it sounds like an excuse, but it's not like I have experience with this." I run a hand through my hair, pushing back the rogue pieces that hang over my eyes. I want her to see me. I need her to know I'm being genuine. "How do you tell someone you're dead? Is there a good way to explain that, somehow, you're in your body, but you don't know why or for how long?"

Skye refills the shot and pushes it toward me silently.

I take it because I'm going to need it to dive into the dark truth of it, that I'm a murderer. "Remember how I mentioned that I'd had a twin sister." Skye nods. "Well, she . . . she killed herself, and I killed the men who drove her to it. I didn't plan it, I just did it. When I found out that they tormented her so relentlessly for months, my hatred for them festered, mixed into a thick, toxic tar with my grief, poisoned my thoughts until I was consumed by the ugliness of it." My throat grows tight and my eyes sting. "You have to understand, I'd been suffering for years. That loss had eaten away at me for half a fucking decade. I couldn't stand the thought that they were going to get away with what they did without consequences—my sister wasn't here to hold them accountable—so I had to." My voice cracks. "I needed them to feel pain like she did; like I have. So, I drove over to their house, this house, and I killed all three of them."

A loud silence fills the room. A guillotine hovers over my head as I wait for her to tell me to stay away from her.

"I know." Skye crosses her arms over her chest. "I looked into you. I went to your house. I met your mother." Her gaze avoids mine. "The reason you did it, I understand—as much as someone who's never been close with their sibling or any of their family can." Finally, she meets my eye. "Had you done it before? Killed anyone?"

My ears are ringing from the bomb she's dropped on me. She knew. And she let me touch her, let me sink inside her, let me hold her down and violently fuck her throat at my mercy? I can only shake my head as my mind tries to catch up with her acceptance.

"Did you enjoy it?" The question is hardly audible as her lips close around it, trying and failing to stop the words.

I spin the shot glass in my fingers. I promised her no more lies. "Yes, I did. It was the first moment of peace I'd known since I found my sister all those years ago." Something softens in her demeanor as I continue. "One of them was my ex. Did you know that?" Skye shakes her head, the onyx hair sweeping over her shoulders. I want to weave my fingers into the inky strands and anchor myself there. "He started tormenting her because I ended things with him."

"You can't know that," Skye says with conviction as she wraps her fingers around my wrist.

"I do. It started a few weeks after I broke it off." The admission I've been avoiding claws its way up my throat and pries my lips open against my protests. "It's my fault she's dead." For the first time in so long, heat coats my cheeks and my vision blurs. I bite my lip so hard, I draw blood. A small penance.

"Aiden," she squeezes my wrist tighter, "it's not your fault. You didn't owe him shit. Someone like that, they don't just suddenly become bitter and vicious, they're born like that. The world is better off without that kind of person." Her brown eyes are a deep well of empathy and I have to blink the tears from my lashes to confirm that's what I'm really seeing.

The truth of her words cast away some of the sorrow that's been clinging to me. I tense my jaw and nod, pulling back the emotions that threaten to spill over. There's something else I need to hear from her, something far more important. "Are you afraid of me?" I don't think she is, but I can't settle the worry writhing through me like a parasite until I hear her say the words. Our games have been fun; I've basked in the murky waters swimming with lust and fear. But if she's afraid of me now, it doesn't bode well.

"No, Aiden. I'm not afraid of you. You've had every chance to harm me." Skye pours herself another shot and throws it back. "What I do fear, is that I've come to crave you." She huffs a humorless laugh. "Despite everything, I've become attached to you. I might even need you."

With the validation of her admission, I ache for her. My own need oozes out of me and clings to my skin. It's replaced the sweat in my pores.

"So, what now?", she asks, her eyes wide with apprehension.

Everything, I want to say, but that's not possible. So I settle for, "Want to watch a movie?"

She laughs. "What?"

A shy smile spreads across my lips. "I just . . . I want some semblance of normalcy. I just want to be with you."

Skye's brow furrows as she studies me. "Sure, we can watch a movie, but this conversation isn't over." She waits for me to nod my concession. "Do you like pizza?" She winces. "Can you even eat?"

"I can drink, so I think so?" I laugh nervously. I honestly have no idea what the parameters are in this situation. I have a body in the technical sense. I can touch, I can feel, I can taste, but I don't know what the limits are. I don't know how any of this is possible. I should be a decomposing corpse, but I look exactly as I did in life down to my clothes and shoes. My fingers find the dangling earring I took as a reminder of Becca. I'm so grateful that I have this piece of her.

Skye stands and grabs the bottle of whiskey, then pauses holding out her hand. It's all I can do not to stumble over myself with eagerness to grab it and never let go. I follow her to the living room she barely uses and sit on the couch with her.

"What kinds of movies do you like?" I barely register the question as she leans down to grab the remotes from the TV stand, her round ass on display. She must have asked me again because she rolls her eyes, walks back over to the couch, and sits a few inches away from me with her legs tucked to her side.

"Something scary." I want to see her happy. I want to enjoy this with her. What I don't think about is the potential awkwardness, given our situation. She watches me out of the corner of her eye for a minute, their gaze catching in a silent conversation, *"Is this weird? Is it wrong?"* Skye scrolling to the horror section is a resounding *"No."* Or maybe, it's a *"Who*

- 292 -

cures?" It's not like anything about us is in the realm of normal, acceptable behavior to most people.

My fingertips itch with the need to feel her soft skin beneath them. I tame them by linking them together and resting my elbows on my knees. My eyes are glued to the screen as she scrolls, but my purposeful avoidance is disrupted when her palm presses against my chest, urging me back into the couch.

"You can relax, you know? Don't make it weird." I laugh and force my limbs to loosen.

Skye selects *House of Wax* and then shifts her attention to her phone. I try not to be nosy but notice that she puts in an order for pizza. We have an hour. A moment of awkwardness flits through me at the idea of having her pay, but then I remember I'm dead. I sink into the cushions, willing myself to relax. Out of the corner of my eye, I watch her style her hair in two braids almost absentmindedly. A vision of them wrapped around each fist as she rides me comes to mind and I quickly try to dispel it before I get too turned on.

Skye shifts, the heat of her is irresistible and I wrap my arm around her, pulling her into my side. All the ways I've ever wanted to touch her wrestle for my attention. I rest my chin on her head as she leans into my lap and I can't help myself from burying my nose against her scalp. It's all I can do to not take a deep breath. I run my short navy nails up and down her bare arm, she lets out a content sigh that nearly melts me into a pool of helpless adoration, but then she rubs her palm over my cock through my jeans. My sharp inhale is the encouragement she needs as she climbs into my lap and wraps her arms around my neck. I'm giddy as she presses against me. I feel like a goddamn teenager again.

Tentatively, her lips press against mine so delicately that I almost question whether I imagine the kiss, but then she continues with more courage. This is different than the other kisses we've shared. She's offering me her softness; a lamb presenting herself to the wolf that won't stop following her. She's letting me take her neck between my teeth and trusting me not to spill her blood in my mouth. It feels like she belongs to me, even if it's just for the moment. Skye's long nails scrape at the back of my head possessively and I moan, letting myself be vulnerable too.

"Don't let go." I nearly beg as my hands palm her ass to pull her flush against me. My fingers slide under the fabric and squeeze, my hands overflowing. Everything about her is so luxurious and plentiful, offering the life and sustenance that was ripped away from me. "Now that I have the chance to tell you, I need you to know, I love these little fucking shorts."

Skye encourages my hands to move as she grinds

against me. I squeeze and rub, memorizing every dimple, but her breasts are competing for my attention. I catch her flimsy camisole in between my teeth, stilling her. "Off." Instantly, she pulls it over her head, freeing her lush breasts. I claim her lips again and cup my hands around them, my thumbs caressing her nipples. She moans into my mouth, and it goes straight to my cock. I don't know what's better, the feeling of her nails digging into my scalp like she's desperate to keep me here with her or the way her back bows to press into my hands.

Skye drags her lips down the front of my neck, sucking and licking. Her other hand undoes my belt and then the button. But as soon as I arch my hips up for her to free my aching cock, the doorbell rings and it's like a bucket of cold water is poured over us as we both freeze.

"Must be the pizza." My eyes catch on Skye's reddened lips as she pulls her top back on and dismounts my lap. "Coming!" she shouts as she rushes to the door.

"Hello again, Skye," a woman purrs.

"Oh, umm, hi," Skye responds nervously. It piques my interest, and I find myself standing and walking into the living room, not bothering to fix my pants.

"Need help?" I ask in feigned innocence as my knowing gaze pins the blond standing in the doorway. The word I want to growl is chipping away at the enamel it's caged behind. My body quivers with the restraint I'm exuding not to take Skye on the floor right in front of the delivery driver who looks at her like she has some kind of claim on her. As if she could ever be anything but *mine*.

Skye tenses, noticing my rigid posture and the way my teeth are set between my tightly smiling lips. She gives a nearly imperceptible shake of her head. "We're good here." She returns her attention to the blond with the preppy ponytail. "Thanks so much, I already tipped in the app." She grabs the pizza and closes the door before the other woman can respond, but based on the shocked look on her face, she expected Skye to be alone—alone and open to extending an invitation.

"Who's that?" I ask, trying to keep the jealousy out of my voice now that the threat is gone. Needing something to do with my hands other than grab Skye, I run a hand through my disheveled hair.

"Oh, she just delivered to me at the, um, other place I tried to rent." Her cheeks redden.

I ignore the painful reminder of her leaving me, but I'm not as successful at clamping down on the possessiveness that's worming its way through the pit of my stomach.

Skye turns to me, mid-bite of her pizza slice, then sets it down when she registers the change in my demeanor. She laughs in disbelief. "You have no right to be jealous. You come and go with zero warning. I had no idea why you left, where you went, or when you'd be back. You can't expect me to have been sitting around waiting." Only she was, and we both know it. Her chest flushes. "We're not in a relationship, Aiden. You're acting like I belong to you."

"You do." I step toward her and cup her cheek. "And I'm going to show you."

Defiant eyes meet mine and I stroke my thumb over her skin, trying to rekindle some of the vulnerability and openness she was showing me before we were interrupted. Finally, she relaxes into it, her eyes turning molten. *That's my girl.* I take my first deep breath in the last few minutes. I should have known better.

"Do your worst." She turns her head quickly and bites my thumb. When I gasp in pain, she sprints in the other direction. It takes me a few seconds to catch up to what she's playing at. *Fuck, I love this woman.*

tastes like bad decisions

CHAPTER TWENTY SEVEN

Skye

August 13th, 2021 - 3:00 AM

My breath stutters as my lungs grasp for the last wisps of air that haven't completely dissipated yet. Playful fear and arousal swim through me in a violent current, the instability making my head cloudy, but I force myself to focus. Every ounce of attention I can gather zeros in on the floorboards creaking beneath Aiden's heavy boots as the weak slats splinter like my composure. I can feel the wood shift under my shins that press into the floor under all two-hundred-and-eighty-plus pounds of me. He's a few feet away, at most, from the hall closet I'm crouched in.

My entire body vibrates with the need for his hands to be on me. As I recall the jealousy in his tone, my clit throbs in time with my racing heart. *The poor organ.* I've put it through so much and we've just begun. Anticipation sears my skin in chills as the seconds tick by. I know what happens when I get caught, and I want it. I want it so badly. I wonder how much he'll torture me before he gives in. He's upset that I wanted to fuck someone else—I remember the couple I called over. It's so damn hard to wait when he was gone so long. I would have done it too, if he hadn't scared them off. A girl like me needs to be fucked and filled and used. It's one of the few things that keeps the worst of my thoughts at bay. Despite that, I did learn to wait for him. I could have had Melissa all over that rental, yet I didn't. *Can't I get a little credit?*

The oppressive presence of him on the other side of that door is a resounding *no*. His need to own me shouldn't turn me on so much but, *fuck*, it does. I press my lips together to suppress an impatient whine. I want his thick cock pumping inside me and filling the aching emptiness I've felt for the last few months until I'm gasping and crying for it to stop. I want his perfectly tailored punishment to bring me to my knees while I beg for mercy. The thought alone has me dripping; my thin shorts are soaked. I clench on nothing and it's everything I can do not to cry out and beg him to fuck me already. The floorboards groan again, mocking me. My chest stills as I hold my breath.

"Come out, come out, wherever you are." His rasping voice sings the words in a distorted tune. The rusted squeak of the handle is the only warning I get before the door tears open and he yanks me forward by my shoulders.

My breasts are spilling out as I'm pulled against him. I can barely stand having clothing between my body and his. I twist in his grip, desperate for friction. Aiden's gray-blue eyes drag over every dip and curve of my fat body with pure desire.

"You want me to touch you so badly, don't you?" He looks down at the way our bodies press together like I'm trying to will him inside of me. "You're such a needy little whore for everyone who comes around here, huh?"

I shake my head vigorously.

Aiden tuts, and his ringed fingers close around my jaw. "Liars don't get rewarded, they get punished, love."

The grounding pressure of his fingertips digging into my cheeks steadies me as my legs shake with need. "You're right. I deserve to be punished. I want it. Punish me, please," I beg as I rub my thighs together.

"Is that so?" He steps back and toys with my braids. "You know, whores like you don't get the fun kind of punishment. I'm going to make you beg and cry, and then I'm going to leave you and your messy, cum-filled cunt gaping and clamping on nothing, even more desperate for me than before."

"I'll take you any way I can have you."

"That's what I like to hear, baby." He tugs the end of my hair. "Tonight, I'll remind you that nobody can give you what I can. I know you better than anyone, Skye." The affirmation is cascading water to my parched soul. "Tonight, you're going to prove to me that you're mine." He grabs my ass roughly for emphasis and I wiggle against him. That earns me a hard slap on my right cheek.

"I will." I squeal in delight. I don't know how he goes from being soft and apprehensive an hour ago to *this*, but it's so goddamn hot. *He's everything I could ask for.* I shove the thought down and stare up into his eyes, eager for more of this twisted game he's playing.

His tattooed hand is around my throat again and I can almost feel the spiderwebs extending from his flesh into my skin, wrapping around and binding me to him as he walks me back into the kitchen. When we finally stop, he shoves me roughly into the thick wooden chair near the kitchen table so hard that my ass makes a clapping sound against the seat on impact. "Sit on your fucking hands." His eyes are so heated with possessiveness that they almost brand me.

I bite my lip, considering disobeying just to see what

he'd do. I can't help it, it's so fun to defy him. He's so sexy when I rile him up. But my curiosity to see what he has planned keeps me silent. I place my palms flat beneath my thick thighs that overflow the seat of the chair.

"That's my good little slut. Now, open those perfect dick-sucking lips of yours. I'm going to fuck your filthy mouth so you can't remember the taste of anyone but me before I even consider kissing it again."

I lick my lips and open them wide. My mouth is watering and I'm desperate to coat his cock in my spit.

Aiden unbuckles his pants quickly, the sound cutting through the tense silence. He tilts my head back and proceeds to ease his perfect cock inside. "That's my girl, so good at taking my dick down your throat." Tears stream down my heated cheeks but I don't wipe them. He needs to see that I'm focused solely on his pleasure.

I rub my tongue along the underside of his shaft as I bob my head up and down quickly. Desperate to force him over the edge as quickly as possible so I can feel him inside me, I hollow my cheeks and suck diligently. My eyes are locked on his as I milk his cock with everything I have, my tongue and throat working in unison. No longer able to comply with his command, I pull my hands out from under me and cup his balls and his head drops back in ecstasy. I memorize the look of bliss on his beautiful features. With his full lips parted in pleasure, that line of tension between his brows, and his long lashes resting on his sharp cheekbones, Aiden looks like a rendition of some holy figure.

His hips start to rock steadily. "Fuck, little wraith. How are you so perfect?" He loses himself momentarily to the satisfaction, praying to me instead of the other way around, but we're not done with our game. I want to repent for the perceived offense of daring to look at anyone but him. I yearn for the brutality.

Digging my nails into his thighs, I regain his attention. Aiden's eyes widen, darkening with that feral desire that suits his fine features and his hips stutter. A few seconds later, he pulls out of me and hot cum sprays all over my chest and stomach.

The heat banks in his eyes and his limbs relax ever so slightly. "That's better,' he says breathlessly. "Let me look at you." Grabbing my braids, he pulls back my head until our gazes meet. "Now tell me. Who do you belong to?" There's a heavy demand in his voice I can't possibly ignore.

"You," I say as I swipe a finger across my chest and lick the cum off.

This earns a pleased smile from him. Warmth spreads through me at the sight. "Such sweet words, but they're not enough. *Show me* what belongs to me."

I stand, rubbing my thighs together as I sway my hips. With shaking fingers, I peel off my cum-covered top, slowly letting the straps slide down my shoulders before pushing the stretchy fabric over my hips and onto the floor. I let him get a good look before I start to rub his cum from my stomach up over my hardened nipples.

"You're testing my patience." A hungry edge sharpens his voice and his eyes are a chilling grey. "Let me see that needy pussy."

I loop my fingers through the lacy sides of my black thong and drag it down my wide hips, over my low-hanging stomach, and then my thighs. When I kick them off my toe, he catches them and brings the fabric to his pierced nose, inhaling the wetness that's soaked through the thin material. I'm transfixed as his pupils dilate and his gaze turns predatory. Like a hungry wolf, he approaches me with determination, ready to sink his teeth into me. I'm the disillusioned lamb who's willing to be caught in his jaws.

"Open up, sweetheart." His voice is all grit. I slowly part my lips, but he doesn't wait. He shoves my panties inside, scraping his knuckles against my teeth. I'm grateful for this little taste of him.

"Not another word from you until I say so." Aiden

pinches my nipples painfully. Eager to please, I nod in silence. "Well, look at that, my little slut is learning." A cool hand gently caresses my cheek and I lean into it. "Now, bend over the table like my good girl."

Wetness leaks out of me at the command. My body is getting ahead of itself. I want him to fill me, but I know better than to beg just yet.

"Look at that desperate cunt clenching on nothing." He's behind me in an instant, forcing my legs apart. Aiden's words are punctuated as he slaps my pussy.

I sink my teeth into my lip to stop me from crying out. My legs are shaking with the restraint it takes not to react. My mind is unraveling as the mental image of him slamming into me from behind consumes my every thought. I've missed him all these months. Once wasn't enough. I *need* him.

But it's not his cock that pierces me, it's steel. A sharp, burning sensation starts just below the curve of my ass cheek and ends mid-thigh. I follow the pain as it comes back down at an angle, stopping halfway then angling back up. It continues in a straight line back to the middle of my thigh. His unsteady breath pants against the open skin. "Have I ever told you how much I love these thick fucking thighs of yours and the way I fit between them?" After a brief pause, the stinging agony starts again in one long vertical line.

I inhale deeply around my panties as the metal leaves my burning skin and he steps back. I choke on a sob as I revel in the throbbing heat that lingers. He doesn't give me much recovery time. A minute later he's crouching behind my right leg and the blade cuts across my skin again. Down. Diagonal. Up again. Then there's a new line that branches off into three short horizontal cuts.

Aiden grabs my chin and turns my head so I can look him in the eyes. My gaze catches on the sheers he holds in his hand, the ones he seemed to have his suspicions about the first time we met. I should have known that would come back to bite me. He takes a few steps back to admire his work and lets out a contented sigh. "There we go. Now you're all mine, little wraith." His tongue licks along the tender skin. "That's the taste of victory." Aiden's forehead rests just below the words as he strokes my legs. "From now on, I'm the only one who gets to *touch* you, to *fuck* you, or to *cut* you. Is that understood?"

I nod weakly. There's no room for debate. He's staked his claim, and not just on my body, but on my soul. Nobody can give me the pain I crave quite like he can. *Not even me.* He doesn't try to sweet talk or fuck it away; he takes ownership of it so I can take a break from bearing the weight of it myself. He doles out the sharp words and inflicts harm like it's natural for him, but I suspect it's something he's embraced all for me. That makes it even better. Warmth spreads through me as I melt against the table I'm still bent over.

My thoughts are cloudy as I try to remain conscious through the throbbing and stinging writhing through my legs. I'm faintly aware of the blood trailing down my thighs in webby veins that tickle my overly sensitive skin.

I hear him mumble as my eyes flicker closed.

"Isn't that a fucking sight to behold? You've never looked more beautiful." A phone camera shutters. Once. Twice. A third time. Then he's standing in front of me. Calloused fingers wrap around my chin as he tilts my head up. Another photo.

"What are you doing?" I whimper, noticing it's my phone in his hand.

"Don't worry. These are just for you. When you think about hurting yourself, when you consider letting someone else touch you, look at this and see how sated you are crying for me. Remember who makes you feel like this. Remember who you belong to and maybe next time, I'll let you come too."

I manage a nod before I let my heavy eyes slide closed. I'm suddenly so tired as I feel Aiden's arms sliding carefully under my legs and the measured steps he takes as he walks me to the couch. I sink into the pillows and let myself disappear into the sweet respite he's given me.

My little wraith

CHAPTER TWENTY EIGHT

Aiden

August 13th, 2021 – 6:00 AM

Carefully, I re-dress a mostly unconscious Skye, then lay her on her stomach on the couch. Once she's settled, I go up to her bathroom and find a clean washcloth, antibiotic ointment, sterile bandages, and medical tape. I didn't go into this planning to cut her, but it was such a perfect way to claim her, for both of us. Once I clean and dress the words I've carved into her upper thighs, I grab us both a glass of icy water.

Skye takes long gulps, and I sit next to her so she can put her head in my lap. I stroke the wisps of hair that have come loose from her braids.

"The trust you're showing me tonight, right now, is everything. But I need you to tell me the truth, are you okay?"

COME OUT COME OUT

I bite my lip to prevent myself from saying anything else.

Skye twists so she's peering up at me. "Yes. I'm fine."

I raise a brow, my stomach dropping as she gives me that trained answer she's so used to giving everyone else.

"Better than fine, I feel . . . peaceful." She sounds surprised at herself, but she licks her lips and continues. "Will you be honest with me now?" Skye waits for my nod. "Do you do this just for me?"

I study her, trying to understand what she's asking.

"I mean . . . is this all role play for me? Or is this how you usually are?"

I smirk, understanding now where she's going with this. "In life? I was definitely a true switch and I liked to experiment with everything. Now, I don't know. All I know now is you. And with you, I need to know you're mine. I'm not the same Aiden I was when I was alive. I guess, in part I am, but I'm so disconnected from the person that I once was. In death, I find it easier to give in to my more primal urges. There's nothing suppressing them anymore." I twist the silver ring on my pointer finger. "But if you're asking if this is all for you, then yes, it started out that way. Now, the ownership I need over you–over your pain–is equally selfish. It's an escape for me, a role I get to fill. It gives me purpose, something I've desperately needed since I died."

"So, what, do you want to fix me, then? Am I project for you?" Defensiveness creeps into her tone.

"Fix you? No baby, we're both too far gone for fixing. I want to take our messy pieces and create our own little fucked up jigsaw puzzle." I brush my thumb against her pouting lips. "You have all the pieces I need to complete the hollow frame I've become."

Gingerly, Skye turns to her side so she can face me. Her warm brown eyes search mine. "You don't want to change me?"

"Never. What I want is to slip into the web of your mind, reach into the spaces where you hide your thoughts and help you take on your inner demons. I want to ease your suffering, but I would never begrudge you for it. I'll be right there in the pits of your personal hell with you."

She averts her watery gaze, and I don't force her to meet mine, allowing her to focus so she can process everything, but I do link my fingers through hers to hold her attention. She *needs* to hear this. She needs to *believe* it. "You never need to hide your darkness from me." The pad of my finger catches the first tear that breaks free, and I press it to my lips, closing my eyes to savor the sweet essence that is her. She tastes like the finest sorrow. "I may be a ghost, but it's you who haunts me. The way you look at me. The way you trust me despite everything. The way you cry out my name like it'll save you. The way your pussy clenches around my cock before you give yourself over to me completely. The way you look, praying to me, when you're on your knees. Everything about you is what I crave, and it's been just out of reach."

She gets up to her knees, wincing slightly when the bandaged skin of her thighs presses against her calves. Once we're face to face, she keeps her eyes downcast but rests her forehead against mine. "Will you leave again?" Her eyes shut, her way of guarding herself from my answer.

"I don't know; I think I'll have to. I don't understand why I'm only able to be like this sometimes. I wish I could control it. I want to be able to promise that it'll be like this forever. But even when I'm not able to feel you and you're not able to see me, I'm here. You're not alone anymore. We're still in this together." I kiss her forehead and hold her face between my palms. "You're mine, little wraith. As long as you're here, we're together."

With a small nod, Skye wraps her arms around my neck and buries her face in my shoulder. I hold her tightly against me, savoring every breath that sends chills of need over my skin, every pounding beat of her heart, and every touch of her fingers against the nape of my neck. There will never be enough moments like this. After a while, Skye falls asleep, and I simply hold her. This is the best day I've had since I've died; I don't want it to end.

But eventually, she shifts in my lap, rubbing her eyes and grabs for her phone. The screen lights up and it shows that it's two in the afternoon.

"I need a shower," she mumbles into my neck.

"Can you walk?" I stroke one of her messy braids.

She nods, presses a kiss to the tattoo at the center of my throat, and stands, her legs unsteady at first.

I follow her up the stairs and start the water while she takes some pain medication. Binx wraps his way around my legs, and I take the opportunity to pick him up, clutching him to my chest and scratching behind his ears.

Skye gives me a quizzical look when she returns.

"We're friends." I shrug and put the cat back down. I only have eyes for Skye right now. She goes to remove her clothes, but I grab her hand and pull her toward me as I lean my back against the bathroom counter. "Let me do it." I run my fingers along the hem of her top, then pull it over her head. Next, I carefully remove her shorts and panties, avoiding the bandages on the back of her legs. "These need to come off too. Lean over the counter." My cock twitches awake as she does as I ask and looks over her shoulder to watch me gently pull the gauze off each leg. I want to touch the lines I've carved into her skin. I want another taste of the affirmation that she's mine. But they need to heal first. Instead, I skim my fingers up the sides of her legs and over her hips, then wrap my arms around her stomach and pull her back against his chest. Finally, I get to show her what I see—us, *together*.

Her smile is shy but lights up her entire face. We look fucking good together and she knows it.

Skye looks up at me in our reflection. "You know, this would be an even better picture if you were naked too."

I laugh easily, a sensation that feels foreign. I go to undo my belt, but she turns and stops me. "My turn." Skye's fingers slide beneath my shirt and she pulls it over my head. Her eyes roam over every exposed inch of my skin, from the defined planes of my stomach to the tattoos that adorn my toned arms. When she's looked her fill, she finishes undoing my pants and I kick them off. Next, she tugs down my briefs, freeing my cock. "You're beautiful," she says reverently.

Not a single partner in my entire life has ever looked at me like she is right now. For once, I'm speechless.

Taking my hand, she pulls me into the shower with her, and pushes me so I'm under the spray. When I try to trade her places, she puts a hand on my chest. "Aiden," my name on her lips is my favorite song, "when is the last time you let someone take care of you?" Her question is simple but there are dozens of emotions playing in her eyes.

I can't answer, so I don't fight her.

"Turn around for me." I do. She strokes over my shoulders, down my arms, and along my torso as she washes me with the watermelon-mint soap that's her signature scent. I melt against her touch, her care. My eyes droop under the hot water, the comfort of which I haven't felt in forever. The minutes pass and I simply exist as I soak in the feeling of Skye's hands and the beating water. Between the warmth and the reassuring pressure, some of the humanity returns. It's a herculean effort to keep my hands to myself as I lean against the wall and watch Skye wash herself.

She's absolutely stunning. My girl is perfect and I'm grateful to revel in it. Too many people write off the sad girl as too hard to love. But it's so easy to do, because she needs it the most. The mistake they make is not being her safe space. If you can be that, you'll be rewarded with the most honest and raw moments. By accepting her, she'll open her heart to you in a way that will change your world. The thing about people who've had to wander the dark alone is they will always hold the guiding light for you without an ounce of resentment. If you're lost, they'll plunge into the depths and lead the way out just so you're never left to the loneliness they've come to know too well.

COME OUT COME OUT

When I'm around her, the reality of my fate is bearable. I remind myself to focus on that comfort instead of the potential that we might be pulled apart again soon, but it steals several minutes from me.

Once we've dried off, she tosses something at me. It's a pair of her joggers and that black crop top with the pink barbwire heart. "What's this?"

"I figured you might want to wear something different for once." A blush spreads across her cheeks. "I know you can't take it with you, when you, you know, but I thought . . ."

"This is," my voice cracks at the thoughtfulness of the small but not insignificant comfort she's offering, "it's perfect, thank you." I pull the joggers on, then slide the shirt over my head.

Her cheeks darken further and she tucks her hair behind her ear shyly.

"What? Do I look ridiculous?" I laugh.

"Definitely not, ridiculous." She closes the distance between us and slides her hand up my exposed abdomen. "You look so cute in your slutty little crop top."

I grab her ass firmly, pulling her against me. "Keep teasing, and I'll show you slutty." I bite into the side of her neck and she squeals while pushing her way out of my arms.

"Come on," she says through a big yawn. "I need to lay

down for a bit."

I follow her to the bed, and she puts on the movie we didn't finish. As soon as she lays down, I pull her against me, determined to savor every second I can feel her skin against mine. I kiss her shoulders, her neck, and her hair, trying to chase away the panic that's stirring to life within me at the thought of losing this.

My Binxie boy

CHAPTER TWENTY NINE

Skye

August 13th, 2021-- 11:30 PM

When I blink my eyes open, it's dark in my room except for the silver stream of moonlight and the glowing TV screen. I stiffen when I no longer feel Aiden wrapped around me, but I roll over and am relieved to find that he's there holding Binx on his lap. My boy is purring loudly, perfectly content. I stroke his silky fur as I gaze up at Aiden. "I'm sorry I fell asleep."

"Don't be. You needed it."

I nod in agreement and wrap my arm around his waist like he's always belonged to me. Binx jumps down, not interested in competing for attention right now.

"Skye," Aiden starts.

COME OUT COME OUT

"Hmm?" My pulse picks up when his muscles tense beneath me.

"I know things are complicated," Aiden pauses to swallow thickly, "but I'm so glad I found you. I don't know what I'd do without you."

I open my mouth to reply, but he holds up his hand.

"I know that all of this is new to you. I've had almost a year and a half to learn everything about you, to fall for you. I don't expect you to feel the same, but I just want you to know, you're more important to me than I can properly express. You don't need to say anything, I just wanted to tell you that." Aiden pulls his lip between his teeth and uncertainty swims in his eyes. I don't know how to respond, but I can show him how much I appreciate the sentiment. I straddle his lap and bring my lips to his. It only lasts a minute before he flips us so he's on top.

"I need to taste you," he says desperately as he positions himself between my thighs. "This pussy," his expression is pained as he licks up my center, "is so fucking perfect, just like you." His tattooed arms wrap around my thighs as he buries his face against me and begins tenderly licking and sucking. I can't take my eyes off of him as he circles my clit with his talented tongue. It's like he's studied a map of my body the way he teases me with such expertise. My head is swimming as I become drunk off the slow pleasure he's building.

"You'd look even prettier with my fingers inside you, don't you think?" His hushed voice vibrates against my sensitive cunt, and I nod vigorously as I stare down at his gorgeous face buried between my thighs. All I care about is that he doesn't stop. So slowly, one finger enters me and it's all I can do not to buck my hips. Aiden patiently works another one in and then a third. I tweak my own nipples as he pumps in and out of me with lavish strokes. When he finally adds a fourth, I squirm at the stretch but adjust quickly. My panting breaths grow faster as he speeds up his movements. And when he presses his palm against my lower stomach, my legs start to shake uncontrollably.

"Just like that. Don't stop, Aiden." He sucks my clit sharply in response. Combined with his fingers filling me, I barrel into the orgasm that's been taunting me. "Oh, fuck."

Aiden works me through it and slowly eases one finger out at a time. With a final lick that sends a jolt through my limbs, he crawls over me and kisses me, letting me taste myself. I pull him down against me, enjoying the feel of his body on mine. Everywhere our skin meets is hot with need. I've been touch starved for him.

When my breathing returns to normal, he kisses down the side of my neck and I stroke his hard cock between us. As he lines it up with my entrance, I wrap my legs around his waist and encourage him to drive into me.

"A perfect fit," Aiden says mostly to himself as he thrusts into me again. "I could never get enough of this, *of you.*"

I squeeze my lips shut tightly, trying to prevent myself from refuting it. He will get tired of me, they all do. My gaze drifts to the dresser where my empty vial sits. Despite how good this is, *because of how good it feels to be with him*, I find myself wanting to escape, needing to run from the inevitability of him leaving again. As if he can read my mind, Aiden's cold fingers grip my chin, bringing my attention back to him.

"Skye," he sounds panicked, his words urgent, "listen to me, I'm not going anywhere, okay." He starts thrusting hard and fast, like he's racing against time itself. "I'll still be here even if you can't see me. Tell me you'll stay here with me." The last word is choked out as his body tenses. He presses his thumb sharply against my clit, scattering my thoughts as I try to respond.

"Okay," I manage to grit out. The sensations whipping through me are dizzying as I hurdle toward a second orgasm.

"Promise me." Aiden gasps out as he cums inside me. I can barely feel him anymore as I unravel. "Skye, answer me." His hands are a faint touch against my skin.

"I promise."

He pulls out of me and shoves his fingers inside of me immediately, holding his cum in my fluttering pussy. My eyes fly open at the foreign, cold sensation just in time to catch a fading glimpse of him. I'm left panting and empty as what's left of our night together leaks between my thighs. My throat grows tight while I try uselessly to catch my breath. I press my hand over my mouth to keep it all in, but the magnitude of what an emotional whirlwind the last twenty-four hours has been is unleashed like a flood.

Happy

August 14th, 2021 – The Next Day

Having everything I've been running from over the last few months finally catch up with me is disorienting. It's one thing to know Aiden is dead, that he's a ghost, and it's another to see the proof before my very eyes. But there's no more denying that I had feelings for him. There had always been *something* about him that felt *right*.

Acceptance is a balm for a part of myself that's been long neglected. Like any abandoned thing, it demands that I feed it.

On sore legs, I stand and head straight for the bathroom to turn on the shower. While the water heats up and the steam builds, I add yesterday's date to my phone, confirming the pattern I've suspected. Before I set down my phone, I quickly purchase notebooks and pens—I can't believe I didn't think of it before. *Because you were keeping your distance, Skye.*

That's not possible anymore.

When I return to the bathroom, I'm welcomed with, *Good Morning.*

"Good morning, Aiden."

Are u ok?

"Just a little sore." I stretch reflexively.

Shower. Movies after.

I nod, a smile tugging at my lips as I undress and get in. There's a true comfort in knowing he's here, even if he's not physically with me, and for once, I feel like I can be here too. I never understood what people meant when they talked about wanting their partner around all the time, but I think this is the closest I'll ever get.

As we spend the day in bed, Aiden's company is a comfort, but it isn't intrusive. I don't feel suffocated by the mask I'm forced to wear around everyone else. I can breathe deeply; I can drop the act and feel freely.

Despite the peace he brings me, simply having him there quickly becomes insufficient. When the notebooks and pens are delivered, I nearly trip down the stairs with the quickness I take them to retrieve them.

Returning to my room, I hop on the bed with more enthusiasm than I've felt in years. I toss one of the notebooks beside me with a pen on top. "Look, now we can talk whenever." I speak with the assumption that he's next to me at all times. He told me himself that there's nothing except me in his world.

I watch, transfixed, as the pen becomes vertical and the notebook opens. I know it's him and yet it's still difficult to wrap my mind around.

Clever. He writes on the first page.

I light up under the praise and proceed to write in my own notebook. It's unconventional, but honestly, it's so much easier to communicate this way. I've never been a big talker, always struggled to organize my thoughts that way. I'm not an elegant, confident speaker like Aiden. However, writing? It's so natural for me. All the things I've wanted to ask that I had difficulty phrasing easily make their way onto the page. Aiden doesn't even complain about my too-close-together, sloppy letters.

He told me I was perfect as I was, it's something I don't think I can ever let myself believe, but I do feel accepted as we sit here in contented silence, having the most engaging con-

COME OUT COME OUT

versation I've ever had. I didn't know it could be like this with someone.

tastes like bad decisions

CHAPTER THIRTY

Skye

October 31st, 2021 - Two and a Half Months Later

    It's incredible how much Aiden and I have in common, which makes him the perfect person–or ghost, I guess–to spend Halloween with. We lay sprawled out across the blankets we've padded the floor with inside our fort we built as the sun went down. Binx stares up at the orange fairy lights I hung along the front, content as can be with our arrangement.

    I feel a little guilty eating the candy and popcorn all to myself–it must suck to miss out–but Aiden assures me he's just happy to be spending it with me.

    And you alone. He adds on the crowded page of the notebook.

    It feels like so long ago that everything changed on this

very day when Aiden snapped and decided that I would be his or no one's.

They were so scared. I laugh about it now.

As they should have been. I was fucking pissed that they just took off without you. What if I was some kind of demon or something? I can see the anger beneath the surface in the jagged edges of his usually smooth letters.

I'm really glad you're not. I laugh again at the ridiculousness of this conversation.

Me too. The pen drops, but rises again moments later. *If anyone ever tried to hurt you, they'd think I was one though.*

I shake my head and turn my attention back to the TV. "Wait, okay, pay attention. This is one of the best parts." I use one hand to grab a fistful of popcorn and reach the other over to Aiden's general vicinity. As I settle back into the movie, I imagine his hand placed on top of mine. It's not perfect, but this is our new normal.

Happy

December 25th, 2021 - Two Months Later

"Don't peek!" I shout from the bathroom. I know I won't be able to tell either way, but it's the principle of the thing. I wait several seconds and then I fling the door open and kick one red-stocking-clad leg out. A second later, I come around the corner and lean against the frame. "Merry Christmas, Aiden." I walk toward the bed and peer down at the notebook he's scribbling in. Is it weird that I now look at pens fondly?

Merry Christmas, Skye.

"I figured since it didn't really make much sense to get you a gift, I wanted to get you . . . something." I gesture to the red satin lingerie set I'm donning. "I couldn't quite bring myself to wear the hat, but you get the point."

Aww, come on, I want to see the hat.

"Fuck off." I roll my eyes even though I can't help the grin that's plastered on my face. "Now sit back and enjoy your gift." I bring my hands to cup my breasts, the smooth bralette teases my nipples, making them harden and I slowly slip it over my head. "Have you been naughty or nice?" I taunt as I crawl up on the bed then run my fingers up my thighs, raising the tiny matching skirt until my pussy peeks out just slightly.

The pen scribbles across the paper at near-lightning speed. *Naughty.*

I wouldn't expect anything less as I sit up on my knees and shimmy the skirt further up my waist. Ever so slowly, I slide a finger through my center to gather the wetness that's already dripping from me and draw circles around my pulsing clit. I stare straight ahead where I can see the indent in the bed and pillows. I love knowing he's watching me as I touch myself.

Go on, little wraith, get yourself off. He writes. *I want to watch you fall apart with my name on your lips.*

I sink a finger inside me, but it's not enough. I follow it with another for a few minutes while my other hand massages my breast. As I work myself up, I fall forward on the bed, careful to position myself so I'm still looking in Aiden's direction. I add another finger then bring my other hand down to toy with my clit, alternating between rubbing and pinching. I start to grind my hips down against the fingers inside me as I chase the orgasm that's so close yet so far.

I read Aiden's next note through fluttering eyelids. *That's right, baby, fuck yourself for me just like that. Give all those fingers to that greedy pussy of yours and make yourself come.*

I attempt to work the fourth finger in there, but just the tease of it sends me over the edge. "Oh, fuck, Aiden, I'm coming," I cry out as I ride my own hand with reckless abandon.

When I finally come down from the high of my orgasm, I rinse off in the shower, then hop back in bed with a heavy sigh.

I miss you. I scribble into the notebook.

After several moments, he replies. *I know, but we'll see*

each other again soon.

You don't know that. I write back.

It has to be true, little wraith. But in the meantime, there's so much we still don't know about each other. We can make the most of what we have.

I decide I don't want to fight when this is the first decent Christmas I've had in a really long time. *I suppose.* Neither of us writes anything for a while, both lost in our thoughts, but then I realize he's right; there are some very important things I don't know about him. *When's your birthday?*

Skye, I'm dead.

Okay, and? I want to know your birthday, don't be weird.

I'll tell you mine if you tell me yours. You're the one who doesn't celebrate it, which will be changing, by the way.

I scoff, but my curiosity gets the better of me. *July 19th.*

Of course, you're a cancer.

Don't think you're getting out of this.

Fine. June 6th.

Once again, I really hope I'm wrong about my suspicions of how this all works. I would love to spend his birthday with him.

Hey, get out of your head. I'm not going anywhere. And this, right here, with you, is all I need.

COME OUT COME OUT

Happy

February 8th, 2022 - One and a Half Months Later

As difficult as it has been for me to admit to myself, the last few months with Aiden have been some of the happiest of my life. Feeling seen is addicting. I don't even try to fight my growing dependency, I throw myself into it, not caring what the cost will be. I get my fix when we divulge our secrets between the pages. Between work, our hours of sharing our thoughts on paper, and more masturbation than I ever thought possible, it becomes the foundation of our new normal. And for a while, it was enough. I've taken everything he can give me and I'm grateful for it, but at some point, like every addiction, it was no longer enough. Hunger for a bigger fix begins to gnaw at the edges of my contentment until it's infected with this insatiable need for more of him.

My brain has started demanding even more and it has me thinking about the future. In any other context, the alarm bells would tell me it's way too soon, but our circumstances are anything but conventional. I already know how Aiden feels; he wants to be with me, despite the obstacles that are clearly in our way. And I want to be with him too, but I also want more.

Would you die for me? I scrawl the question across the page and turn my notebook slightly toward where the indent of Aiden sits just to my left.

I'm already dead. The letters are unsteady, confused.

Right, but theoretically?

Yes. Aiden writes without hesitation.

I take the answer for the reassurance I need and file it away, then change the conversation to his family. I want to know more about his sister. *Do you think Becca is like you?*

Aiden follows my lead, giving me the intimacy I crave. *I don't know. Part of me wishes that she was still in this world, but the other part of me wouldn't wish this existence on anyone. I'm lucky to have found you, Skye.* I wait for what feels like forever for him to elaborate. *If she's alone, if she's not able to reach out to my parents or anyone else, then I hope not.*

We sit in silence while I mull the weight of his words over. I should change the subject to something happier but now that we've started down this path that my train of thought has led me down so many times, I can't help myself. Apprehensively, I scribble the question I can't hold back anymore.

Is this enough for you?

When he doesn't answer immediately, I worry he won't respond at all, but then he writes, *Yes. I'll take anything I* can get with you.

It's a reminder of how fleeting my own happiness is. Must I ruin everything? Can I not be grateful for what I do have? My frustration distracts me enough that it takes me a minute to realize he's written something else. I tilt my head to read the slanted letters. *Is it not enough for you? Do you not want to be with me?* His fear thickens the air around us.

Of course I do. All I want is to be with you, but I want more. Once or twice a year isn't going to cut it. I don't want to be without you.

We don't know it'll always be this way. He responds stubbornly.

I do. It's time to fill him in on my suspicions. *You only get to be here in your . . . body . . . on Friday, the 13th.*

Are you sure?

Yes. I scroll back to March 13th, 2020 on my phone's calendar and show him the dates.

The truth sits between us for several moments, but he finally writes, *What are you saying, Skye?*

I want to be with you. All the time. He knows me enough to know what I'm saying, but I understand his apprehension, so I spell it out for him. *I want to become a ghost, too.*

No. The letters are thick. Even in the dim light of my bedside lamp, I can see that the paper is nearly torn through.

I'm ready to die, Aiden. I let out a sigh like I'm trying to explain something obvious to a child. *My entire life has been leading up to this. I'm not asking for your permission.*

The bed shifts and then a faint chill that I have to concentrate to register brushes my arm. Months ago, it would have frozen me in fear. Now, I crave these moments. I watch expectantly as letters form one by one on the open page.

Please just wait until I can be there with you. It's only a few months.

"Okay," I say out loud as I take out my phone and look up the next Friday the 13th, and then put a note in my calendar under *May 13th, 2022: Death Day.*

I add a tombstone emoji for a little flourish.

No matter what happens, I'm going through with this. I know it's the right thing for me, for us. I've had time to think about this and now I'm setting my plans in motion. Step one: make sure Binx is cared for. We'll still be able to be together, but I won't be able to go out and get him the things he needs, which is why I looked up Melissa Pierce and found her number. She's sweet, she knows where I live, and I know she works hard for her money. It's a perfect solution. I shoot off the text and hope she agrees.

It's Skye. You've delivered a few things to my house. I add after a second.

COME OUT COME OUT

Oh, trust me, I remember you. She responds immediately. *Hello, beautiful. Kicked that asshole to the curb?*

Ha ha, no. But I have a job for you, and it pays well.

I'm listening. She replies.

If I pay you $3,000, will you come to my house every few days and check on my cat, bring him food, and make sure he has what he needs?

Ummm, abso-fucking-lutly. Damn, I didn't know you had money like that. For how long? A valid question.

Just a while. I'm going on a trip starting May 13th. I'll text you the updated details and transfer the money before then. A little white lie, but I wrote a note for Melissa. When she reads it, I know she won't abandon him. Besides, eventually, someone will move in, and they'll take over; nobody can resist him, he's too cute.

Cool, sounds good. Added it to my calendar. Her confirmation allows me to fully settle into the peace I've made with this decision.

While my mood notably lightens, Aiden's presence is distinctly heavier.

Come out, come out, wherever you are

Chapter Thirty One

Aiden

February 15th, 2022– One Week Later

An expiration date has been set on my little wraith's life. I need every moment I have to convince her that this is a terrible idea. I'll do everything I can to prevent losing her. I risk angering her as I take our conversation sideways; she needs to understand what a bad idea this is. *You might not even end up here with me.*

What are you talking about? She lets out a frustrated sigh, then continues writing, *Yes, I will. If I die here, I'll stay here, like you did. It's just what makes sense.*

Three other people died here in this house with me that night, except they're nowhere to be seen. I scribble furiously. Panic makes the letters barely legible; she has to read it twice through squinting eyes.

They didn't die here. She writes matter-of-factly.

What do you mean? I think I would know. I respond.

Skye rolls her eyes. *Two of them died in the ambulance. The last one . . . Richard, I think? Died at the hospital.*

How do you know that? I wonder if my mom told her. My chest tightens at the thought of her as guilt sours in my stomach. How little I've thought of my mother's grief is shameful.

Skye pen-tapping her notebook steals my attention away from the shocking realization. I lean forward to read. *I read it in the news articles.* She stands, grabs her laptop, and types something lightning-fast before turning her screen to me. As I read, she slowly scrolls down the page.

There it is, in black and white. The "Spark Notes" version of the night that changed everything. I sit with the new information for several minutes, so many questions are now answered. It's a small reassurance, that even if she does something rash, she'll still be here. But it doesn't change the fact that I've been fighting to keep her alive all this time, I can't bear the thought of her ending her life to be with me. She deserves so much more than this existence has to offer.

GONER

April 15th, 2022 - Two Months Later

It's been two months since Skye mentioned her death to me and I've been doing everything I can to make her see how much I can fulfill her like this if she just lets me.

We've even picked out sex toys together, like the one I'm using on her right now. While she can't feel my touch, I can still pleasure her this way.

I stroke my cock as I drive the intricately ribbed pink and green monster dildo that's inspired by one of her favorite romance books into her. We've been building up to this one with its thick shaft that's enhanced with all kinds of fun for her pleasure and I'm enjoying putting it to good use almost as much as she is. Each time her pussy clenches around it, I imagine it's my cock buried deep inside her.

"Right there. Mmm, fuck, yes." Skye cries out as she rubs her clit. That's my queue to pick up the pace. I match the strokes of my fist to the tempo. Her back arches and I recall the delicious taste of her skin on my tongue when I've sucked and licked on her pretty dusky pink nipples. I don't realize I've stopped working the dildo in favor of thrusting into my hand until Skye speaks.

COME OUT COME OUT

"Is it hard to focus when you hear me whining and begging for you and you can't sink inside me?" She taunts cruelly. She's been pushing me like this every chance she gets. Thinking she can change my mind with the temptation of getting my cock wet more often is short-sighted. I've grown to be a patient man.

But since she wants to be mouthy, I hold the dildo still inside her and return my attention to my throbbing dick.

"Aww, don't be mad." She begins shifting her hips, trying to fuck herself on the abnormally shaped silicone. "I miss you, too. I miss the way your perfect cock fills me." As if on cue, she clenches around it. My fist moves faster as I chase my release. Skye pinches her nipple with one hand and her clit with the other, while she makes every obscene noise I've ever heard in porn. She's playing dirty, so I can too. I slowly pull the dildo from inside her; her pussy grips around it but I don't stop.

"Aiden," she calls out in frustration, and that's what sends me over the edge.

I consider leaving her gaping and wanting, but I decide to give her a choice, setting the monster cock on the floor and holding it at the base.

"Are you fucking serious?" she huffs. Doubling her efforts on her clit, she tries to finish, but she can't deny that she wants to be filled. Skye slams her fist against the mattress before standing and walking over to the dildo. Her eyes are narrowed in a glare as she lowers herself to the floor and hovers over it. I tease her entrance with the tip before lowering it again. "You're a fucking assho—" her words melt into a moan when the thick tip of it enters her as she sinks down on it.

    Satisfied and eager to enjoy my retaliation, I sit down right in front of her, tighten my grip on the watermelon-colored toy, and watch as she desperately fucks herself inches away from my face. Who's winning now? I get a front-row seat and she can't even see me. Skye's husky voice fills the room as she whimpers and gasps with abandon. It's a bittersweet symphony.

    I swallow thickly as I watch her move up and down, tits bouncing, thighs jiggling, mouth parted. Such a pretty picture she's painting for me. I'm overcome with the urge to fuck into her throat but stifle the unfulfillable desire. I'm just lucky to watch my little wraith cry and writhe as she gets closer and closer to the edge, the toy disappearing into her faster and faster in flashes of vibrant color that further accentuate that pretty pussy that's slamming down on the base I hold in my hand. I can't feel her, but it's a goddamn erotic sight if I've ever seen one.

    "Oh, fuck, I'm so close," she confirms my suspicions.

Come Out Come Out

I know my girl's body almost as well as my own. I close my eyes in satisfaction and let myself enjoy the harmony of her panting, accented by the wet suction of her cunt trying to devour the lifeless silicone. It all comes to a crescendo when her orgasm hits her with my name on her lips. "Aiden, Aiden, Aiden," she recites my name in a plea that she thinks will change my mind.

It won't.

I open my eyes to take in the shaking mess she's become—hair disheveled, slick sweat coating her ample body, pussy dripping, and most importantly, her skin flushed the softest red with exertion. She's so full of life like this, I can't take that from her.

My little wraith

CHAPTER THIRTY TWO

Aiden

May 12th, 2022 – One Month Later

The numbers *11:55* blink up at me from Skye's phone screen as she checks the time eagerly, as anxious to prove her theory as I am.

Nervous energy is palpable, nearly filling the room to bursting as we wait those five minutes, neither of us needing to communicate. I'm too preoccupied with fear. I can't let her do this, I won't.

When I feel the warmth of the air and the thumping of my heart, I know it's finally the thirteenth.

Skye's eyes go wide and her head whips back to her phone. 12:01 am. "Fuck," she gasps as her hand presses to her heart, "I'll never get used to you just appearing."

Come Out Come Out

I laugh half-heartedly, panic setting in. It takes me another minute to adjust to the feeling of being in my body. It feels heavier than usual with the tension in my muscles and the stress forcing my heart to pump quickly.

"Ready?" Skye asks, excitement lighting her eyes as she hops off the bed. "I am. I'm even wearing my favorite outfit." I turn to face her; she does look good in the all-black ensemble. I let my gaze linger on the mini skirt she's paired with the cropped tee featuring a happy pill graphic on it, with fishnets and her platform boots. But when my attention moves to her hand, I flinch, the glint of silver catching my eye. She's holding a goddamn knife. And not just a simple bread knife, it's the largest one she owns.

I can't think of anything to say other than, "Do you have any idea how badly it hurts to die by knife?" A phantom ache flares in my side. "I would know. It's not a pleasant way to go." I try to dissuade her as I form a plan in my mind.

"Hurting is part of the fun, isn't it?" Her brow furrows as she looks me over. "I thought you understood me?", she says hotly before flicking her bangs out of her eyes that are dark and determined and framed by perfect winged eyeliner.

Unease swims through me as I take in her scowl. She's on the defense, which I'm not used to. I need to catch her off guard. I take a step closer and she tenses, but she watches me intently as I press my finger to the tip of the blade. "What are you going to do with this, little wraith?" I step closer, until the long, sharp edge is pressed against me. "You're going to stab yourself and then make me watch you bleed out?" I look down my nose at her, my piercing momentarily catching the light. "Have you thought about what happens if you don't go deep enough? If you have to stab yourself again when you're shaking and weak? What if it doesn't work?" My thumb runs between the seam of her matte black lips and we stare at one another for several seconds before she bites down and digs her teeth into the skin. It hurts but it's the moment of distraction I needed to grab her wrist and force it back until she drops the knife. I reach down and grab it before she can.

"Give it to me, Aiden. I'm doing this and I'm not asking for your permission. This is my decision to make." Her throat works up and down as she tries to fight the tears that rise with her anger.

"That's the thing," I reach forward and turn Skye so her back is pressed against my chest and her arms are bound beneath the one I have wrapped around her. With a bit of difficulty, I walk us into the bathroom and flip on the light. "It's not just about you."

Overpowered, Skye's anger bubbles over, and the tears she was fighting begin to fall. "Aiden, please. I want to do this.

You *know* how badly I want this."

I ignore the way her plea pulls at my heartstrings and wedge her between my body and the bathroom counter. "Take off your shirt."

"Aiden," she starts, but I press my hips forward.

"Take it off now, or I'll mess up that beautiful hair and makeup you spent all that time on," I threaten and she obeys. "You're so pretty when you cry for me. Cheeks flushed, mascara running, and those sad brown eyes—fucking exquisite. So beautifully, alive." I inhale the scent of her before I lean down and pin her flat against the countertop. I use my other hand to pull down her skirt, black mesh panties, and fishnets. When she's naked enough for what I want to do to her, I make sure she can't move by slipping my non-dominant hand around the nape of her neck, my fingers putting pressure on the sides so she has no choice but to look at me.

Holding her gaze, I bring the knife to my lips and lick the blade, then proceed to run it down the column of her throat. My cock jumps at the harsh way she swallows against the cool kiss of the sharp tip. I draw it across her collarbone and down her right arm, increasing the pressure so a shallow cut opens from the top of her bicep down to the side of her outer wrist.

Her eyes roll back and she gasps. She's such a whore

for her own suffering. I lighten the pressure once again as I drag the blade down her torso and hips. When I reach her upper thigh, I halt the descent and turn the knife so the pointed end is pressing into the skin. I twirl it in time with her needy pants then drive it in, just a little bit. Scarlet blooms from the injury and my cock strains against my pants as her nipples harden. She shifts her bare legs together, trying to create friction.

"Do you still crave the pain, Skye?" I punctuate the question with another dig of the knife into the meat of her thigh. "Do you like how it hurts?" I'm hypnotized by her agonized expression in the mirror as she nods. "If you'd just stop being stubborn and fighting me every step of the way, I can give you exactly what you need, just like I promised." I kiss down the side of her neck, my lips resting over her erratic pulse. "Let me show you that I can be enough. I can make our time together everything you want and need, even if they're few and far between. I'll fulfill all your fantasies and I won't even make you beg this time." I resume my path with the blade, dragging it against the plush, sensitive flesh of her thigh until I find the space where her thick legs meet her pussy. I pause for several seconds to revel in her muffled whimpers.

Flipping the blade, I rub the handle along the front of her cunt, coaxing her to open her legs. When she rubs her ass into me to spur me on, I tighten my hand on the back of her neck. "Don't move." I release her and step back to admire the faint scars on the back of her quivering thighs. *Mine.* I've never seen something so glorious.

"Get up on the counter." I sweep everything that clutters the space between the two sinks onto the floor. She's so deep in her lust that she climbs up without protest. "Press your palms against the mirror." She does, but I'm not quite satisfied. I push between her shoulder blades until her breasts are smashed up against the reflective surface and she's forced to turn her head to comply.

"I'm going to fuck your needy hole with this." My threat is punctuated by the blade sliding down her bare spine. I flip it in my hand once again when I get to her tailbone and bring the handle to her pussy. Skye shifts her legs farther apart and arches her ass out. "Such a desperate little slut for this knife. I might get jealous." My other hand grips her ass cheek and lifts, giving me a stunning view of her dripping cunt as I run the black plastic along her center with the lightest touch.

Skye rocks her hips. "Put it inside me already, fuck."

I laugh bitterly. "Don't worry, little wraith, I'm going to drive it into you again and again until my hand is covered in everything your sweet pussy has to give me. I'm going to fuck this macabre fantasy out of your pretty head."

Whatever protest she was going to make is cut off as I glide the first few inches of the handle inside her needy hole. My hand wraps around the blade, covering the intersection of steel and plastic, so I don't actually injure her. A little bleeding won't hurt me, after all. Her legs open further and shake violently as I ram it inside her over and over. She's gradually lowering herself onto the knife in shallow bounces as she tries not to slip in her precarious position.

"That's my girl, so desperate to be fucked and filled by me. Go ahead and touch yourself." Her fingers find her clit and she harshly rubs the swollen bud. I continue to thrust the knife handle into her while I take in the gorgeous mess I've created. Her breasts are reddened from the pressure of being flattened and tugged against the unforgiving glass. Her brow is furrowed and her mouth is dropped open, just waiting for my dick. I take in her voluptuous ass as it moves up and down with each roll of her hips. She's a fucking goddess.

Ready to reward her for her cooperation, I kneel on my knees and run my tongue between her cheeks as I speed up the steady stroke of my wrist. I lick the tight rim of her hole and it shatters her weak hold on her composure. As she orgasms, she gushes down the handle, coating my hand. I pull back and watch in a daze as she drips down the blade. *Fuck, I'm about to cum already.*

Come Out Come Out

Standing, I remove the knife and wrap my arm around her stomach, dragging her down from where she shakes and gasps, utterly spent. "On your knees, baby." Still a bit disoriented, she staggers to her knees. I undo my jeans with one hand while the other holds out the knife that's glinting and slick. "Lick it clean." Carefully, she presses her tongue to the flat slide and collects the evidence of her orgasm. My fist is tight and punishing as I stroke my cock. When she finishes, I toss the knife in the sink and run my dick between her lips. She welcomes me inside eagerly, her tongue swirling and massaging my length.

A groan rumbles in my throat and I gather her hair in my hand, holding her steady as she milks my cock so hard she's bound to suck out my soul. *How fitting since she already possesses it.* The thought soothes the raging ache within me and I cum down her throat in hot bursts. She drinks it all down with a smile on her face.

When I finally tug her head back, she releases it with a pop and stands to her feet, pulling up her skirt, panties, and fishnets. Her lips slam against mine in a victorious kiss that makes me even more lightheaded. It's so distracting that my reflexes are too slow when she pulls away, grabs her top and the knife, and takes off at a run.

Fear slices through the hazy pleasure that gripped me

seconds ago.

"Skye, get back here, right fucking now." Anger at my foolishness mixes with fear in a sickening cocktail that turns my stomach as I pull my pants up and chase after her. "This isn't a goddamn game. You're going to be in so much fucking trouble when I catch you." As I start down the stairs, I catch a glimpse of her black hair. I take them two at a time.

When I get to the bottom of the stairs, I stop to listen to where she's snuck off to. "Come out, come out wherever you are, little wraith." It's silent for several moments, but then I hear her trip and something clatter on the counter. I follow her into the kitchen. My arm wraps around her waist just as her fingers clutch around the back door's handle.

"No," I yelp. She brings the large knife gripped in her left hand into my upper thigh in one swift swing.

I cry out in agony and she tries to grab the knob once again, but I tug her back against me. Desperate to escape my clutches, she lurches forward and hits her head on the door, her face bashing through part of the window and glass shatters everywhere. I pull her back into me and she sways on her feet. A few seconds later, she crumples into my arms, unconscious.

Everything slows down as I watch blood start to flow from the wounds she's sustained. There's a large gash across

COME OUT COME OUT

her forehead and tons of cuts from the glass on her beautiful face, yet worse is the huge piece of glass sticking out of the side of her throat. On autopilot, I tear off my shirt and press it against the wound and gently turn her head to the side. I stare at her punctured throat, unsure whether I should pull it out or leave it, my gut says leave it until I have something better to staunch the bleeding. I run to get bandages, my leg pouring blood that I'm not concerned about across the floor. I'm already dead, it doesn't matter how much blood I lose tonight, I'll be fine tomorrow. But Skye, she can't die. *Not like this.*

My Binxie boy

CHAPTER THIRTY THREE

Skye

May 13th, 2022 – The Same Day

When I come to, I'm laying on the kitchen floor with Aiden's shirt under my head. The pounding in my skull makes it difficult to keep my eyes open but I look around from where I lay. Everything fucking hurts and my face is wet. Disoriented, I rub my forehead. I pull my arm away only to find it coated in bright red. My head spins as I register the amount of blood on the shirt. Panic seizes me and my breaths come quick, only they're cut short with an excruciating pain in my neck. I raise my hand to feel it and there's something big and sharp sticking out. I immediately start to violently shake. I try to call out but moving my throat at all is excruciating.

Aiden is nowhere to be seen. A trail of blood leads out

of the kitchen and I finally remember that I stabbed him in the leg. I know he's already dead, but I can't help but worry, even though I can't do anything.

"Aiden," I force myself to take the discomfort as I call out in a frail, quivering voice. Everything is eerily silent for several seconds but then I hear his boots pounding down the stairs. I sag with relief when he enters the room.

"You're hurt, let me help you." He presses a towel against my head and cautiously touches the thing in my throat with his other hand. The white-hot pain that erupts makes my vision blur. I let out a pathetic whimper as the world narrows and everything goes black.

Happy

It's still dark inside the house when my lashes flutter open, but I can make out the shape of Aiden kneeling next to me, arms resting over one bent knee as he watches me with a distraught expression on his face.

I try to speak but my throat is so dry that only a rasp comes out. When I shift to sit up, Aiden's hand presses against my sternum holding me down.

"Don't move, you're bleeding a lot." He reaches up on the island and grabs a glass of water. Aiden guides me up just slightly so I can drink. The movement makes me want to scream.

I'm covered in a cold sweat and struggle to sort out my thoughts. I let my head fall back against the soaking fabric. "I don't want to play anymore." My voice is barely recognizable, the words weak and shaky. Tears blur my vision as I watched him carefully. He remains silent, rocking back and forth while he spins one of the thick silver rings that adorn his fingers. His hair is sticking up everywhere; he must have been tugging at it frantically. Even in my hazy state, I can see the indecision running through his mind. When his steely eyes collide with mine, I know he's made a choice.

"You've been running for your fucking life nonstop little wraith, and look what's happened when you stopped watching where you were going. You've run right off the cliff." Tears crash over his lashes from the raging storm in his eyes.

"And what if," I take a wet, ragged breath, but force the words out, "what if I wanted to fall?" I have to pause to breathe through the pain. "What if I'm finally ready to jump off the cliff and take refuge in the dark embrace of the water below?" I swallow hot coals and continue, "What if I tell you that I never want to come up for air again?"

A choked sob escapes his trembling lips. "I was supposed to keep you afloat. You might have stopped kicking, but I would have kicked enough for two. I don't care what kind of storm we're facing. I was devoted to doing anything to keep you alive."

Using the little strength I have left, I dig my nails into the inked skin of his arm. I don't let go until he looks me in the eyes. "Aiden, the game is over. It's how it was always supposed to be."

"Shh, little wraith," he pushes the wet, clumped hair away from my face, "don't forfeit just yet."

"I'm not forfeiting," I cough and it's thicker than it should be. "I won; you're the only prize I ever needed."

Come out, come out, wherever you are

Chapter Thirty Four

Aiden

May 13th, 2022 – 11:45 PM

I'm dead and she's always had one foot out the door, what chance did we ever stand at a happily ever after?

It was unwise of me to hope that I could convince her to stay. Maybe it was even unfair. The last few years play through my mind as I stroke the side of her face.

"Aiden," her voice is so quiet.

"Yes?"

"It's all over." She laughs and gives me a content smile.

"I'm so sorry." I bring her hand to my lips and kiss it.

"Don't be. I'm ready. I promise." She holds my gaze and I take in the soft relief in her features. The peace in her voice is pattering rain on the tin roof of my guilty conscience.

COME OUT COME OUT

The cool relief of it sweeps through me, but the lump in my throat is keeping me from speaking.

"I have one more thing to ask of you." She squeezes my hand with the little remaining strength she has. "I want to feel you inside me like this one more time." Each word is a monumental effort.

"Skye," I start to protest.

"Please, Aiden." Her voice is fading quickly.

I stare in disbelief as I try to wrap my mind around her request. Is it worse to deny her dying wish or to fuck the woman I love while she dies?

"Please," she repeats. The need in her voice is something I can't deny. I want her to have the peace she's seeking as she slowly slips away.

Gently, I pull down her fishnets then panties and I can't miss how soaked they are. It's the confirmation I need that this is the right choice. Freeing my cock, I lay myself over her, careful not to rest my weight on her. Slowly, I thrust into her inch by inch then drag myself out. I repeat the motion, trying not to jostle her too much. She presses her thighs around my waist urging me to go harder. There's barely any pressure, but I comply, pumping into her with slightly more fervor. One of her hands grips the hair at the back of my head and her lips claim mine possessively. The jagged glass scrapes against my own throat, but all I can think about is how this is the last time her lips will ever be warm on mine again. I cling to that fleeting feeling like one would watch their last sunset.

The room fills with the sounds of our hushed panting, the light slapping of our skin, and our lips colliding in desperate kissing. Skye's shaky cries join, "Yes, Aiden, right there, baby." The words slip across my skin like the finest silk, causing chills to erupt following their caress. "This is perfect. You're giving me everything I need." Her words are muffled by gurgling now.

When her shaking legs slip from around me, no longer able to clench, her fingertips flutter in my hair and I take that as a sign and guide my ear down to her lips. "Aiden, I love you." The proclamation is punctuated by a grotesque sinking sound and her gasp. Every muscle in my body freezes and I drag my reluctant gaze to look at Skye as she stutters her last breath.

Her vacant expression is punctuated by a slight curl of her lips. Adrenaline pulses through me and I force myself to sit up and slide out of her. My stomach tumbles as I take in the knife she plunged into her side—we now have matching wounds—but I can't tear my eyes away from her.

"Skye," I cry out. "Skye, please, no." I pull her body against mine and sob into her already cooling skin. I hold onto my girl with every ounce of strength I have, but I quickly realize it's just a body, just empty flesh. It doesn't feel like her, it's missing the most important part. *Skye's not in there anymore.* Her blood soaks through my clothes, chilling me to the bone. I lay her down carefully and brush the shaggy bangs away as I close her eyes.

Binx is meowing his fucking face off, his distress matching my own, and I reach a hand out in an attempt to comfort him. He ducks under it and begins rubbing his head on Skye's. His cries grow louder in protest of the truth we both know. *She's gone.*

Tears pour down my face and even my nose is leaking as I continue to unravel as I stare at the culmination of the ending I'd always known was coming but couldn't accept. There was no other way this ever would have gone, just like Skye tried to tell me. I should have prepared better for this outcome, but it feels like the world has been ripped from beneath my feet and I'm being swallowed up whole by my worst nightmare.

"Please, please, please, please," I chant, pressing my eyes closed. "Not again. I can't do this again." I choke on the words, coughing and sputtering; I'm drowning in my fear of what comes next. I don't know what will happen to me if she's not there waiting for me on the other side.

tastes like bad decisions

CHAPTER THIRTY FIVE

Skye

May 14th, 2022 - A Few Minutes After Midnight

For several minutes, it's as if my soul is being torn in half. On one side there is so much pain it's like fire is shooting through my veins and melting me from the inside. But now that I'm on the other side, all I know is the exquisite pleasure of peace. I'm weightless in a way I never could've imagined. For the first time in my life, everything is quiet.

Slowly, I become aware of Aiden and every point where his body presses tightly against mine. Awe strikes me as I take in his appearance, he looks completely normal to me. Almost everything does, I don't know what I expected. A dull, gray landscape, perhaps? The house feels a bit dimmer, my senses dulled to the world around me, except for what matters most, Aiden. He feels whole and sturdy in my arms. Our bodies are bound here by whatever fate brought us together in the first place.

"I thought I lost you." His red-rimmed eyes are wide with grief that would destroy me if I didn't know that everything was okay.

"Never." The weight of the commitment I've made to him sinks in. It feels like I'm finally home. I take his hand and hold it tightly, giving him a squeeze of reassurance that I'm right here with him and I'm not going anywhere. "Everything is how it was always meant to be. It's just me and you now." I press my fingertips beneath his chin and force him to meet my gaze.

"Skye, I need you to be honest with me." He quickly averts his eyes.

"Always." If I had a heartbeat, it would be pumping violently. He's making me nervous.

"Are you okay?" Aiden asks uncertainly through a loud sniffle. "Do you regret it?" The anxiety floods out of me because this is such an easy question to answer.

"Not one bit." I wrap my arms around his neck and pull him toward me for a kiss. He melts into me. His hands claw underneath my shirt, digging into my back like he's trying to crawl inside of me so I can't leave him ever again. The last few minutes were transformative for both of us. For the first time, he feels heavy and I'm eager to bear that weight, to be the one who's strong for him. I've been looking forward to this moment, but he's been dreading it and it's all catching up to him.

I play with the hair at the nape of his neck and his shoulders begin to relax under my touch. "I feel better than ever, actually." It's the truth. For Aiden, this may have been an endless purgatory; he didn't have a choice. For me, this is what I've wanted for as long as I can remember. "I want you to hear me when I say this," I lean back just enough to be able to meet his eyes as he continues to clutch onto me. "You're not alone here anymore, Aiden. You'll never be alone again. You'll never have to worry about losing anyone again. This is the beginning of our forever."

Something I've said breaks through the shroud of loss that was suffocating him. He nods vigorously and wipes at his face with the lower half of his shirt. I stand completely still as he closes his eyes and breathes deeply–the calming habit from life is unnecessary but it still seems to help him to center himself. When he finally looks at me again, happy tears flow over his lashes, and he kisses me like his lips are the only thing that can keep me here. "I love you, Skye. You're everything I've ever wanted."

COME OUT COME OUT

"Do you know what you are to me?" He shakes his head. "You're everything I *needed*. My grim reaper who took my restless soul by the hand and led me into the bliss of death." I stroke my nails through his hair, pushing the unruly strays back so I can see his painfully gorgeous face reflecting everything I feel right back at me. Our entire story unfolds there in the curve of his lips and the red splotches that disrupt his otherwise perfect skin; there's sorrow, desperation, grief, solace, and most importantly, the love that bloomed in that forbidden space between life and death. It's fucking beautiful. It's more than I ever could have hoped for.

"So, what now?" Aiden asks as he cups my cheeks.

I smirk, because this is the final step in my plan. Stepping out of his embrace, I reach for the real gift I bought when I did my online holiday shopping. I hold my ring in between my fingers and look over the engraving.

On the top of the silver band, it reads, '*Yours eternally*' in a handwriting-style font.

On the inside, it says, '*Your little wraith*' with a small black heart at the end.

"What is that?"

"My promise to you." I hold my hand out for his and slip it into his ring finger.

"Fuck, you thought of everything, didn't you?" He

laughs as his eyes become watery again. He stares down at it for several seconds before shifting his attention to the many other rings that adorn his hands.

I lace my fingers between his. "You don't have to part with any of them, I know you're mine."

Aiden shakes his head, easy laughter spilling out of him like I've never heard before. It's intoxicating. I watch, confused, as he twists one off. "This is too fucking good," he says as he slips it on my finger.

I look down and I can't help but laugh because it is. *Perfect.* I squint as I stare down at the tiny etched scythe and the barely legible words *'dead inside'* in script. Affection blooms in my chest where my still heart sits. He really does see me. "This is like something straight out of one of my romance novels." My smile is so wide that my cheeks start to ache. I can honestly say I've only experienced this kind of joyful pain a handful of times in my life.

Binx meows his approval from the floor between us. I smile down at him, unbelievably grateful that I didn't have to say goodbye to him. *Yeah*, death is already off to a better start than anything I could have ever imagined.

Aiden leans down and kisses my hand, where the ring now sits proudly. "Yeah, Skye, just like that."

EPILOGUE

June 1st, 2022 - Two Weeks Later

    We stand shoulder to shoulder as we look out the window of my old bedroom that's been cleared out by my family. It was weird seeing them here, grieving over me, it was like they were really seeing me for the first time. I'd let them go a long time ago, but it didn't mean I didn't feel for the loss they were experiencing. I didn't regret it though, I'd finally found someone who didn't look away from my pain, something they could never give me. We were all free now.

    I lay my head on Aiden's shoulder and hug Binx against me as we watch the same movers I used walk in and out of the house, unloading the two trucks that sit in the drive. They seem tense looking around everywhere as they take trip after trip inside. Then there are the two women unloading their own cars. One has long brown hair that cascades around her in waves, stopping just above her wide hips. Aiden and I have set our sights on her. Both our gazes track her every step as she unpacks load after load. She's fascinating with her hopeful brown eyes and the mosaic of tattoos that cover her from neck to ankles. The other has a vibrant red pixie cut that curls around her ears and frames her round face. She's stunning but we've agreed we both prefer brunettes.

It's a bit inconvenient when a muscular man with black hair runs up behind her and embraces her. A boyfriend isn't ideal, but it's not a problem. There are two of us, after all. Our eyes meet and we share a knowing smile. This will be so much fun.

Acknowledgements

Jack,

Thank you for your encouragement. I know this story changed SO MUCH from the original plot, but you were the first person who made me believe in this idea, and I can't tell you how much that means. You've always been a safe space for me to word-vomit book concepts–many of which will die in our dms . . . RIP. You've just been such a big part of my journey–from helping me find a community with your readers to feeling confident in my random ideas. I appreciate your friendship so much.

A. Vrana,

Thank you so much for volunteering to alpha! I can't begin to tell you how grateful I am for your thoughtful feedback. Rewriting this entire book was so daunting, but you were so patient and helpful the entire time. You really helped me rework this story into something I can be proud of and I'm so appreciative.

Angie,

Where would I be without you? You're such an invaluable part of my process, I can't imagine doing this without you at this point. Thank you for getting this story and pushing me to make it the best it can be.

Shannon,

I'm so glad we were able to work together on the formatting for this. I love your creative mind and the vision you had for this book was so perfect. More than the professional aspect of this book, I want to take a second to thank you for your friendship and support. You're such an incredible, thoughtful person and I'm so glad we found each other amongst the chaos of the clock app.

The earliest A.O. followers,

Deciding to start over with this book has been terrifying and humbling. To those of you who followed me over from A.C.M. and the readers who found me in the earliest days and decided I was worth the follow, THANK YOU. It's a slow climb, but I just want you to know that every like, comment, and moment of excitement has meant the world to me.

Jules,

You won't read this, I mean I really really hope you don't read this one, but it only feels right to acknowledge that you are the one true Nirvana fan in this family and I am but a humble casual fan.

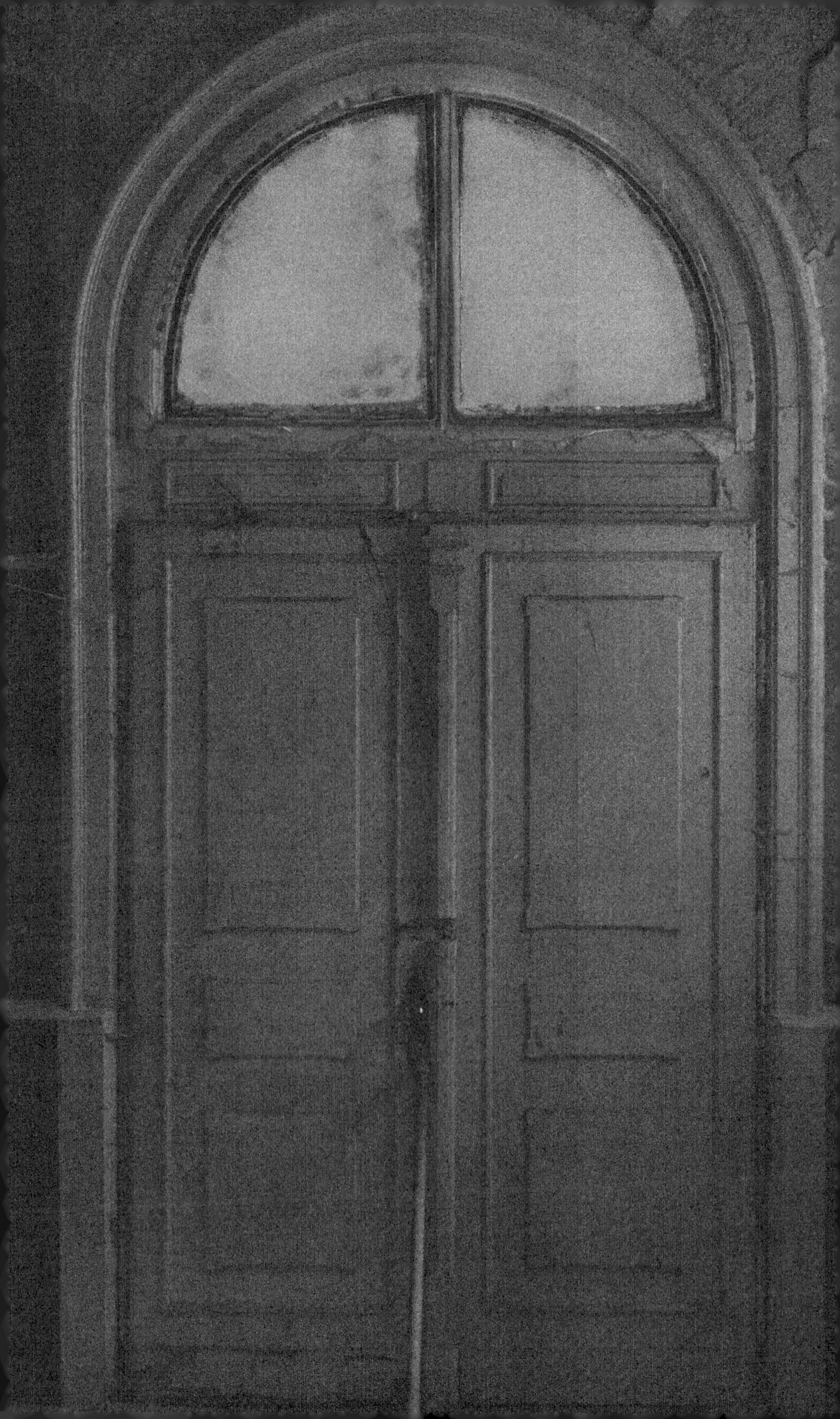

About the Author

Alexia Onyx is a dark romance and horror author who loves exploring the dark side of humanity. In her books, you can expect to find plus-size/fat representation, queer relationships, and mental health themes.

Alexia lives in sunny San Diego but mentally, she's somewhere cold and rainy. She's a little obsessed with Halloween, her adorably plump cat, and bubbly water, which she truly does need to survive. When she's not writing, you can find Alexia surrounded by her fall-scented candles while hiding from the world with her latest read, scream-singing along to her favorite songs, or gleefully curating playlists and mood boards for her next book.

Keep up with her latest releases by following her on TikTok or Instagram at @alexiaonyxauthor.

More from Alexia Onyx

Warmer, Colder (Haunted Hearts Book Two) - Coming 2024
Light as a Feather (Haunted Hearts Book Three) - TBD

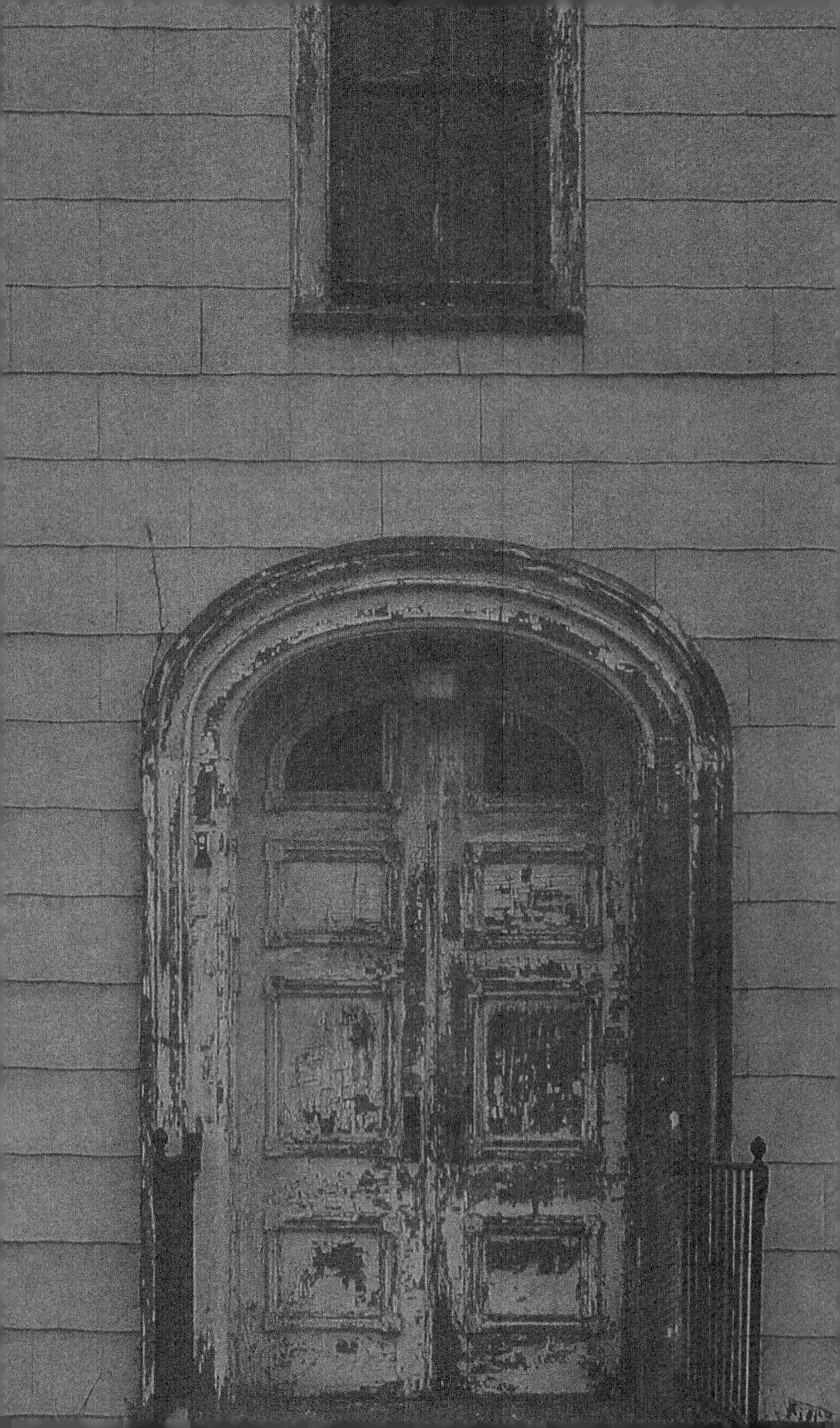

CW By Chapter

Note:
This breakdown starts at chapter 1,
the prologue is not included.

1. Loss/grief, finding a dead sibling after suicide (described in detail), murder, gore, blood, cops, stabbing, death
2. Death, grief/loss, references to suicide, blood, abandonment, (minor) anti-religious rhetoric
3. Haunting, cutting, masturbation, voyeurism without consent
4. Breath play, voyeurism fantasy, unprotected sex, sex while under the influence
5. Chasing, unprotected sex, sex in a dangerous place with risk of serious bodily injury, CNC/role play
6. Self-harm, negative self-talk (non-body related), references to alcohol misuse, memories of overstimulation, isolation
7. Masturbation, drug abuse (cocaine), self-harm (cutting), speculation of suicide, possessiveness, FMC hooks up with someone other than the MMC
8. Haunting activity
9. Mentions of anxiety and depression, cocaine use, self-harm (razor blade/cutting), attempted drowning
10. Discussion of suicidal ideation, death, drug misuse
11. Degradation, chasing, edging
12. reference to dead family member, spitting, potentially life-threatening sex, unprotected sex
13. Sensory overstimulation
14. Feelings of abandonment
15. Sexual fantasies about someone other than the MMC
16. Break-in, self-defense, predatory landlord
17. N/A
18. Masturbation
19. Discussion of depression
20. Cocaine use, self-pity
21. Remembering loss, despair
22. Vomiting (non-pregnancy related), discussion of murder and death
23. Grieving mother, discussion of children who have passed

away, reference to murder
24. Rough blow job
25. Unprotected sex
26. Jealousy/possessiveness
27. Degradation, Humiliation, Jealousy/possessiveness, Mutilation (cutting/carving), (fake) slut shaming
28. Unprotected sex
29. N/A
30. References to addiction, mention of suicide
31. Large, non-human dildo use
32. Knife play, penetration with an object
33. Head injury, bleeding out
34. Sex with an injured person, grief, self-inflicted wound, death
35. Death

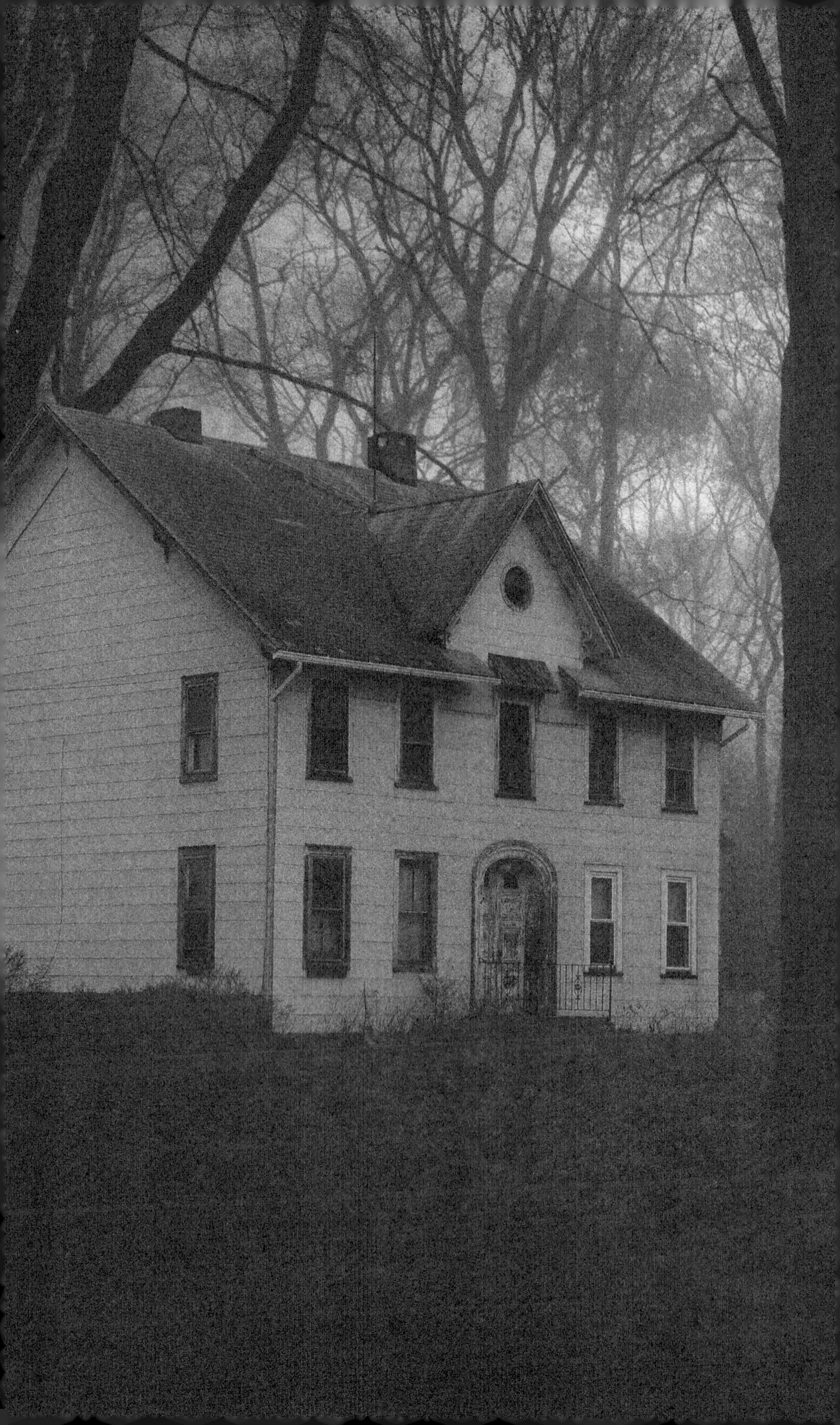

Black Cat Statistics

As a lifelong cat lover, it breaks my heart that black cats are still very misunderstood and often fall victim to harm done by humans. I'd like to share a few facts about black cats with you:

- Black cats have experienced some of the highest rates of euthanasia
- They have the lowest rate of adoption of any cat color
- They are often victims of pranks and abuse due to superstitions

Black kitties could use so much more love in the world. If you'd like to find more information about black advocacy or adopt your very own furry friend, here are some resources.

- [Black Cat Holistic Rescue](#) (California)
- [Black Cat Rescue](#) (Massachusetts)
- [Binx's Home for Black Cats](#) (North Carolina)
- [Black Cat Animal Rescue](#) (Kentucky)

There's also a [National Black Cat Day](#) where you show love and advocate for these adorable animals. Thanks so much for reading!

Printed in Great Britain
by Amazon